Child of Earth and Sky

www.penguin.co.uk

Also by Menna van Praag

Men, Money and Chocolate
The House at the End of Hope Street
The Dress Shop of Dreams
The Witches of Cambridge
The Lost Art of Letter Writing
The Patron Saint of Lost Souls

The Tale of the Sisters Grimm
The Sisters Grimm
Night of Demons and Saints

Child of Earth and Sky

Menna van Praag

bantam

TRANSWORLD PUBLISHERS
Penguin Random House, One Embassy Gardens,
8 Viaduct Gardens, London SW11 7BW
www.penguin.co.uk

Transworld is part of the Penguin Random House group of companies
whose addresses can be found at global.penguinrandomhouse.com

Penguin Random House UK

First published in Great Britain in 2023 by Bantam
an imprint of Transworld Publishers

A CIP catalogue record for this book
is available from the British Library.

ISBNs
9781787631700 (cased)
9781787631717 (tpb)

Typeset in 10.5/15pt Berling LT Std by Jouve (UK), Milton Keynes.
Printed and bound in Great Britain by Clays Ltd, Elcograf S.p.A.

The authorized representative in the EEA is Penguin Random House Ireland,
Morrison Chambers, 32 Nassau Street, Dublin D02 YH68.

Penguin Random House is committed to a sustainable future
for our business, our readers and our planet. This book is made
from Forest Stewardship Council® certified paper.

MIX
Paper | Supporting
responsible forestry
FSC® C018179

For Alastair

With great love and deepest gratitude for the splendid gift of your magnificent illustrations for this trilogy.

I'll be forever grateful to the serendipity that caused our paths to cross again!

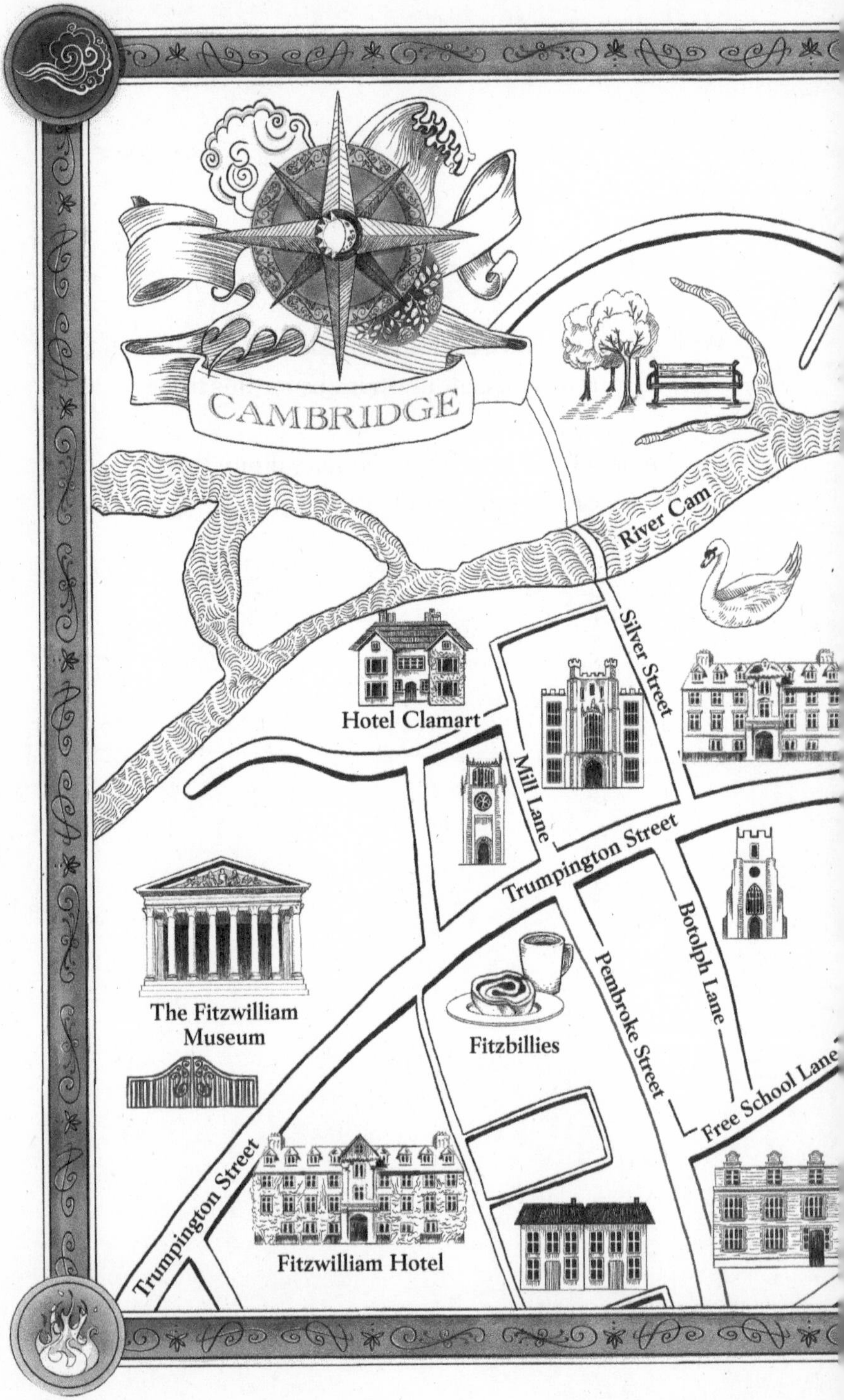
CAMBRIDGE
River Cam
Hotel Clamart
Silver Street
Mill Lane
Trumpington Street
Botolph Lane
The Fitzwilliam Museum
Fitzbillies
Pembroke Street
Free School Lane
Trumpington Street
Fitzwilliam Hotel

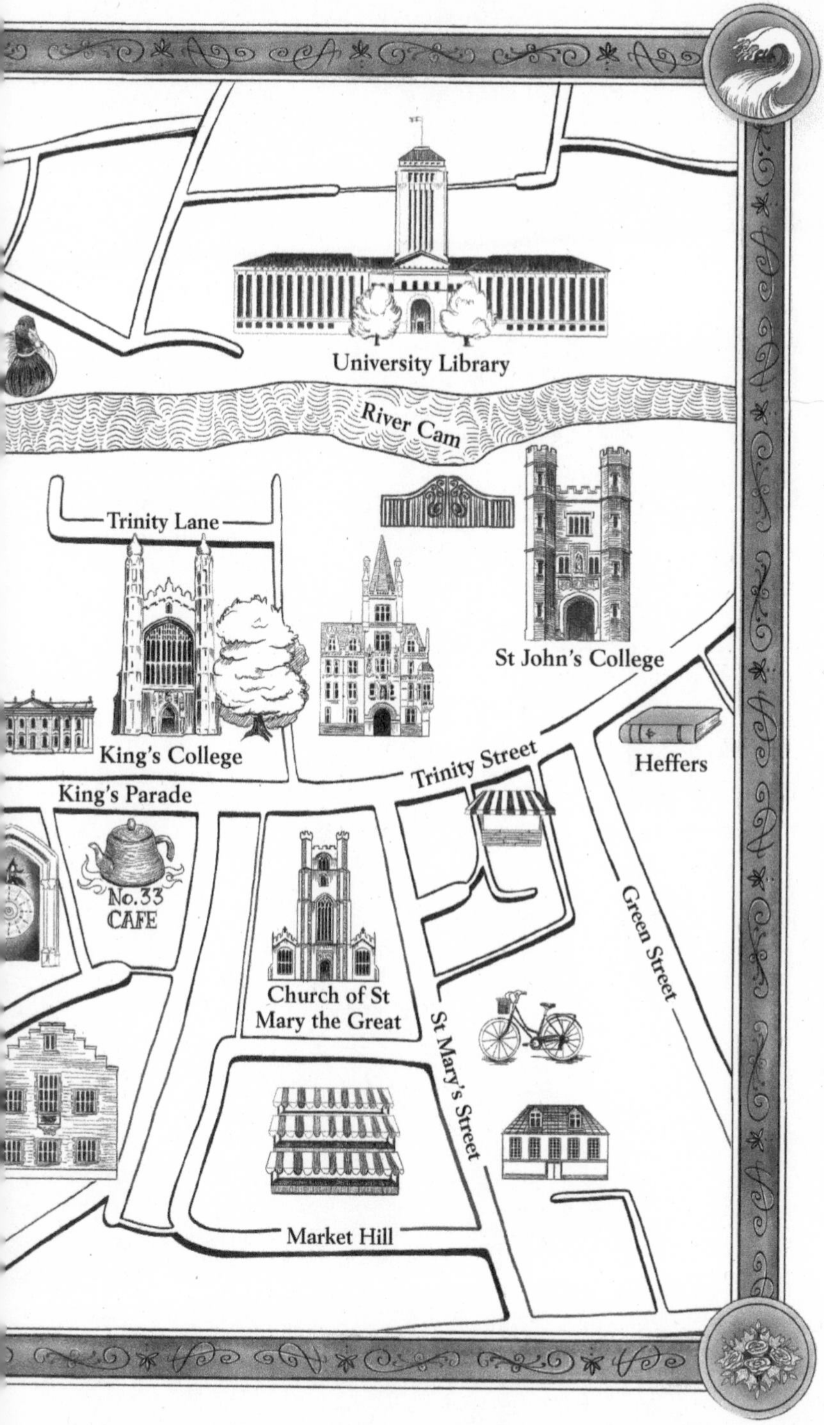
University Library
River Cam
Trinity Lane
St John's College
King's College
Trinity Street
Heffers
King's Parade
No.33
CAFE
Green Street
Church of St
Mary the Great
St Mary's Street
Market Hill

Prologue

It happened three years ago, but Goldie can still close her eyes and relive that night as if it were happening now. It had been a perfectly ordinary evening at first, no whisper on the breeze to indicate what was to come. The unwavering moon hung low in the star-speckled sky, seeming to graze the tops of the towering birch trees, and the rivers that twisted through the forests of Everwhere lay calm.

As usual, the sisters were scattered around in their favourite spots: Goldie perched in the low branches of her treasured oak tree in the glade teaching sisters of earth how to coax fresh green shoots from the ground; Scarlet theatrically setting alight fallen branches beside the lake, to the awed gasps of sisters of fire; and Liyana stood in the middle of the lake, showing sisters of water how to conjure waves and whirlpools from the depths.

They all heard the scream.

For a second, the shock of the scream pinned Goldie to the tree, but then she leapt down and ran, barefoot, across moss and stone, a dozen women and girls following in her wake. Fear rippled along the stream of sisters as they fled from the glade towards the source of the sound. For so long now, Everwhere had been a place of safety, a place to flourish, to find inspiration, courage and spirit. It was a long time since soldiers had roamed the forests; a long time since anyone had any reason to be afraid.

When Goldie reached the edge of the lake, the single scream had spread into a cacophony of chaos: arms waving, water splashing, a hundred wails and shrieks and howls piercing the air. And, at the centre of it all, two women were caught in a relentless rush of water, a frenzied vortex sucking everything into its core.

It took another second for Goldie to realize that one woman was Liyana, the other Scarlet. Her two beloved sisters: one drowning, the other trying to save her. Goldie had already plunged into the water by the time this realization hit, and she swam all the stronger for it, with every aching limb and gasping breath, trying to reach them.

But she was too late.

By the time Goldie reached the centre of the lake it was already calm, having swallowed Liyana into its depths and left Scarlet floating on its surface. Other sisters were already dragging Scarlet to the bank and Goldie followed. She administered the kiss of life – though she barely had breath left in her own body – and managed, with the assistance of her own life-giving touch, to bring Scarlet back from the brink.

As soon as she'd opened her eyes and coughed up the water from her lungs, Scarlet had asked for Liyana. It was Goldie who'd told her. Together they'd held each other and wept, though Scarlet didn't speak another word. Not that night, nor for a long time after.

It took them all a long time to accept what had happened, to understand that Liyana wasn't coming back. At least, not to Earth. They could, of course, still talk to her every night in Everwhere. But it wasn't the same. They couldn't see her, they couldn't hug her; and Liyana couldn't write and illustrate her stories, though she still told them. And for Kumiko – who'd adored Liyana just as deeply as her sisters did, yet, with no Grimm blood running through her veins, couldn't visit her lover in Everwhere – the loss was greatest of all.

If Kumiko was struck down by the deepest sorrow, Scarlet suffered the greatest guilt. She believed that she should've been able to save her sister and, no matter what anyone said, she couldn't let it go. Less than a year later, she fled Cambridge for lands unknown. And, despite every effort, Goldie had failed to locate her sister. And because Scarlet never returned to Everwhere, her disappearance for Goldie was, in some ways, a greater loss than Liyana's death.

3.33 a.m. – the Sisters Grimm

Every night, despite her overwhelming busy daily life running a women's shelter, Goldie spends at least an hour in Everwhere. It was her promise – to Leo, her sisters and herself – that she'd support and grow the community of Sisters Grimm around the world, to strengthen and empower them, to inspire and motivate them, for their own betterment and the betterment of the oppressed and marginalized everywhere.

Tonight, Goldie sits cross-legged on a rotten tree stump. Before her, a large semicircle of women and girls sit similarly cross-legged on the mossy forest floor. No one speaks; they all watch Goldie, waiting.

'Many of you have been here before, some of you are quite new, and a few of you have never been.' Goldie's voice echoes round the circle of oak trees – an audio effect assisted by her two dead sisters. And, as she speaks, the dead tree stump begins to show signs of life: the wood slowly shifting from grey to brown, the flaking bark softening, the new shoots of sapling branches twisting between Goldie's legs, wet bright green leaves unfurling from the fresh twigs. 'But the reason you're here, as I always say, is to find your strength, your power, your ability to be and do whatever it is you wish. To be at the mercy of nothing and no one, to triumph over all obstacles, especially your own doubts.'

Applause rises into the air and Goldie takes a breath. The number of Sisters Grimm gathering in Everwhere has been increasing with each passing year; sisters have been spreading the word, for they know there's strength in numbers. Lately, every month or so Goldie must uproot the trees and expand the circle. Tonight, she thinks, the crowd might even exceed five hundred.

As the cheer reverberates through the glade, Goldie gazes down at Luna, who sits cross-legged at her feet, grinning wildly and cheering louder than anyone. Goldie smiles down at her daughter who has, for as long as Goldie can remember, had an astonishing knack of one minute being a little girl and the next an adult. She's been bringing Luna to Everwhere every night (restricting it to Saturday nights once school started) since she was born. In the absence of Leo's physical presence, she'd reasoned that this place was the closest possible experience to being with him. Here, at least, even if she couldn't feel his touch or hear his voice, Luna could at least sense her father's spirit. And, sure enough, Luna had grown to love Everwhere more than any place on Earth. Here she'd learned to walk on moss and stone; she'd learned to set fire to dry sticks with her fingertips, to spread those fires with well-aimed gusts of wind and put them out with focused bursts of rain. Which was how

Goldie discovered that her daughter could control not only one element but them all.

'Tonight, as ever, we're going to practise a series of exercises, both physical and mental, to strengthen ourselves,' Goldie continues. 'So we might better protect the weak and vulnerable on Earth, which must always begin with protecting ourselves.'

A murmur of agreement runs through the crowd, peppered with nods, clapping and the occasional cheer. As usual, Luna does all three. On Earth, Luna is as moody and mercurial as any child, but in Everwhere her adoration of her mother is undiluted and her admiration absolute.

'It's time to get together in small groups – no less than ten, no more than twenty – of sisters who share the same elemental force. Those of you more expert in your skills can support those less experienced,' Goldie says. 'The space will be held, as usual, by myself and my sisters, Liyana and Bea. So no one need hold back their powers for fear of causing harm. On Earth you've been taught to make yourself small, to fit in, to smile, to be pleasing, to swallow your words, to shrink your emotions. In Everwhere you can practise doing exactly the opposite. And we will keep you safe, so let it all out: rage, fear, fury. Let it all out – let yourself go!'

At Goldie's feet, Luna whoops and cheers, sparks flying from her fingertips, fresh ivy springing up at her feet, a wild wind whipping through her hair, faint cracks of thunder and forks of lightning in the sky directly above her. The first Grimm girl to have command of all the elements with ever-increasing, perhaps infinite, power.

Goldie grins at her daughter, internally torn between pride and fear. She wishes, as she does every night, that Leo was here to witness his daughter's brilliance, but she tries her best to be both parents at once.

All this at only nine years old, she thinks now. *What will you be at nineteen?*

Chapter One

3.33 a.m. – Luna

What you've heard is true. The gates. The moon. The devil. For years I thought Ma was telling stories, making it all up, like the fairy tales she whispered to me at night, the ones written by my dead aunt Liyana. I still sit in her lap sometimes, pressed against her warmth while I wait for her words. I always wanted those stories; I loved them because they connected us.

I am a Sister Grimm, Ma would tell me. *And so are you.*

But lately something's changed. I've changed; I'm *different*. Now I don't snuggle with Ma so much because her stories aren't *my* stories anymore. At least . . . I realize now that I'm not just a Grimm; not just a sister but a soldier too. Like my dead father. Half a sister, half a soldier, born from a daughter of earth and a fallen star. At first, I didn't think it mattered, but then I started to notice how Ma seemed a little scared of me. Or *for* me – I'm never sure which. She pretends she isn't, but I know she is. I see the strange looks she gives me when she thinks I'm not looking.

I just wish I knew why.

7.56 a.m. – Goldie

'Luna, come on, we'll be late.' Goldie watches her daughter sitting at the kitchen table, eyes flitting from Luna's face to the untouched bowl of porridge.

'O-kay,' Luna says, scribbling in her notebook without looking up. Goldie's fingers twitch with the temptation to simply feed the last few spoonfuls into Luna's half-open mouth. But she holds back.

'Lu-Lu, please. You need to eat.' The thought of Luna hurtling around the playground on an empty stomach pushes Goldie's hand forward, but Luna's scowl stops her. 'What are you writing?'

Luna regards her mother suspiciously. 'A story.'

'Oh?' Goldie raises a curious eyebrow, trying to gauge the right balance between interest and respectful distance. 'Is it a story Aunt Liyana told you?'

Luna nods, but says nothing.

Goldie waits.

At last, Luna glances up. And, as ever when Goldie meets her daughter's eye, she's pinioned yet again by loss and longing for the man who looked so much like Luna. For her daughter was born in the image of Leo: blonde hair, broad smile, eyes a dozen different shades of green. Often, Goldie is so overcome by a sudden rush of sorrow at the sight of Luna that she has to turn away, force herself to focus on something else. Often, when she hugs her daughter she must do it with her eyes closed.

'Shall I tell you what it's about?' Luna asks, then absently – to Goldie's great relief – takes a spoonful of porridge.

Goldie tempers her grin. 'Yes, please.'

Luna looks thoughtful, as she always does when discussing her stories. It makes her, Goldie thinks, look like a wise old crone. It pleases Goldie deeply that Luna has a love of stories, that she spends so much time chatting with Liyana in Everwhere, taking dictation and often collaborating with her aunt to create tales together. That her daughter is so connected with her sister brings Goldie great joy, softening the edges of her grief.

'Perhaps one day you'll write a book with your aunt and publish it,' Goldie suggests.

Luna considers this, chewing the end of her pen. 'I like that idea,' she muses. 'But can dead people publish books?'

'Oh, yes,' says Goldie, happy to have pleased her daughter. Without thinking, she takes a spoonful of Luna's porridge and, before she knows it, she's taken another. She's not hungry, has already eaten a breakfast of her own, but food smothers the constant sadness threatening to burst forth, while soothing her rising anxiety. 'Plenty of authors are dead.'

Luna brightens. 'Really? I didn't know that. I've never met any other dead writers except Aunt Ana.'

Goldie laughs. 'No, that's not what I meant . . . I – anyway, weren't you about to tell me what the story's about?'

Luna nibbles on her pen again. 'It's about . . . you.'

'Oh,' Goldie says, a little unnerved. 'Really. Well, um, what happens to me in the story?'

Luna's eyes widen. 'I can't tell you that. Aunt Ana told me that writers should never discuss their works in progress. It dilutes the process. Didn't you know that?'

'No,' Goldie admits, charmed by Luna's phrasing. She never fails to be surprised when her daughter suddenly transforms from a girl into an adult. A few months ago, the school had informed Goldie that Luna is a prodigy, not that she was surprised. *You should see what she can do in Everwhere*, she'd thought. 'I didn't.'

'Well.' Luna folds her arms. 'You should.'

'All right.' Goldie nods. 'Noted. Now, will you please at least have one more mouthful of porridge?'

'Okay, okay,' says Luna, ignoring the bowl and returning to her notebook. As she writes, Luna absently reaches out with her free hand to rub the leaves of the juniper bonsai tree in the middle of the table. Instantly, the little tree's leaves perk up like a cat's ears, then begin to turn a lighter shade of green. Goldie watches, marvelling at her daughter's power. She's never been able to do anything like this, especially not so effortlessly. To elicit growth and transformation takes focus and concentration. *Effort*. Yet Luna does so much without even being aware of it.

Goldie glances at the clock. 'Right, let's go.' She stands, lifting the bowl and polishing off the remaining porridge on her way to the kitchen. Luna, head down over her notebook, doesn't move.

'Luna, please.'

Still her daughter ignores her. Goldie feels irritation rising and tries to suppress it.

'Lu-Lu, come on, we've got to go.'

Nothing.

'Luna!' Goldie snaps, losing the battle. 'Now! We'll be late!'

With a theatrical sigh, Luna snatches up her school bag, stuffs her notebook inside and stomps off in the direction of the front door.

'It's raining!' Goldie calls after her. 'Coat!'

On the table, in the wake of Luna's huff, the bonsai's leaves flutter as if blown by a sudden breeze. Goldie watches as, one by one, the leaves shrivel and drop from their branches onto the tablecloth.

They live in the little flat above the women's shelter and must pass each of the eight residents' rooms to leave the house. The rooms aren't always occupied, but it's rare that one lies empty for more than a few days. If the women and children are already up and milling about, this takes a while, but usually Goldie manages to usher her daughter out quickly enough to avoid much delay. If it was up to Luna, she'd stop at every room and engage each occupant in conversation, enquiring as to their well-being, their hopes for the future. It's highly impractical, of course, but Goldie is still proud to see how deeply Luna cares, how she befriends every arriving child. The children are traumatized, to varying degrees, though not as much as the women, who've taken the brunt of the abuse. But, even if they've not been beaten, the children have endured years of suffering. Yet Luna always has a healing effect on them and, after only a few hours of play, they usually come out of their shells, a little stronger, a little happier.

If Luna had been an ordinary nearly-ten-year-old, Goldie would never have considered raising her in a women's refuge, but it became apparent soon after Luna was born that she was very far from ordinary. When she'd slipped out onto the hospital bed after the final agonizing push, the midwife who'd caught her had let out a little cry of astonishment. When she'd rested the baby on Goldie's chest, the dazed new mother had gazed down at the triplicate scars of crescent moons and stars etched on her daughter's shoulder blade. The first time Luna suckled at Goldie's breast, her throat glowed as if she'd just swallowed sunlight. Sparks showed at her fingertips as soon as she uncurled her tiny fists; she'd created spontaneous waves in her bathtub whenever Goldie bathed her, and inadvertently set fire to flammable objects so often that Goldie had to start hiding toys, and especially books.

Every day while Luna is at school Goldie spends time with each of the women – all Sisters Grimm – encouraging them to come to Everwhere, where she can reinvigorate their strength, teaching them skills and powers they didn't know they possessed. A volunteer therapist comes one day a week and a few retired women help with the day-to-day running of the shelter. But Goldie does far more than anyone else. Sometimes she wonders if Luna might resent it, but she seems only to relish it.

'Do you have everything?' Goldie asks, as they reach the school gates.

'Yes, Ma,' Luna says, glancing in the direction of a gaggle of chattering girls. 'I've got everything. I'm fine. Okay? Now—'

'I wish you'd eaten more,' Goldie says. 'What about a biscuit before you go in?' She starts fishing through her coat pockets. 'I'm sure I've got—'

'I told you, Ma, I'm *fine*.' Luna starts to pull off her coat, an unnecessary accessory even though Goldie insists on it, since rain always seems to slip off her anyway.

'All right, all right, I'm just . . .' Goldie leans in to kiss Luna's head, but her daughter dodges the kiss and slips away to join her friends.

'Mrs Clayton? May I have a word?'

Goldie turns to see Luna's teacher looming behind her.

'Oh, hello, Ms Walker,' she says. It seems silly to address her like this; she's not *her* teacher, after all, but Goldie is never sure what else to say. She's also lost the will to tell Miss Walker that she's not married and, even given that impossible eventuality, she certainly wouldn't become a 'Mrs' anything. Swallowing the desire to lecture the teacher on the finer points of feminism, she smiles. 'How lovely to—'

'Mrs Clayton,' Miss Walker interrupts, never one to waste time on pleasantries. 'We need to talk about Luna. Will you . . .'

Goldie's porridge-heavy stomach lurches. Miss Walker keeps talking, but Goldie doesn't hear a word. She refocuses.

'I'm sorry, what did you just say?'

'I said –' Miss Walker looks irritated at being forced to repeat herself – 'will you be able to attend a meeting with myself and the head teacher at four p.m. tomorrow?'

'Yes, of course.' Goldie thinks of the sparks at Luna's fingertips. Of her ability to make things grow and, more worryingly, wither. Her tendency to levitate ever so slightly whenever she's excited. Has she done this in school? Do they *know*? 'But . . . I wonder, um, might you be able to give me some idea what it's about in advance? Should I be concerned?'

Miss Walker pauses. And in that moment – seeing the tightening of the teacher's jaw and the concern in her eyes – Goldie realizes that she shouldn't simply be concerned; she should be scared.

Chapter Two

10.28 a.m. – Goldie

'Social services?' Teddy repeats the words for the dozenth time, perhaps attempting to erase reality with a reverse conjuring spell. 'But . . . why?'

'I told you, I don't *know*.' Goldie wipes her eyes ineffectually with the back of her hand. She's trying not to snap at her brother, who's been nothing but kindness since she collapsed in tears on the dilapidated sofa of the communal living room – the one usually reserved for receiving new arrivals to the refuge – providing her with endless cups of undrunk tea and plates of uneaten biscuits. Not even a chocolate Hobnob could take the edge off at a time like this. 'They wouldn't tell me,' she says again. 'I suppose they don't want to give me advance warning or any chance to prepare a defence. Surprise is their mode of attack.'

'Then why did the teacher tell you?'

Goldie crosses her legs under her and reaches for a cushion to hug. 'No idea.' She shrugs. 'An uncharacteristic bout of kindness? Maybe they have to give just enough notice to be sure you're available but not enough that you can leg it.'

Teddy considers this. 'And she didn't even give you a hint as to what it might be about? They don't call in social services for nothing.'

Goldie, who'd been plucking a stray thread from the

cushion, now glares at her brother. 'No shit, Sherlock,' she snaps, forgetting her resolve. 'I know that. And no, I've been going over the conversation again and again, and the bloody woman didn't give me a single fucking clue as to why they want to take Luna away from me, all right?'

Teddy sighs. 'Oh, sis.' He stands from his chair, steps round the coffee table and sits on the sofa beside his sister. It sags beneath his weight, an unwelcome reminder that the refuge is in dire need of renovations and repairs. The sofa is the least of it. 'Don't jump to the worst. They're not going to—' He tries to pull Goldie into a hug, but she shrugs him off.

'They're not going to sit me down for a cuppa and a chat, Ted.' Goldie clutches the cushion. 'This is the fucking social services. It's their job to take kids away; don't be so naive.'

'Come on, Gee-Gee,' Teddy says, hoping to soothe her with the pet name he'd called her before he could say her name. 'They take kids from abusive, neglectful parents.' He slips his arm around her shoulder. 'And that's the last thing you are. Quite the opposite, in fact.'

Goldie blinks at him with puffy eyelids. 'What's that supposed to mean?'

'Well . . .' Teddy treads carefully. 'I mean . . . you're the flip side of neglectful, aren't you? You spend half your life taking care of Luna and the other half taking care of the women and children who come to the shelter. No one could accuse you of—'

'Maybe that's what they're concerned about,' Goldie interrupts. 'That a women's refuge is an unsafe place to raise a child. After all, they've got no idea that this place is protected by . . . spells and the strength of our sisters. If I told them about us, about me, they'd lock me up and throw away the key.'

'I don't think they do that sort of thing anymore,' Teddy suggests. 'It's not the nineteen-fifties, thank God. Anyway, if they did lock you up, you'd only need to escape to Everwhere and never come back. Speaking of which, Luna could do the same if they took her a—'

Goldie starts to sob again, gulping air and spluttering words. 'Wh-what the hell are you t-talking about? I-I can't raise Luna in Everwhere – how would I educate her? What would we eat? And we'd never see you again for a start, let alone the fact that I can't abandon the shelter – that's the most stupid thing you've ever said. We wouldn't survive a week in Everwhere. You might as well say we could run away to the Amazon!'

'Sorry,' Teddy says, abashed. 'I didn't mean . . . I was only trying to be helpful.'

Goldie drops her head into her hands. 'I know, I know, I'm sorry. It's not your fault. It's just, I'm just . . . terrified. I've spent the last nine years doing everything I can to protect her and now . . .'

His arm still over her shoulder, Teddy tries again to pull his sister into a hug. He wants to hold her as she once held him, when he was small enough, comforting him after their mother died, taking care of him every day since. This time she lets him.

'Look, sis, you're the most loving, dedicated, all-consumingly caring mother I've ever encountered – you put our mum to shame. There's no way anyone is going to take little Lu-Lu from you. And, if they try, I won't let them. Okay?'

With her face pressed into her brother's chest, Goldie nods. But she's still terrified and she doesn't know what to do.

'I just wish Leo was here,' she sniffs. 'He *should* be here.'

'I know,' Teddy says sorrowfully. 'I wish he was too.'

11.57 p.m. – Goldie

Goldie sits with her back pressed into the corner of the sofa in her own flat, Liyana's Tarot cards in her lap. A large glass of red wine rests on the coffee table beside an already half-empty bottle. Luna is asleep in her bedroom, but Goldie knows there's no point in going to bed since she won't sleep tonight. In a feat of Herculean strength she'd managed to pretend that nothing was wrong, had acted (almost) normal with Luna, and if her daughter noticed anything strange she didn't say anything. Goldie forced herself not to squeeze Luna tight, nor stare at her for too long, though she was desperate to do both. She forced herself to chat and smile and make jacket potatoes with baked beans and cheese (Luna's favourite) as if life was perfectly normal and she wasn't teetering on the edge of a nervous breakdown.

But as soon as Goldie was alone and free to hurl herself headlong into said breakdown, she did. Three hours later, after devouring a tub of ice cream, a plate of Hobnobs and half a bottle of wine, while simultaneously working her way through an entire loo roll, Goldie feels nauseous and exhausted. Her stomach hurts, her head hurts, her nose hurts, her eyes hurt. But what hurts most of all, as always, is her heart.

Glancing down at the Tarot cards, Goldie feels a pang of longing in her bruised heart for her sisters. She'd once thought that a body could only hold so much loss and sorrow before it simply imploded and the unfortunate soul died of a broken heart. But she's since learned that the human body is cruelly strong and able to absorb what seems an unbearable amount of pain and yet still keep functioning.

'Oh, Ana.' Goldie strokes a finger over the facing card: the Three of Cups. *Friendship, camaraderie, celebration.* 'I wish you were here. I know, I know.' She sighs, continuing as if Liyana were sitting beside her now. 'I can visit you in Everwhere; I can talk with you whenever I wish. But it's not the same. No one reads the cards like you . . .'

A lump rises in her throat as her thoughts pass, immediately and inevitably, to Scarlet. The sister she can't even speak to, let alone see or touch. The sister who might be living in Australia, or dead, for all she knows. Yet, if the latter, then surely Scarlet's soul would return to Everwhere and Goldie would find her there . . . So Goldie still holds out hope that one day she will meet her missing sister again.

After thinking of Scarlet, Goldie's thoughts don't pass to her beloved Leo, because they never really leave him. Her awareness of his absence, and her longing for his resurrection is ever present, and a portion of her mind always dwells on him, like a tune she can't stop humming. Goldie's love for Luna's father is the soundtrack to her life.

Absently, her hand slips from the cards and into the pocket of her hoodie. She pulls out a small crystal skull. The stone is black but flecked with starbursts of white, its chin protruding with carved teeth, and its deep eye sockets, though empty, seem to be watching. It belongs, along with the Tarot cards and a small wooden statue of Mami Wata, to Liyana. However, since she has no use for material things in her current form she bequeathed them to Goldie. All Liyana's illustrations had remained with Kumiko, who'd generously given Goldie and Luna a small collection before returning to Japan to live with her parents. Now and then, Kumiko sends Goldie texts: most recently a short video of herself and her new girlfriend. They looked happy and Goldie had felt glad for them although, deep down, she'd also felt betrayed. After three years frozen in grief, Kumiko had moved on, and Goldie, grieving for nearly a decade now and still nowhere close to letting go, couldn't help but think it'd been too soon.

I'm pleased, Liyana had said when Goldie finally plucked up the courage to confess the contents of the text. *Really I am. I love her deeply and I certainly don't want anyone I love to suffer.*

'You're not jealous?' Goldie had asked.

Liyana laughed, the sound of a river rushing over rocks. *Of course I'm jealous. I might be dead, but I'm not a saint!* She paused. *But that doesn't mean I don't want her to fall in love again. So I know, given that Leo loved you more than life, he would want the very same for you.*

Goldie shakes off the memory as she gazes at the little stone skull. 'You're a curious one, aren't you?' she says, almost expecting an answer. When none comes, she sets it down on the cushion beside her and returns to Liyana's cards.

'Yes, I know,' Goldie says, as if her sister were sitting beside her. 'You're with me in spirit.' She reaches for the glass and takes another gulp of wine. 'It's a shame spirits can't drink booze – not that you're missing anything; it tastes like piss – but I feel like such a loser drinking alone.'

With a sigh, Goldie shuffles the pack, then deals five cards onto the coffee table. The Lovers: a man and woman, attired in heart-embroidered clothing, embrace as they stand atop a swan that flies over a field of flowers. A parade of sprites dance joyously around them. *Love, partnership, trust*. Judgement: a baby mermaid sits in the cup of a flower, held aloft from the ground between two decorated trees that grow together into a canopy over the child. *Rebirth, resurrection, awakening, mental clarity*. The Moon: a purple-haired wolf standing at a river's edge howls up at a fat yellow moon. Towering white trees flank the river, their trunks encircled by a pair of two-headed snakes. *Prophetic dreams, illusions, the unconscious mind*. The Five of Wands: four winged, sharp-toothed, long-beaked creatures with snaking tails clash their wands like swords in battle. A fifth, filigreed wand rises up between them. *Discord, conflict, struggle*. The Tower: a growling stone beast guards the crumbling tower, flames roar from the windows, licking the sky. Blown by a ferocious grey wind, vultures soar above the people tumbling to their deaths. *Loss, sudden change, devastation*.

Strangely, the words that follow the pictures materialize unbidden in her mind, as if Liyana is indeed with Goldie now, whispering into her ear, telling the story. It is a story of love and loss and something strange and terrible to come – but exactly what isn't clear. The story is only told in broad, abstract terms, painted with great sweeping brushstrokes so that Goldie views it through a fog and the general effect is muted. Still, in its wake she's left with a bitter, unshakeable sense of foreboding. Which can only mean one thing. Social services are going to take her daughter away.

'Oh, Luna.' Tears fill Goldie's eyes again, blurring her sight. 'My Luna.'

Of course she can't sleep, not after that. So Goldie sits on the sofa, plucking at threads in the cushion while gazing mournfully out at the fat yellow moon hanging just outside the kitchen window.

If only Goldie could sleep she could travel to Everwhere, talk with her sisters, seek comfort and reassurance. But she'll have to wait. So she thinks of Leo and imagines how it would feel to have him beside her now. To touch him, be held by him, weep against his chest, kiss him . . . Although the loss of Leo has smoothed over the years to an acute ache that sits in the centre of her ribcage like a hand always pressed to her back, a little extra weight on her heart, sometimes it will suddenly constrict her chest. Goldie imagines that her love and longing for Leo is like a pendulum in a clock. It's what keeps her ticking. Without it, she would simply stop.

If she loses Luna though, the person she loves more than anything or anyone, her one remaining piece of Leo, Goldie knows that she won't be able to live. The body may be able to contain a great deal of sorrow, but losses are too great for anybody to bear. Even a Sister Grimm.

Chapter Three

3.59 p.m. – Goldie

Goldie barely slept last night and now feels as if she's dragging herself through quicksand and blinking through fog. It's been years since she's been up all night, not since the early months of breastfeeding Luna, and even then she'd usually snatch twenty minutes' sleep now and then. But last night all she did was clutch the cushion, stare at the moon and weep.

When Luna woke just after six o'clock, Goldie had tried vainly to pull herself together and make breakfast and, mercifully, Luna had been so consumed by her own thoughts that she hadn't noticed her mother's puffy eyes and clumsiness. Goldie had crawled through the rest of the day, avoiding her usual visits to the shelter's residents, closing her office door and telling Teddy she was engaged with meetings. Then she'd plunged her face in cold water, applied copious amounts of concealer, put on her most motherly outfit: baggy tweed skirt (necessitated by years of emotional eating), cream knitted jumper and brown suede shoes.

Then, with pounding heart and shaky step, Goldie had walked to Luna's school.

Two days ago: 11.45 a.m. – Luna

She had felt him watching her from across the room. And Luna found, as she focused on the increasing heat of his eyes on her back, that she could feel his emotions too: concern, worry, fear . . . And then, when she really tuned in, she could hear his thoughts: *Who the hell would do such hideous things to a little girl? Isn't her father dead? Not her mother, surely not? Unless, perhaps, she's involved in a religious cult, or something unnatural* . . . It was interesting, this recent ability to hear other people's thoughts – though frustratingly it didn't apply to her mother or aunts, or any of her Sisters Grimm.

Luna turned then, swinging her bare legs over the balance beam, to catch her gym teacher's eye. Mr Barnes stood across the hall, helping Alice Jago climb back onto the pommel horse while staring at Luna with barely concealed horror. Luna glanced down at her left shoulder to see that her T-shirt had slipped a little, revealing a few of her scars. Her heart sank. Usually Luna took precautions to ensure that no one saw her scars, being especially careful in changing rooms, avoiding strappy dresses even in the height of summer, wearing a wetsuit in the swimming pool, citing sensitive skin. But this time, foolishly, she'd forgotten. That morning she'd forgotten to pack her T-shirt for PE and had borrowed Alice's extra one, forgetting that her friend was two sizes bigger.

Mr Barnes, after checking Alice was safe, beckoned Luna over. When she didn't budge, he starting crossing the gymnasium towards her.

'Shit,' Luna muttered. 'Shit.'

If only she could transport herself to Everwhere right now. If only it was night, if only she was asleep or had access to a nearby gate. But there were no special gates on the school grounds and the sun was high in the sky.

A moment later it was too late. Mr Barnes was standing before her.

'Luna, I'd like you to come with me, please.'

Luna blinked innocently. 'I've not finished my routine yet.'

'That doesn't matter,' he said, voice soft with sympathy. 'I'd like you to come with me right now.'

Luna gripped the balance beam with both legs. 'Where?'

Mr Barnes hesitated. 'We need to pay a visit to the school nurse.'

4.03 p.m. – Goldie

Although she wants to sink into the floor, Goldie perches on the edge of the hard wooden chair with an obsequious smile fixed on her face. She *hates* visits to the head teacher's office, since they make her feel thirteen again instead of nearly thirty. And Goldie was in her own headmaster's office *a lot* at thirteen. For lying, stealing, truanting, shirking her homework, plagiarizing other students' homework . . . And then, a year later, her mother died and she'd had to raise Teddy alone and things had only grown worse. Thankfully, Luna has been an impeccable student – a prodigy, so her teachers say – so Goldie has avoided the office until this moment.

Goldie had been expecting to face a panel of social services interrogators, but the room holds only her and the head teacher, Mr Gillies, who, although Goldie has been sitting in the chair for several long minutes, continues to shuffle papers on his desk. Finally, unable to stand the wait any longer, Goldie coughs and Mr Gillies looks up.

'Ah, yes,' he says, as if he's only just noticed her presence. 'Thank you for coming, Mrs Clayton.'

Goldie nods.

Now Mr Gillies coughs. He's a short bespectacled man, bearing more than a passing resemblance to a hobbit. And Goldie can tell that he's as embarrassed by the situation as she is scared, which helps to ease her fears just a little.

He coughs again, then pulls a handkerchief from his pocket and begins to wipe his glasses. 'So, um, I've asked you here to talk about Luna.'

No shit, Goldie almost says. *And here was I thinking you were about to ask me out on a date*. Instead she nods thoughtfully, patiently resisting the urge to reach across the desk and strangle him. She remembers her own headmaster as an ogre of a man, tall and terrifying, in whose presence one might very easily faint or cry. Mr Gillies, on the other hand, is a soft, bumbling figure permanently clad in hand-knitted cardigans.

'Well . . .' Mr Gillies returns his glasses to his nose, then clasps his hands together, as if about to beg Goldie's forgiveness. 'The thing is . . . The thing is this . . .'

Out with it! Goldie wants to scream. *Out with it, for fuck's sake!* Instead she says, in what she hopes is a calm, controlled tone, 'Miss Walker led me to understand that you'd, um, called in . . .' She falters, as if saying the words will conjure them into the room. 'S-social services.'

'Well, yes . . .' Mr Gillies examines his fingernails. 'That is to say, we've informed them, but . . . perhaps I should explain why we . . . So, Luna was participating in a physical education class a couple of days ago. And, well . . .' He stops and takes a deep breath. 'It seems that . . . It seems that . . .'

He takes another deep breath. Goldie grips the arms of the chair, thinking it's lucky she isn't Scarlet or the chair would be aflame by now.

'Well . . .' Mr Gillies gathers himself, ready to take another run at it. 'Well, it seems that Mr Barnes, the physical education teacher, observed something rather unusual that gave him great cause for concern . . .'

Goldie exhales, filled with sudden and glorious relief. 'Oh! Yes, of course, now I know what it is you're worried about.'

'You do?' Mr Gillies looks slightly shocked, as if he'd been expecting Goldie to deny everything. 'Well, in that case—'

'Yes,' Goldie interrupts, before the situation escalates. 'You're talking about the scars on her back, aren't you? Naturally, they've raised concerns before.' Goldie smiles sympathetically. 'Mr Barnes isn't the first to see them, though Luna has always done her best to cover them up. She's embarrassed – you know what kids are like.'

At this, Mr Gillies nods a little wearily, as if he only wishes he didn't.

'But the fact is,' Goldie hurries on, 'she's had them since birth. The doctors were unable to explain them at the time but wrote a full report testifying to the fact that Luna had been born with the scars and that there wasn't any external cause.'

Goldie sits back in the wooden chair, awaiting the head teacher's bumbling apologies. When he says nothing but instead looks increasingly mortified, Goldie feels her stomach drop. In a vain attempt to act as if everything's fine, she starts to stand.

'Well, if that's everything, then I suppose I'll be—'

But Mr Gillies gives a slight, regretful shake of his head. 'No, please sit, Mrs Clayton. I'm afraid that's not all.'

In spite of the dire circumstances, or perhaps because of them, Goldie feels a flash of annoyance at his dual assumption that she's married and has taken her husband's name. She wants to shake him and shout, *Did the feminists fight for nothing? What century do you think we're living in?!* Instead she rights herself in her chair, assumes another fake smile and takes a deep breath, trying to calm her racing pulse.

'I'm sorry, Mrs Clayton,' Mr Gillies mumbles, eyes cast down as if he wishes his desk would swallow him whole. 'But, as I was about to say . . . I'm aware of the previous involvement with social services and—'

Goldie takes another deep breath, but it's no use. 'There was no "involvement", Mr Gillies,' she snaps, feeling that she's already a defendant in court. 'Any concerns that might have arisen were allayed by the doctors at the time and nothing has arisen since. I'd presumed social services would have access to such files, so I fail to see why the issue is being raised again.' Folding her arms across her chest, Goldie hopes to hell that her little speech has resolved this ridiculous issue.

Mr Gillies nods slowly. 'Yes, I understand that, Mrs Clayton,' he says, as if trying to placate a hysteric. 'And I'm certainly not suggesting that there was anything untoward back then . . .'

Goldie sits forward again, heart still thumping. 'I should hope not.'

'Indeed not,' he says, not taking his eyes from the papers on his desk. 'But this time it's different.'

Goldie tries and fails to calm herself. 'H-how so?'

'Well . . .' Forcing himself to look up, Mr Gillies fixes his gaze on a spot on the wall above Goldie's head. 'The thing is this . . . So, we compared what Mr Barnes witnessed with the photographs taken at the time of Luna's birth and there has been an, um, significant increase in the number of scars since then. She was born with three, yes? And now it seems she has five. An increase of, um, sixty-six per cent, I believe . . . so . . .'

'F-five?' Goldie stammers. *How did she not know this? How could she not have seen it?* Luna is a very private person, certainly: dressing herself since the age of four, not letting her mother bathe her since turning eight, never parading around the flat naked as Teddy used to do until he hit puberty. Even then, it's horrifying to Goldie that she hadn't noticed Luna's scars were spreading. But, more importantly: what the hell is happening to her?

Oblivious to Goldie's panic attack, Mr Gillies nods solemnly. 'So, you . . . you see why we needed to contact the authorities.'

Goldie grips the edge of the chair till her knuckles turn white. 'Or you might have come to me first to discuss it before escalating the matter and potentially causing a catastrophe out of nothing.' She narrows her eyes and drops her voice. 'Unless, of course, you're suggesting that I am scarring my own daughter?'

Mr Gillies stares at his desk, a deep blush rising in his neck. 'Now, now, Mrs Clayton, let's not jump to conclusions. It could equally be another child, or perhaps Luna herself. Which is why an investigation must be opened into the matter. After all, even if it proves to be the latter, self-harm is something to be taken seriously—'

'Yes, it certainly should be taken seriously, but not in an atmosphere of threat and interrogation. How effective do you think that will be?' Goldie stands. She needs to see Luna right now, needs to hold her girl tight and never let her go. 'I've had just about enough of being treated like a criminal, Mr Gillies. I want to see Luna. Where is she?'

'Please, Mrs Clayton, please sit.' Mr Gillies clasps his hands. 'That's not what's happening here. We've only arranged for you and Luna to be interviewed separately by social workers on Monday. I'm sure you'll agree that's a perfectly reasonable response to the situation.'

'Perfectly reasonable?' Goldie shrieks. 'Perfectly reasonable?'

'And until that time,' Mr Gillies ploughs on, 'we ask that you don't discuss the matter with her. If you try to influence or prepare Luna's answers, they will be able to tell and you'll only create an environment of suspicion, which, I'm sure you'll agree, it would be better to avoid.'

'As opposed to the environment of trust and confidence that you're creating,' Goldie says, eyes hot with tears. *Do not cry, do not cry, do* not *cry.* 'I – I . . .'

And then, despite all her resolutions, Goldie descends into incoherent hysteria. The head teacher watches as she sobs and shrieks, swelling his office with storm clouds of despair. Hiding behind his desk, mumbling calming noises and waving his handkerchief vaguely in her direction, he gazes longingly at the clock, wishing it was already six o'clock and that he was strolling by the river with his Highland terrier, Binky.

4.33 p.m. – Luna

Ma isn't telling me something. I can tell by the way she walks too fast and avoids meeting my eye. When I ask her what's going on, she only says, 'Oh, nothing, don't worry. It's fine, I'm fine.' Like all adults do whenever they think you're too young to know stuff. It's probably got something to do with stupid Mr Barnes and that stupid school nurse. I refused to show them anything, told them they couldn't make me, that it was an issue of privacy and human rights – that shut them up – but it didn't matter. It was too late. He'd already seen enough.

Chapter Four

12.33 a.m. – Goldie, Liyana & Bea

Goldie sits in the boughs of her favourite tree, listening to her sisters chattering away with their life advice. Rather, she's half listening to them and mostly worrying about Luna, biting her lip, kicking her feet out, twisting her hands in her lap. *Why are the scars multiplying? What the hell is happening?* So far, neither of her sisters has come up with an adequate answer – certainly nothing that would placate social services – and Goldie is, though she knows it's unreasonable, feeling increasingly frustrated.

Before I forget: I've got a story for Luna, Liyana interrupts herself. *Did you remember the notebook?*

'I did,' Goldie says, pulling herself away from her thoughts. 'Meaning I had to drag myself out of bed and walk to a gate to bring this thing, instead of just falling asleep.'

So why didn't you let her come? Liyana asks. *I thought Saturday night was—*

'She needed to sleep,' Goldie says. 'It's been a bit of a stressful week, don't you think?' She sighs, suddenly irritated. 'So, you going to tell me this story or not?'

Bea's laughter splits through the air, startling a nearby raven that lifts itself from a higher branch, beating its wings with annoyance. *No pressure then, Ana. But it had better not be shit, or you'll incur her sisterly wrath.*

Goldie looks up, eyes narrowed. 'What are you gabbing about? I'm not wrathful.'

Of course not – what was I thinking? You're tranquillity itself.

'It's not my fault I'm churned up,' Goldie retorts. 'You would be too, if you were being interrogated by social services on Monday morning.'

Bea laughs again, a sound like the snapping of twigs. *Oh, sis, you know it doesn't take anything more than the wind changing to stir me up. I was born wrathful.*

'That's nothing to boast about,' Goldie says. 'You've got a helluva temper.'

I do and I'm proud of it. All women should have one. Men do and no one judges them for it – but we're raised to be sweet, pretty, meek. And vulnerable. It's dangerous. Anger is self-protection. Anger is a feminist act.

'Yeah.' Goldie sighs. 'That's your excuse and you're sticking to it.' Still, she can't help but think of the women at the shelter and how much better their lives would've been if only they'd been taught to stand up for themselves earlier.

'Why don't you have any idea where Scarlet is?' Goldie changes the subject. 'I thought you were all-seeing, all-knowing. Yet you can't find our sister.'

We can only see those who are unaware they're being watched, Liyana says. *Not those who are hiding. And she is definitely hiding.*

'It's not fair,' Goldie says, conscious that she sounds like a petulant child. 'That she escapes, leaving the rest of us to hold the fort, to spend our lives, and deaths, taking—'

This elicits Bea's laughter again.

'—taking care of others, while she's gallivanting around the world doing God knows what.'

I hardly think she's living the high life in Rio, Liyana counters. *More likely the poor thing is riddled by guilt, addicted to meth, sleeping in a gutter somewhere.*

'Oh, come on!' Goldie snaps. 'Don't be so dramatic.' Though, in truth, she's often been left sleepless when imagining such fates for Scarlet herself. 'Anyway, I'm only saying . . . it's not as if I didn't feel . . . I was consumed by guilt too, you know. I wanted to run away, or crawl into a dark hole for a while, but I couldn't, could I?'

How many times do I have to tell you? Liyana says. *It wasn't your fault. Nor Scarlet's. I don't blame you; I never have.*

'I know.' Goldie plucks at the bark of the tree and thinks, with a pang of longing, of Leo. 'I know. But . . .'

You could get away if you hadn't decided to be such a bloody martyr. Bea's voice is sharp as the point of a stick pressed to the neck. *Having Leo's kid was a curious choice, but I get it. Still, no one made you open a women's refuge. And now you're moaning about how overwhelming it is – what did you expect?*

'Thanks for the sympathy.' Goldie scowls. 'And I'm not a martyr. I—'

You spend your life helping others and never ask for any help yourself, Bea retorts. *You're the very definition of a martyr. And I'm warning you, you won't be able to—*

'The world is in crisis, if you hadn't noticed,' Goldie interrupts in turn. 'We need everyone to take care of each other. If everyone was as selfish as you, we might as well bring on the apocalypse right now!'

Selfish?! A twig snaps from the tree and scratches Goldie's cheek. *Who's spending her afterlife supporting the empowerment of every stray sister who comes here? Eh?*

'That's only cos you're stuck here,' Goldie grumbles, hand to her cheek. 'If you were alive, you wouldn't waste five minutes of your precious time helping anyone!'

Bullshit!

Stop it! Liyana's words crash like a great wave upon the shore. *Stop it, right now. What's got into you both? You're supposed to be two of the most powerful sisters in this life and the next, this world and the other, and here you are, acting like a couple of toddlers fighting over a toy.*

'She started it,' Goldie sniffs, calmed. 'When she killed the man I loved.'

Oh, that's hardly fair. Liyana's voice is soft now, like surf lapping on sand. *She'd been brainwashed; it wasn't Bea's fault any more than it was your fault for not saving me.*

'I suppose so,' Goldie huffs, rubbing the welt on her cheek where the twig had drawn blood. 'I concede she's not pure evil now, but she's still mean as a snake.'

And you're a mess of martyrdom, Bea huffs back, *headed straight for a nervous breakdown. And what good will you be to anyone then? I tell you, martyred mothers are the worst, no fun at all.* She blows a conciliatory warm breeze across her sister's face. *When was the last time you had fun?*

Goldie folds her arms, silent.

That long, eh? I thought so.

'I have fun,' Goldie protests. 'I have plenty of fun.'

You do? Bea's laughter cracks through the glade. *Doing what? Watching crap on Netflix with a bottle of wine and a tub of ice cream?* She pauses and the wind whips up. *When was the last time you laughed? When did you go out by yourself? Or on a date?*

'Shut up.'

It's been twelve years.

'Eleven and a half.'

A light rain starts to fall. *I'm afraid I'm with Bea on this,* Liyana whispers. *It's time.*

A sudden rush of indignation floods Goldie's bloodstream and she jumps down from the tree, notebook in hand. 'I came here for comfort,' she says sharply. 'Not a fucking lecture.'

We're only saying, Liyana tries again, *that you need to start doing some things for yourself, or you're headed for burnout. And perhaps you should learn to be a little more selfish. Is it selfish, after all, if it's for the greater good?*

Goldie starts walking, already wishing herself back to Earth, already picturing the gate: the ornate disused entrance to the Botanic Garden on Trumpington Road. She can already feel herself fading at the edges, with her sisters' protests swirling around her like smoke, when the thought comes unbidden: *If only I was Scarlet, if only I could disappear. Just for a moment. Just for an hour, a day, a week, a year . . .*

This floods Goldie with guilt – what about Luna? What about the women whose safety is in her hands? And she suppresses it, so quickly and completely that, in the next moment, it's as if she'd never had the thought at all.

7.28 p.m. – Goldie & Luna

'I've got a story for you,' Goldie says. After storming off last night, she'd returned a few minutes later to apologize and ask Liyana to share the story, writing it down to recount later. Determined that their final evening together before the interrogation will be special, Goldie's been waiting all day to tell Luna this tale.

'All right,' Goldie says, snuggling down into bed beside Luna. 'Are you ready?'

Luna nods, her feet tapping under the duvet with excitement. Goldie swallows a smile, then takes a deep breath and assumes a solemn tone.

'There was once a girl, luminous as a star. She was born between one world and another, fashioned from fire and ice, moonlight and fog, blood and bone. She was a child of the earth and the sky. And her name was Estella—'

Luna sits up. 'That's my middle name.'

'I know.'

'Is she *me*?'

Goldie cups her daughter's chin. 'Why don't you wait and see?'

'O-kay,' says Luna reluctantly, snuggling into Goldie's armpit. She waits. 'Go on then, you can carry on now.'

'Thanks for the permission, sweetheart,' Goldie says. 'But now you've made me lose my place.' Returning to the notebook, she feels her daughter roll her eyes. 'All right, all right, give me a minute—'

Luna sighs. 'Do you have Alzheimer's?'

Goldie looks down at Luna's upturned face, frowning. 'What?'

Luna sighs a deeper sigh. 'You know, the disease when you forget everything because you're so old.'

'Hold on.' Goldie laughs. 'I'm not *that* old.'

Luna emits a disbelieving huff. 'Ma, you're *thirty*.'

Goldie gives her daughter a squeeze that is mostly affectionate. 'You say that like I'm three hundred and thirty-three.'

Luna gives a little shrug, as if suggesting that there's hardly a great deal of difference between the two figures.

'Anyway,' Goldie protests. 'I'm not thirty till next month.'

'All right, Ma, you're still very young – if that makes you feel better? Now, can you please get on with the story?'

'I *am* still young,' Goldie mutters. 'And if you'd shut up for a second, I would.'

Luna sighs again, then mimes zipping her mouth closed and throwing away the key.

Goldie kisses the top of her daughter's head, catching sight of the scars on Luna's left shoulder: the elaborate etchings of crescent moons and stars that so closely resembled her father's marks. Goldie closes her eyes and tries not to think of what's coming tomorrow. Will Luna be angry that she hasn't mentioned it? Goldie dearly hopes not.

'So, where was I? Oh, yes . . .' She refocuses on the notebook. 'Once there was a girl called Estella . . .' She skips ahead, thinking of Leo. 'She was born after a fire witch and ice witch fell in love and—'

'Were they lesbian witches?' Luna interrupts. 'Like Aunt Liyana?'

'No, sweetheart.' Goldie smiles. 'Not this time. This was a girl witch and a boy witch. They were sworn enemies and—'

'Why?'

'Why, what?'

'Why were they enemies?'

'I don't know,' Goldie admits. 'They'd been enemies for so long, the fire witches and ice witches, that no one could remember why.'

'That's silly,' Luna says. 'It doesn't make sense.'
'I know. Most fights don't.'

The Child of Fire and Ice

There was once a girl, luminous as a star. She was born between one world and another, fashioned from fire and ice, moonlight and fog, blood and bone. She was a child of the earth and sky. And her name was Estella.

Estella was a rare, almost inconceivable thing: a daughter of elemental opposites. Her parents met a year before she was born. He was a fire witch; she was an ice witch. And, though their covens were sworn enemies, they fell in love. When the ice witch became pregnant, no one believed that the fire witch could be the father – since it was impossible for these two elements to combine.

Thus the fire witch became embattled in many duels defending his lover's honour. And, in the last of these, he was killed. The grief sent the ice witch into labour, and when the baby was born everyone could see the impossible on the girl's face: she was indeed a daughter of fire and ice.

As the child grew, her mother started noticing strange and curious things. Estella would burn herself when she sucked her thumb, causing blisters so she couldn't suckle; her subsequent frostbitten screams shattered the glass of her mother's scrying mirror. On especially hungry nights, every window of every hut in the village cracked.

As time went on, Estella couldn't pass a day without causing some fresh disaster, either to herself or her neighbours. Soon her mother, fearing for Estella's life, set a spell to trap her daughter's magic inside a silver box. She buried the box in a deep pit in the heart of the forest, enchanting the spot so that no one would ever discover it. Every night she told Estella stories of malevolent trees that snatched lost children and fed on their hearts, of wicked crones who lured children into gingerbread houses and cooked them in pots, of maniacal huntsmen and feral wolves and greedy trolls that dwelt under stone bridges and gobbled up anyone who dared cross over.

The ice witch's tactics worked and Estella was always too scared to venture into the forest.

Years passed until, one day, the ice witch had almost forgotten what she'd done. After hundreds and thousands of happy, uneventful days drifted by, she stopped telling Estella of all the fabricated horrors of the forest and told her other stories instead. Stories of love and adventure and magic.

So it was that one day on her way home from the market Estella reached the two paths that both led home – one through the fields and one through the forest. Estella had vague memories of childish stories that had kept her away from the forest all these years, but today was midsummer: the sun fell through the trees, a gentle breeze danced with the wildflowers, a blackbird's song filled the air and all at once the forest seemed a beautiful and bewitching place.

Once in the forest, entranced by playful squirrels, plump mushrooms and delphiniums of the deepest blue, Estella was soon drawn from the path and – like a homing pigeon – eventually came to the glade where her mother had buried the box. Only, the box was no longer buried, having over the years worked its way – inch by inch, root by root – out of the pit.

Now it sat on a cushion of moss, rusted and dirty.

Waiting.

Estella set down her basket, brimming with mushrooms and flowers, and stepped across the cracking twigs of the forest floor. A faint warning, in her mother's voice, rose from the depths of dark memories. Estella dismissed it and, bending down, picked up the box.

The moment she opened it, all of Estella's magic flew out.

Sadly, being so many years without her magic, Estella was unable to contain the force that suddenly swept into her chest, and the united violence of fire and ice instantly knocked the spirit from her body. And she would have died if her mother – seized by a sudden intuition – hadn't that moment snatched up her scrying mirror and screamed out an incantation, casting a spell drawing on the earth and transforming her daughter into an ash tree.

Every day at dawn the ice witch visited her daughter, knelt over her roots and wept, lamenting her own foolishness and Estella's terrible fate. Her spellbound tears fell with the tree's leaves as they united in grief. Every summer solstice the tree burned spontaneously and fiercely, scorching the surrounding woods. Every winter solstice it turned to ice, freezing every living thing it touched.

Fearing the enchanted tree, no one ever went into the forest again. Everyone thought that this proved the dangerous impossibility of combining elemental opposites such as fire and ice. Only the ice witch knew the truth. But, of course, no one would listen to her.

8.59 p.m. – Goldie

Perched on the end of Luna's bed, Goldie watches her daughter sleep. *I'm being watched too,* she thinks. And the thought makes her shiver. Since Friday, the spectre of social services has loomed perpetually at the edges of Goldie's thoughts and she knows that she won't sleep tonight, despite aching with exhaustion. Nor will she rest, nor think on anything else, nor settle, until the interrogation is over. What will the outcome be? And how will she explain the multiplying scars? How can she, when she doesn't know the answer herself?

Chapter Five

11.12 a.m. – Luna

'Did your mother ever hurt you?'

'No.' Luna scowls. 'No, I already told you a hundred times. No!'

The social worker, Miss 'call me Olivia' Gibbons, sits forward in her chair. 'Yes, I know,' she says, her voice ever softer and more syrupy. 'But children will often protect their parents. Even, sometimes especially, those who've been abused.'

They've spent the past hour together, sitting on the floor doing a rather tricky puzzle, while Miss Gibbons gently quizzed Luna about her home life. Finding that this line of investigation yielded no results, she escalated to direct questioning.

'Yes.' Luna grits her teeth. 'I bet, but I haven't been abused!'

'I hear what you're saying.' Miss Gibbons presses her hands together. 'But—'

'But you *don't* hear me,' Luna snaps. 'Or you wouldn't keep repeating that, would you? So it seems like not only don't you listen but you're also a bloody idiot to boot. Either that or you're just being obtuse.'

Olivia's eyebrows shoot up and her mouth drops open, before she quickly regains her composure. 'I – I'm surprised that you seem to know such adult language. Do you— Are you exposed to a lot of that at home?'

Luna narrows her eyes, looking up from the puzzle. 'What language do you mean? You've never heard the word "obtuse" before? Well, the *Oxford Dictionary of English* defines the word as "annoyingly insensitive or slow to understand". Also—'

'I know what it means,' Olivia says, giving Luna a tight smile. 'Your teacher told me you were clever.'

Luna slots the last piece of the puzzle into place. '*Prodigy,* I believe is the correct terminology.' She folds her arms, defiant.

'Yes.' Olivia nods, lips thin. 'But you're still a child. Even if—'

'Even if I'm cleverer and more knowledgeable than you'll ever be.' Luna gives the social worker an innocent smile.

Miss Gibbons sits up straighter. 'I'm not here to fight with you.' Her voice is sharper now. 'I'm here to help you—'

'No,' Luna says, feeling the heat rising in her hands. 'You're here to take me away from Ma.' She slides her hands under her legs so the social worker can't see the sparks at her fingertips. 'That's what you're doing.'

'No,' Miss Gibbons echoes her. 'I am here to assess the situation and write a proposal for your care that will be in your best interests.'

'Then why aren't you listening to me?' Luna snaps. 'I *told* you what's in my best interests: to stay where I am. I love Ma and she loves me. You could look for the rest of your life and you wouldn't find a better ma in the whole world . . .' Luna feels tears spring to her eyes and blinks them back – she will not allow this stupid woman to see her vulnerable. 'She's strong and soft and stupidly overprotective and, and—'

'I'm very pleased to hear it, Luna.' Miss Gibbons sits back in her chair. 'But then why can't you tell me how you got those scars?'

11.33 a.m. – Goldie

'She was born with them. The midwife present at her birth confirmed the fact.' Goldie nods at the file the social worker is clutching. 'I'm sure you'll have a full report in there, along with the doctor's notes and case studies.' Goldie takes a deep breath, trying to calm down. 'I was never under any suspicion, as well you know.'

She sits across the table from him in a dingy little room that's barely big enough to fit the table and two chairs. The walls are white and scuffed, the plastic furniture is peeling at the edges. The whole effect is monumentally depressing, which echoes Goldie's feelings entirely.

'Yes.' Mr Clarke nods. 'Yes, I've read all the documentation. But, as *you* know, the reason we've reopened the case is due to the observations made by Luna's teachers.'

'Yes,' Goldie repeats, feeling the urge to bite her thumbnail – a nervous habit – but, with great effort of will, she suppresses it. If he thinks she's nervous, he'll think she's guilty. 'Yes, I know. You've already told me. And I've been through it a million times in my mind – I've not stopped thinking about it since Friday. I don't understand how it is that the scars seem to be . . . spreading. But I can only assume that there must be some sort of medical reason – we don't know how she got the scars in the first place, after all. One doctor postulated that they might have been caused by abnormalities in the womb; another said it might be a birth defect.' Goldie gives a little shrug as she thinks of Leo and the real reason for Luna's scars. 'And if—'

'Perhaps,' Mr Clarke says. 'But that doesn't explain why Luna now has more scars than she did, does it? She was born a long time ago, Mrs Clayton. And there has been no change in all that time until now. Yes?'

'Yes. No. I don't know.' Goldie wishes that Teddy was sitting on her side of the table. Hell, right now she'd take a total stranger off the street, just so she wasn't facing the scrutiny of Mr Clarke alone. 'I-I can't be sure,' she admits. 'Because I very rarely see Luna undressed. But, whenever it happened, I-I think it's not improbable that, if . . . that this birth defect is a skin condition that has lain dormant and is suddenly flaring up now. You know, in the same way that eczema is triggered by stress.'

'Yes,' Mr Clarke persists. 'But no one's suggesting that the scars are akin to eczema. Surely you aren't suggesting that birth scars spread.'

Goldie shrinks in her chair, feeling like a mouse being eyeballed by an owl. A mouse with nowhere to hide. 'I don't know, Mr Clarke,' she says weakly. 'I'm not a medical professional. Perhaps Luna should be seen by experts before you start accusing—'

'No one's accusing anyone of anything,' Mr Clarke interrupts. 'And you can rest assured that all due diligence will be taken in our investigations.' He pauses. 'Have you considered that fact that if you – or some other person – didn't harm Luna, that perhaps she harmed herself?'

Goldie swallows. How can she get out of this? How can she survive this interrogation when she cannot come up with a plausible lie and she cannot tell the truth? If she told

Mr Clarke the real reason for Luna's scars – her magical father – then she'd be in even worse trouble than she is right now. So what the hell *can* she say?

'No,' Goldie says. 'She wouldn't do that. She's not unhappy and, anyway, she doesn't have any access to razors or knives.'

'Are you quite certain?'

'Yes.'

'So you know everything that your daughter is up to at all times?'

Goldie dearly wants to say 'yes' again, but knows she can't. The owl has extended its talons and she has no defence. 'No, of course not. But nor does—'

'So it's not inconceivable that Luna has been self-harming under your care, is it, Mrs Clayton? That perhaps she obtained the razor from a friend at school, or some such.'

'Yes,' Goldie concedes. 'I suppose that's conceivable.'

Mr Clarke nods – *one–nil* – then returns to his file. 'I understand that Luna's father left before she was born, so—'

'He didn't *leave*.' Goldie bites the word. 'He died.'

'Oh, of course,' Mr Clarke says without feeling. 'So it's only the two of you at home?'

Goldie nods.

'And how do you manage with that set-up?'

'Are you saying . . .' Goldie slides her thumbs under her thighs and suppresses the urge to scream. 'Are you suggesting that my daughter is self-harming because I'm a single mother?'

'N-no.' Mr Clarke stutters. 'No, of course I'm not suggesting anything of the sort. I'm simply saying that raising a child is challenging and I'm asking how well you're coping. Do you have any support? Employees? Friends? Neighbours? Grandparents? Godparents?'

With a pang, Goldie thinks of what Bea said and deeply wishes she could say, '*Yes, yes, yes, I have all those people and more*.' Instead, she takes a deep breath, trying to inject a single name with as much power as an army. 'I have a brother, Teddy. He runs the refuge with me.'

'Ah, yes.' Mr Clarke fixes the spotlight of his gaze upon her. 'You run a refuge housing women and children who've been made homeless by domestic abuse, is that right?'

Goldie nods.

Mr Clarke scribbles in his file. 'And, I imagine, this refuge takes up a good deal of your time, yes? It's not an ordinary job with reliable, predicable hours . . .'

Goldie grits her teeth. 'If you're suggesting, Mr Clarke, that my vocation means that I neglect my daughter, then you're wrong. My brother and a few of our voluntary staff take care of everything out of hours. I'm only on call while Luna is at school. I drop her off, I pick her up. Every day, at eight thirty and three fifteen. I don't put her in before- or after-school care. We do her homework together, we cook dinner, we watch TV. We do all that boring, normal, predictable, reliable stuff. Just like any other family.'

As she talks, Mr Clarke scribbles this down. When he finishes, he looks up. 'But you and Luna live in a flat above the refuge. Isn't that correct?'

'Well . . .' Goldie succumbs to the urge to chew her thumbnail. 'Yes. We do. But she is never involved with any of the residents and never witnesses any of the incidents. And if you—'

'How can you be so sure of that?' Mr Clarke leans forward, elbows on the table. 'Given that you're not entirely sure whether or not your daughter is self-harming?'

Goldie bites into her skin, wincing. 'I'm sure,' she says. 'She's never unsupervised at the refuge.'

'Only in your flat.'

Goldie sits forward. 'Much as I might like the reassurance of monitoring my daughter's every move,' she says, voice quivering, 'I'm sure you'd agree that children are entitled to some privacy. And Luna is a very private person.'

'Do you think that is because she's hiding the effects of her self-harm?'

'I – I . . .' Goldie stutters, desperately fighting the urge to cry. 'I think . . . we shouldn't jump to conclusions before, before . . .'

'Don't worry,' Mr Clarke says. 'We'll be doing a thorough investigation before we put forward conclusions and suggest appropriate courses of action. Meanwhile, I'll ask you again: do you really think that a women's refuge is an appropriate environment in which to raise a young girl?'

12.58 p.m. – Teddy

'You don't *know* they'll take her away,' Teddy says. 'Not for certain.'

'I do,' Goldie sobs. 'I do . . . Not only because I just *know* but because what can I say? There's no adequate lie that'll save the situation and I can't tell them the truth. So what the hell am I supposed to do?!'

Having spent the past hour desperately grappling for answers and coming up with nothing, now Teddy is silent.

They're sitting in Goldie's office, side by side on the floor, leaning against the wall. Which is where Goldie was when he'd knocked on her door and found her – surrounded by a sea of snotty tissues.

'Tell me what I can do to help,' Teddy says, both to fill the silence and because he can't bear it when his sister cries. 'Please.'

Goldie reaches for the rapidly dwindling supply of tissues and blows her nose again. 'Nothing,' she says with a heavy sigh. 'There's nothing you can do.'

Not for the first time, Teddy feels the inadequacy of his position – the pathetic human with not a drop of Grimm blood in him – like a punch in the stomach. 'There must be *something*.'

Still sniffing, Goldie is quiet, ruminating. Teddy sees the moment the idea strikes her. He waits to see if she'll share it with him.

'Can you hold the fort here for a few days?'

Teddy nods. 'Yeah, of course.' He pauses, still waiting. But when she says nothing – just stares at the carpet – he plunges in. 'Sis, there's something I have to talk about.'

'I might need to go away for a little while,' Goldie says, not hearing him. 'I know I shouldn't take Luna out of school for long, and of course I don't want to leave the women here, but you'll be able to handle everything for a while, won't you? Because I can't let them take Luna away. I just can't.'

'Yes, but . . .' Teddy trails off, trying to digest what she's just said. 'Where are going? You can't just run away, not anymore. You'll be found in an hour. Everything's digital, everything's tracked, you can't possibly hope to make it ten miles before—'

'Not here,' Goldie says thoughtfully. 'But we can go to a place where nothing is digital and no one can find us.'

Teddy frowns. 'I don't know . . .' And then he does. 'No, wait! You can't go *there*.'

For the first time that day, Goldie smiles. 'Why not? Ever-where is the perfect place. Luna and I can come and go from here to there whenever we please. No one can stop us and no one can find us, except for other sisters, and I hardly think—'

'No, wait,' Teddy says again. 'That's madness. It's absolutely crazy. You—'

'Maybe,' Goldie ploughs on, increasingly animated. 'But what other choice do we have? You said it yourself – it's not like we can go on the run here, and anyway—'

'But perhaps they won't take her away,' Teddy tries lamely. 'Or, if they do, you can still visit her, can't you? And it won't be forever, so—'

The look of pure rage on Goldie's face stops him in his tracks. She has dropped the tissue in her hand and is staring at him as if wishing to do him harm.

'Visit her? *Visit* her?!' She spits out the words. 'You have no idea. No fucking idea.' Her voice pitches dangerously towards hysteria. 'Luna is my daughter. My *daughter*. She's my . . . everything. She's all I have left.'

Of Leo.

The words hang in the air, unspoken. But Teddy hears them as clearly as if Goldie snapped them at him. And, just when he thinks she is about to scream or hit him, she starts to cry again.

'Fuck,' Teddy mutters. 'Sis, please, I'm sorry. I didn't mean – I'm an idiot, ignore me. I understand, I do. I mean, I know I don't have kids, but I know what it is to love someone more than anything else in the world.' Tears spring to his eyes and he kisses the top of Goldie's head. 'That much,' he whispers into Goldie's hair, 'I do know.'

Eventually, Goldie looks up, wipes her nose on her sleeve and gives her brother a half-smile. 'You *are* an idiot.' She ruffles his hair.

'Absolute,' he admits, relieved. 'Grade eight. First class.' He offers a tentative smile. 'Forgiven?'

She nods. 'Forgiven.'

'Thank you, then, please, promise me this.'

'What?'

'Promise me you'll try to think of a way you can solve this in a way that means I'll get to see you and Luna again, okay?'

Goldie sniffs again. 'I promise.'

Teddy nods, pretending to believe her. 'Just don't do anything really stupid,' he says. 'And, before you do, tell me first. Okay?'

'All right, little brother, I will.' Goldie reaches for his hand and squeezes it tight. 'Thank you.' She pauses, remembering. 'What was it you wanted to tell me?'

Teddy regards his sister blankly, his heart starting to race.

'You said you wanted to talk to me about something, didn't you?'

'Oh, that,' Teddy says, as if it's nothing, as if he's only just remembered. 'It's not important. It can wait.'

11.59 p.m. – Luna

Of course I didn't tell that stupid woman anything. What an idiot, thinking she could trick me into saying stuff about Ma. What an idiot, thinking it was her when actually it was me. I didn't tell her that sometimes I do things and don't understand afterwards why I've done them. And maybe every week I'm overcome with these sudden rages and I want to smash up everything in my room. Sometimes I want to scream at Ma when she really won't leave me alone, but other times she says or does something and I want to hug her so tight I might squish her. My feelings are so *much*. Too much. It doesn't make sense. Why can't I be like Uncle Teddy, always so calm and kind? Is it because I'm a Grimm? Or is it just my own fault? I don't know. Lately, it's been getting worse. Lately, to calm myself down, I've been doing things to myself that Ma wouldn't approve of.

But now the scars on my back have started to itch and burn, sometimes so badly I feel like they're being newly branded onto my skin. I have a strange feeling it's a sign something bad is coming, and the badness, whatever it is, will happen on my birthday. I'm not psychic or anything like that, not like Aunt Ana, but I still can't shake it. And every day it grows stronger, like a time bomb counting down to the day I turn ten.

Twenty-one sleeps.

The thought scares me and I want to tell Ma, but then I worry that if I speak my fears aloud, then it'll make them real. So instead I try to squish them down and, whenever they threaten to bubble over, I take a razor and carve it into my skin till my blood runs free. Which makes me feel a bit better. I got the idea from a history book I read at school a few weeks ago about doctors using leeches to let blood from their patients who were hysterical or ill. At first I thought it the stupidest thing ever, but then I tried it and it worked. I mean, it doesn't cure me of sickness or anything like that, but it does make me feel better for a few hours or days. And then I just have to do it again.

Chapter Six

Everwhere

It is a place of falling leaves and hungry ivy, mist and fog, moonlight and ice, a place always shifting and always still. It never changes, though the mists rise and fall, the fog rolls in across the shores and sea. But the moonlight never ebbs, the ice never melts, the sun never shines. It's a nocturnal place, a place crafted from thoughts and dreams, hope and desire. It's lit by an unwavering moon, unfettered by clouds, illuminating everything but the shadows. It's an autumnal place, but with a winter chill and hue. Imagine a forest that reaches between now and forever, with ancient trees stretching high towards the marbled sky and an infinite network of ancient roots reaching out to the edge of eternity.

The entrance to this place is guarded by gates, perfectly ordinary if rather ornate gates, that now and then transform into something extraordinary. And, if you've got a little Grimm blood in you, you might just be able to see the shift.

Walking through a gate, you'll step onto moss and mud. Go carefully over the slick stones as you begin to find your way. Reach out to steady yourself whenever you need, palm pressed to the bleached moss that blankets every trunk and branch. Soon you'll hear the rush of water, a vein of the endless river that runs on and on, twisting through the trees, turning with the paths but never meeting the seas.

It's a while before you notice that everything around

you is alive. You feel the hum of the earth beneath the soil, the breath of the trees in the rustle of their leaves, the murmur of the birds in flight. As your eyes adjust to the light you'll see marks on rocks, crushed patches of leaves, slips in the mud. *Footprints*. Others have been before and now you're following in their footsteps. You wonder how many have preceded you, which paths they took and where they went. And so, you walk on . . .

Stick to the path, let your instincts lead you to the others, just as they will be led to you.

3.33 a.m. – Everwhere

The girl's body isn't visible for long. Almost as soon as she's taken her last breath, her spirit is engulfed by the mists and her soul sinks into the soil. Her death is only the matter of a moment. No one, except the one who ended her life, is there to witness it. After that, there is no trace. Indeed, the only evidence of the kill is the white leaf. The first of its kind in over a decade.

It falls from a single spot in the sky and drops into a river to drift away, unseen.

Chapter Seven

Three years ago: 5.45 p.m. – Scarlet

The night Liyana died, Scarlet returned from Everwhere and walked, in a roundabout way, from the gate to the bus station. She had no particular plan in mind, she simply wandered in a daze through Cambridge and found herself there.

Scarlet sat for a while, as the night slowly drew back its shadows and allowed the light to seep in. When she looked up again, the first bus of the day had pulled into the station. Without thinking, without looking at the destination, Scarlet stuck her hands into her pockets and pulled out a ten-pound note. She had nothing else: no phone, no ID, no purse. She'd left all that at home.

But it didn't matter. Nothing mattered anymore.

Ten pounds was just enough, it turned out, for a single ticket to Oxford. It even left her with enough change to buy a can of Coke and a packet of crisps. The seat beside her was free and she laid them there, thinking she'd be hungry at some point during the four-hour journey. She certainly should've been ravenous, given all she'd just been through. But she wasn't. And when she finally alighted from the bus in Oxford – after the multiple stops and diversions – she stumbled into the empty station in Jericho and left them behind.

Scarlet wasn't hungry for a long time; for the first time in her life she didn't think about food, didn't keenly anticipate her next meal nor plan what she might prefer. In the sharp aftermath of loss, the cavernous pit of grief and the gnawing ache of guilt, all desire left her – and, with it, joy. Instead, Scarlet merely survived, though without any particular intention of doing so. She simply found that, one day after the next, she was still there. Still breathing, still walking, still blinking out at the surroundings.

Oxford, it turned out, was (almost) as beautiful as Cambridge, if rather more modern and decidedly less quaint. Nevertheless, the ancient stone, elaborate spires and ornate gates of its university colleges bestowed a fairy-tale hue upon the city, which, under normal circumstances, would've enchanted and entranced Scarlet, but which now passed largely unnoticed. She saw it all as she walked past – Scarlet found that she couldn't stop walking – but hardly noticed the difference between the dirty alleys behind the Covered Market or the Westgate shopping centre and the illustrious cobbled paths winding around the magnificently domed Radcliffe Camera. She simply noted it all with the same uninterested gaze and walked on.

It wasn't until several days of fasting and walking, when Scarlet's usually plump body was flattening down, her curved stomach hollowing out, that her thoughts turned to food. Not the delicious food that she'd been used to in her other life – the one where she had sisters and friends, where she worked in a café and believed she deserved happiness – but simple sustenance, whatever was available that'd fill the void. Taste didn't matter, nor nutrition; such concerns were luxuries she could no longer afford to consider. Only when the ache of hunger grew so fierce that it vied with the ache of guilt did Scarlet realize, if she wanted food, she first needed money.

Oxford was a beautiful place, but it, like all cities, had its insalubrious places. She found them quite by accident. Her endless wanderings had eventually and inevitably taken her to the darker parts and deeper ends of the Cowley and Iffley Roads, and even then a plan didn't present itself until a car slowed alongside her and a man enquired from within: 'How much?' So she told him. In her past life, Scarlet would have been horrified, would've screamed and harangued him. But to the benumbed woman she had so swiftly and completely become, it seemed only that Fate had stepped in to offer her a solution to her current predicament. And so she took it.

It was over quickly. She successfully insisted on a barrier of latex between them – and she found that she was easily able to remove herself from her body and imagine herself elsewhere for the duration, so the mark it left upon her was more a scratch than a wound. That first time enabled Scarlet to buy food enough to fill her empty belly and rent a room for the night so she could sleep a few hours in safety, then wash the stink of sweat and dirt from her skin.

It seemed a fairly acceptable transaction, and so she carried on. Just often enough to eat and sleep. No one hurt her. Some tried, but didn't succeed. Those men left with souvenirs from the encounter: burns on their bodies that scabbed and turned to scars. Scars that led, in some cases, to awkward questions. For others, the scars simply remained as reminders to think twice before raising their hand to a woman.

1.18 p.m. – Teddy

In snatched moments of free time away from the refuge, or whenever he feels the levels of antagonism towards men bubbling over, Teddy visits his favourite haunts. In the summer months this is Jack's Gelato on Bene't Street; in the winter it's Fitzbillies on Trumpington Street. Now, it's the little gelateria that draws Teddy. He looks forward to studying the daily changing menu at leisure and eavesdropping on the babbling brook of customers.

Teddy had discovered the place quite by accident one day when he'd seen the snaking queue stretching past the Eagle pub – infamous as the location where Watson and Crick supposedly set down their discovery of DNA. Though, as his sister was often at pains to point out, the Nobel Prize committee and history had neglected the one woman integral to the discovery: Rosalind Franklin.

'Bloody typical,' she'd bemoan. 'Just like Jocelyn Bell Burnell, Esther Lederberg, Chien-Shiung Wu . . .' At which point, Teddy usually stopped listening. Not that he's not a feminist. How can one work in a shelter for battered women and not be?

Today, Teddy slips past the queue swelling the pavement and shop to head for the nook at the back. He's already slipping into the enclosed booth before he realizes that the bench on the other side of the table is already occupied.

'Oh, sorry, I didn't—' He stands again.

The young woman looks up. 'That's okay. No one's sitting there.'

'Are you sure?' Teddy asks. 'You don't mind sharing?'

She shrugs her assent and, after hesitating, Teddy sits. Working in the shelter has made him acutely aware of respecting women's personal space. He's seen how easily men violate it, often unintentionally, owing to the fact that women are often willing to please others over themselves, to say 'yes' when they want to say 'no', to smile when they wish to scream. What he's supposed to do about this, Teddy has yet to figure out.

While studying today's menu – its delectable offerings of dark chocolate and gochujang; yuzu, beet and coconut; cardamom and rose – he glances surreptitiously at the girl. She looks about his age, early twenties, possibly younger. And—

'What are you looking at?'

Shit. Teddy stares intently at the menu, before turning his gaze back to her. 'Sorry?'

She looks at him, one eyebrow raised. 'You were studying me.'

'Oh no, I wasn't . . . I mean – I was only trying to decide what to have. So many choices and the decision-making process isn't aided by the daily changing of flavours.'

She smiles and he sees now just how strikingly beautiful she is: dark skin, natural afro springing up like a halo, large dark eyes and a smile that might illuminate the cosy booth as brightly as any light.

'See,' she says. 'You're doing it again.'

Shit. He wants to evaporate. 'I'm sorry, I didn't . . . It's not you. It's your . . . dress. I was admiring its elegance. You don't often see haute couture on these streets.'

'Oh, yeah?' She gives him a wry smile, as if she can see right through him.

Teddy flushes. Today will definitely be a three-scoop day. 'No, really. I . . . I used to . . . Well, I wanted to be a clothes designer once, so I always notice these things.'

She grins, as if daring him to make a fool of himself. 'What is it, then, that you admire so much about my dress?'

'Well . . .' Teddy struggles to find adequate language

under the full beam of her attention. Then, finally, he does. 'Well . . . I love how the green of the yoke complements the blue of the bodice, and how the decorative top stitch highlights the collar . . . The subtle ruching at the cuffs makes for a nice understated embellishment, along with the use of lapped seams at the hem . . . I've also always favoured the princess seam over the use of darts.'

She stares at him in shock. Then bursts out laughing.

'I told you so,' he says, ridiculously delighted at having made her laugh, even if she is laughing at him. 'As a kid, I read the biography of every designer I admired. My sister bought me a sewing machine for my thirteenth birthday and I taught myself edge stitch and embroidery and . . . all that. I never played video games; I designed batwings and Bardots, swing dresses, shifts . . . I would've gone to Saint Martins but . . .' He trails off, embarrassed. 'My sister asked me to help run her shelter. And she'd done so much for me, so I couldn't say no.'

'Oh.' She regards him curiously. 'That's very kind of you.'

Teddy shrugs. 'Hardly. She raised me after our mum died; she was only thirteen. She gave up any kind of future for me, so it's only fair I return the favour.'

She considers this, licking her ice cream thoughtfully. 'I suppose so. But that's awfully sad.'

Teddy shrugs, suddenly embarrassed. *Why on earth is he confessing the entire contents of his heart to a complete stranger?* He's desperately trying to think of something sensible and normal to say when, abruptly, she stands.

'Oh, shit! I've got to go! I've only got half an hour for lunch and my boss will kill me if I'm late.' She glances at her phone. 'And I'm already late.' Then she glances at Teddy, meeting his eye with a look of sympathy and affection. 'I'm so sorry.'

Teddy watches her go, hurrying out of the nook in a sweep of linen and silk, taking her smile and an unfinished cone of blood-orange sorbet with her. It's a few moments before Teddy returns to the menu and then, after studying the sumptuous selection of flavours for several minutes, makes the unprecedented decision to forgo gelato altogether.

2.39 p.m. – Goldie

The letter arrives that afternoon – Royal Mail rarely manage to deliver anything before lunchtime – she knows what it is before she's even picked it up, before she's turned it over, before she's ripped it open. She certainly doesn't need to see the official blue crest to know it's from social services. It lies there, on the mat, among the bills and takeaway menus, as if emitting a radioactive glow.

Goldie stares at it for a while, wishing it would gather all its swirling ominous portent and implode. But the letter remains, pulsing its silent warning. Waiting to deliver its devastating decision, waiting to execute its fatal blow.

Cambridgeshire County Council Social Services
Shire Hall
Castle Hill
Cambridge
CB3 0AP

Dear Mrs Clayton,

Following our preliminary interviews with yourself and your daughter, Luna Clayton, along with the evidence presented by Mayfield Primary School and the witness testimony of Mr G. Barnes, we ascertain that there is enough evidence to open a case file into the fitness of Mrs Goldie Clayton to continue in her role as primary caregiver to Luna Clayton.

In the first instance we have been authorized by the local authorities to implement further investigations into the possible causes behind the minor's two additional bodily scars on her upper right shoulder blade that have developed since birth. For this matter she will be under the purview of Mr Tristan Lane, a dermatology consultant at Addenbrooke's Hospital. An initial consultation has been arranged for 10th June at 9.20 a.m. Mrs Goldie Clayton will be expected to accompany her daughter to the appointment but will not be permitted to attend with her. Ms Olivia Gibbons will act in the capacity of caregiver for the duration of this appointment.

When Mr Lane has submitted his initial conclusions, we will invite both parties for additional interviews, to be undertaken separately. Prior to this appointment, you are asked to remain at home and are not permitted to leave the country for any reason.

As we discussed previously, you are strongly advised not to communicate with your daughter on this, or any other, matter pertaining to the ongoing investigation. Failure to follow this advice may result in Luna Clayton being taken into temporary care. If you have any queries, you may contact your case worker, Ms Olivia Gibbons.

Sincerely,
Mr Daniel Clarke

Goldie knew it was coming. She'd been almost certain. But anticipating the fall of the axe doesn't dull the pain of the blow. When it comes, she drops to her knees and weeps.

Chapter Eight

3.33 a.m. – the Sisters Grimm

'You need to breathe more deeply, Alba,' Goldie says. She's finding it extremely difficult to focus, to think of anything else but the letter, and yet she must. 'Try five deep breaths before you leap, all right?'

On the ground, a sister in her early twenties – built like a bird, with long thin brown hair and a smattering of freckles – pulls herself up with a groan.

'Like everything in life, it just takes practice,' Goldie assures her. 'But you'll be flying above the forest before you know it.'

A whoop of delight sounds from above and everyone else in the glade looks skyward to see Siobhan, another daughter of air, who's not been practising half as long, swooping through the trees as if flying is the easiest thing in the world. Alba studies the forest floor, crestfallen.

'That'll be you by the end of the week.' Goldie takes a deep breath, dragging her thoughts away from Luna, who's sleeping safely and soundly in her bed, and back to the girl who needs her help. 'If not tomorrow night.'

Suddenly the whoop of delight shifts into a cry of alarm.

'Remember – call out Bea's name if you're falling,' Goldie shouts, cupping her hands around her mouth to throw the words higher. 'She'll give you an extra breath of wind to take you up again!'

'Anyway . . .' She turns back to Alba. 'There's no rush. You can take as long as you need. It's safe now for you to practise your skills and develop your strengths. Soon you'll be braver and stronger than you've ever believed possible.'

Alba touches the fading bruise on her collarbone, grimacing slightly.

'Once you can fly in Everwhere,' Goldie promises, 'you'll be able to do anything you put your mind to on Earth.'

If only, she thinks, *it was that easy.*

If only the same was true for me.

5.33 a.m. – Liyana, Scarlet & Bea

After everyone else has left, Goldie stays. It's only now, when she's no longer in her leadership role, that Goldie can admit how scared she is.

I know it seems bad right now. Bea's voice is the flap of a raven's wing. *But remember, you always fear the worst. You worry too much. It doesn't mean—*

'I know,' Goldie says, for once conceding that her annoying sister is speaking the truth. 'But that doesn't mean I'm not right – hypochondriacs still get cancer, you know.'

You're not going to get cancer. Liyana sprinkles a gentle rain atop Goldie's head. *Trust me, that much I know.*

'It was a metaphor.' Goldie rolls her eyes. 'And I don't care if I get cancer; I just don't want them to take Luna away.'

Stop jumping to the worst-case scenario. She's not even seen the specialist yet.

'And what's going to happen when she does?' Goldie starts pacing. 'He's hardly going to conclude that it's a medical issue, is he? I mean, how could it be? Either it's magical, or she's self-harming, or . . .' She trails off, unable to think of anything else. 'Well, either way, it's not going to have them throwing out the case file, is it?' Goldie stoops to pick a stone from the ground and rubs it between her fingers. It serves to soothe her a little. 'I just wish we could stay here. Safe and sound, where they can't find us.'

We'd love that too. Liyana's voice is the rush of a nearby river. *But would it be fair to her? It'd be fun for a few weeks, but then what will you do? Raise her feral? Take her away from her uncle and her friends? What about when she hits puberty and—*

'Yes, all right, all right,' Goldie snaps. 'I get it. It's insanely impractical. But can either of you think of a better idea?'

The united sigh of her two sisters blows a cool breeze through the glade. Above the trees, ravens swoop and caw. In the branches of a silver birch, a blackbird starts to sing. Leaves rustle. Twigs crack. The river gurgles. Still, her sisters are silent.

'You see.' Goldie stops pacing. 'I told you so.'

11.38 p.m. – Luna

When I wake, I'm crying and calling out for Ma. I'm hot and sticky and shaking. What's wrong? Am I sick? Did I have a nightmare? I can't remember.

'Ma! Maaaa!'

She's at my door before I can take a breath to scream again. She looks terrified. Seeing her face cuts through my fear, almost makes me laugh with relief. I sit up and she's folding me into her arms before I can even open mine.

'It's all right, Lu-Lu, I'm here.' She holds me tight. 'It's all right, everything's all right.'

I bury my face in her chest, absorbing her warmth, the rapid pounding of her heart and I almost believe her. Ma waits while I cry, whispering her promise again and again, holding us both tight till I don't know anymore who's crying and who's whispering and who's trying to convince whom.

'Ma,' I croak. I wipe my nose with one sleeve and my eyes with the other. My throat is sore, my head is aching.

'Yes, sweetheart?' Ma strokes my hair, kisses my forehead. I feel her fear ebb but not evaporate.

I open my eyes. 'I miss Pa.'

'Oh, Lu.' Ma's eyes fill with tears. 'I miss him too. Every day. Very, very much.'

I sniff, wiping my nose again. 'Sometimes I think because I never met him I miss him more, not less.'

'Of course.' Ma cups my cheek, tucks a stray curl behind my ear. 'Of course you do.'

But she doesn't mean it. Ma's a liar, always has been. She tells me all sorts of shit, thinking I'm too young, too naive to notice. She thinks she's the only one who really loved him, the only one entitled to mourn. And she's been mourning since long before I was even born; so, of course, she's the queen of grief. But what Ma forgets is that while he gave her his heart, he gave me his blood. And his scars. She didn't tell me this; it was Aunt Bea who let it slip one night.

Suddenly I pull away from Ma, no longer wanting to touch her, wishing I was with my Pa instead. Without saying anything, I slip back under the covers and turn away.

11.58 p.m. – Goldie

She sits at the edge of Luna's bed until her daughter's breathing deepens and slows. Then she leans over and kisses Luna's cheek and whispers, 'Goodnight,' feeling a sudden rush of love so fierce it almost scares her. The urge to sneak a look at her daughter's scars is overwhelming, but it feels like a step too far. She would snatch up her baby girl and disappear to Everwhere right now, if only she could.

When Goldie finally stands, her gaze falls on the bedside table and Luna's notebook. She has never snooped before, and never imagined she ever would stoop so low. And the only way she can explain what she does next is fear – for her daughter's future – and the desperate desire to know what's going on. Perhaps, Goldie thinks as she picks it up, the notebook might give her some answers. And, though she won't admit it even to herself, she wants to know what's going on in her secretive daughter's life; she wants to prove her sisters wrong and demonstrate exactly how much she's got to worry about.

What she finds isn't concrete evidence, not a diary (as she was hoping) but a story.

The Good Girl

Once upon a time there was a little girl who, though she was often good, sometimes got upset and flew into rages, stamping her feet and shouting. Whenever this happened, her parents didn't ask what was wrong, didn't discuss her feelings; instead they punished her, banishing the girl to her bedroom. Every time she was shut away, the girl sobbed, convinced she wasn't loved and fearing she'd been banished forever.

The girl noticed that other girls were loved for being sweet and kind, for always smiling and playing nicely. So she did the same, behaving as her parents wanted. This pleased them greatly; they no longer shut her away but told everyone – flushed with happiness and pride – what a good little girl she was.

The girl grew into a woman and soon she had a family of her own. The woman loved her husband and, though he loved her too, she was scared to upset him in case he left her. So she was sweet and kind and, if ever she felt frustrated or angry, she suppressed those feelings and felt sad instead. She tried hard never to get angry. The woman behaved in this way with everyone she met, nodding and smiling, always careful not to disagree with or displease anyone.

When the woman was passed over for a promotion, for a younger and more inexperienced man, she said nothing. When her husband left her for a younger but more experienced woman, she only wept. When the politicians refused a living wage to the nurses and teachers but awarded the bankers bonuses and themselves pay rises, the woman did not protest. When the governments of the world ignored the plight of their bleeding Earth, subjecting it to fracking and pillaging, she lamented the climate crisis but did not act. When she witnessed police brutality against innocents, she watched the outcry with awe but did not join the fray.

Until, one day, the woman started sobbing in a supermarket aisle and, though most people ignored her (just as she had tried to do), someone stopped and asked what was wrong. 'Everything,' the woman wept. They talked for a long while, until the person offered some advice: 'Compassion without action creates depression – when you see something's wrong, you must do something about it.' For the first time in a long time, the woman smiled a real smile. 'And anger is not a bad thing,' they added, 'but a necessary thing. You feel it in the face of cruelty, injustice, inequality . . . Anger tells you it's time to act.'

That was the day the woman transformed into a hurricane. All the anger she'd suppressed over a lifetime whipped up into a swirling, twisting, churning storm inside her, until she was a whirling dervish of pure, resplendent rage.

When the dust finally settled, the woman was filled with the strength of a thousand.

Now, she spoke up against abuse and stood up against oppression and fought injustice. She let her anger guide her, with calm clarity, to the places where she needed to act. She was no longer sweet, kind, nice – and powerless. She was clear, true, mighty – and able to change the world.

Goldie has a niggling feeling that she's heard that story somewhere before – at least the first few paragraphs – but then it'd taken a twist and a turn she didn't recognize. And it scared her. She thinks, in the aftermath of reading, of Bea's words after Goldie accused her of having a temper: *I do and I'm proud of it. All women should have one. Men do and no one judges them for it – but we're raised to be sweet, pretty, meek. And vulnerable. It's dangerous. Anger is self-protection. Anger is a feminist act.*

Bea is right; Goldie can't deny it. If only women were raised differently – and men, of course – there'd be much less need for shelters like hers. But still, she's been raised in

this society, with these values, and she can't help but want her little girl to be all the things Bea condemns. With the possible exception of vulnerable. Because, if she's not, it begs the question: what else might her little girl be getting up to behind her back?

Chapter Nine

3.33 p.m. – Goldie

Seven days. Seven days until the dreaded appointment. This fateful day is dangerously close to Luna's tenth birthday, in eighteen days, which somehow just seems to make it all worse. Goldie can hardly think of anything else, is struggling to organize the extravagant birthday celebrations – Luna wants to invite every current resident of the shelter: eight women and five children – and wonders if she'll even still have custody of her daughter by then. What if they act fast? What if this Mr Lane decides that Luna should be immediately taken into care. The thought makes Goldie's heart ache and her stomach churn.

'Ma, Ma!' Luna tugs at her mother's coat.

Goldie blinks down at her daughter, having almost forgotten that she was there. They've just crossed the junction at Chedworth Street, the gates of Mayfield Primary School closing behind them down the road, and are now ambling along Merton Street, veering left.

'I'm sorry,' Goldie says. 'What is it?'

'Where are we going?' Luna demands. 'I thought we were going straight home to the shelter.'

'Oh,' Goldie says, only half listening. 'I thought perhaps we could go to the café today. Special pre-birthday treat . . .'

Luna says nothing, just hikes her rucksack up on her back, trotting along beside Goldie as the bag slips down again, gently bouncing. Goldie glances at her: Luna, looking for all the world like an ordinary schoolgirl. Not a prodigy, not a writer of strangely sophisticated tales, not half-Grimm, half-star. Goldie feels a fierce wave of love and a sudden piercing wish that her daughter *was* entirely ordinary. Not special, not different, not unique, but just the same as everyone else. Entirely unremarkable.

'I'll buy you a chocolate delice,' Goldie says, offering the only thing that's sure to guarantee a positive response. She has it vaguely in mind to try to talk around the subject of the interview with social services and upcoming appointment. Surely she needs to inform Luna in advance, even if she's not permitted to discuss the particulars? And maybe touch on the subject of the story she read, without actually admitting she read it. Anything in the hope of trying to winkle information out of her secretive daughter. She turns right onto Derby Street, towards the Maison Clement café and their delectable treats, which Luna is quite unable to resist.

Luna looks up. 'No, thanks. I'd rather go straight to the shelter.'

'Oh.' Goldie sighs, deflated. 'All right then.'

4.59 p.m. – Luna

'Okay, if Snap's too boring, how about a puzzle instead?'

Luna collects up the scattered playing cards and slots them carefully back into the box. She's sitting on the floor of their newest resident's room, conducting a preliminary interview with her little girl. Luna meets with every child within a few days of them coming to the shelter; she asks them pertinent questions and finds that they usually give her the information she needs. And, since she's a child too, their mothers rarely interfere.

The little girl, Masie, strokes her chin, considering this offer. Luna smiles, waiting. She has infinite patience with the children, indulging them to the same degree that she never does herself, but then Luna has never thought of herself as a child.

'O-kay,' Masie says, as if bestowing upon Luna a great favour.

'Perfect.' Luna laughs. 'Which one? Dragons or goblins?' When her mother established the shelter three years ago, after Aunt Liyana's death, Luna had put herself in charge of choosing children's toys. She banned all princesses, fairies and ballerinas, declaring them a bad influence on girls, a sentiment with which Goldie could only agree. Luna permitted witches, goddesses, female warriors and super heroines. She also insisted that the little library in the common room be stocked with books that promoted female empowerment: *Good Night Stories for Rebel Girls*, *Little Women* (especially Jo), *The Paper Bag Princess* . . . And banning the likes of *Pride and Prejudice*, *Jane Eyre*, *Wuthering Heights* and any such stories that ended with marriages and similar happily ever afters. 'It's not what you want to read,' she'd argued, 'when you've just run away from a violent man.' And, again, Goldie couldn't argue with that.

'Dragons,' Masie decides. 'The blue ones.'

'Excellent choice.' Luna reaches for the box, tipping it upside down. 'Right, let's separate the edges first.'

As they both set about doing so, Luna casts Masie surreptitious glances. The little girl has been in the shelter only a few days, but is already settling in well. Having snuck into Goldie's office and read the file, Luna knows most of what she's suffered. And the anger she feels towards the man who inflicted it fired sparks at her fingertips, so she almost singed the papers.

'Well done! You've found the four corners, the most important pieces,' Luna says, having nudged those pieces in Masie's direction. 'Now we can get started.'

Having eavesdropped on many of Goldie's sessions with new residents, Luna knows the best way to get children to open up. Distraction is the first key: when a person is engaged in something, they're more likely to talk about difficult subjects. Luna finds puzzles, requiring a modicum of concentration, optimal.

'You're very good at puzzles,' Luna says presently.

Masie nods.

'Did anyone teach you? Or did you teach yourself?'

Masie presses two edge pieces together unsuccessfully.

'Try this one.' Luna slips Masie the matching piece. 'It might work.'

'Yes!' Masie exclaims, grinning up at Luna. 'It did.'

Luna smiles. 'Did you do puzzles with your mummy at home?'

Masie shakes her head.

'Your daddy?'

Masie stiffens, hand hovering over the scattering of jigsaw pieces. Luna falls silent too, focusing on fitting blue dragon scales together while humming a tune.

'Mummy and Daddy played their own games together,' Masie whispers. 'They wouldn't let me join in.'

'Ah.' Luna nods. 'Parents can be like that sometimes.'

'I didn't want to play anyway,' Masie says. 'The games always made Mummy cry.'

Luna doesn't make eye contact. 'Did Daddy make Mummy cry a lot?'

Masie sniffs.

'I see,' Luna says. 'Well, I have an idea about that.'

Masie looks up, brows knitted.

'So –' Luna sets down her jigsaw pieces, finally getting down to business – 'would you like me to teach him a lesson?'

Masie ponders this, then gives a single, solemn nod.

'Okay then.' Luna smiles. 'I will.'

Twenty-four months ago – Scarlet

Nearly a year passed before Scarlet found a place akin to home. She was wandering aimlessly along Turl Street, having just spent the past hour aimlessly circling the Radcliffe Camera, when her haphazard trajectory finally intersected with a moment of opportunity. As she ambled past the entrance to Exeter College, serendipity brushed up against her as she snatched the end of a sentence one of the college porters was saying to the other.

'I heard him chucking saucepans about the place when I passed the kitchens just now,' one said. 'Making a right old hullaballoo he was.'

'Not surprised,' the other replied. 'Harry quitting on him on a Parlour Evening, it's not on.' He shook his head. 'These kids, no sense of service.'

'No bloody sense at all,' the other added.

They both laughed.

Scarlet saw her moment and, after a split second's doubt, she seized it.

Students streamed in and out of the entrance, so she slipped into the stream – as if visiting the college had been her intention all along – and in the next instance she was spat out onto the other side. The opulent beauty of the place didn't come as a surprise; she'd lived most of her life in Cambridge, after all, and had become (almost) used to the juxtaposition of these magnificently ornate, sprawling medieval buildings planted all over the otherwise ordinary town. As if some conquering king had scattered grand stately homes at every turn for all his dukes and earls.

Hurrying along the cobbled pathways crossing the quad, Scarlet tried to intuit the location of the kitchen. Since the dining halls usually sat in the centre of the colleges, she could reasonably suppose the kitchen would be adjacent. She darted through a stone archway and along a stone corridor to emerge into another quad, this one lined with flower beds of golden marigolds, the surrounding walls lush with purple-headed wisteria that hung in heavy canopies of blooms over the marigolds beneath. Scarlet wanted to slow down and soak it in but didn't dare. She darted beneath the rows of leaded windows that glittered above her, past the ancient wooden doors, gateways to student and tutor rooms, with lists of names painted in fine letters on placards beside the doors.

A ramp led up to the next corridor, a rare modern addition to the ancient place, and as Scarlet stepped up she heard a voice behind her.

'Miss!'

She glanced back to see the shorter, stouter porter striding towards her. 'Miss!'

She hesitated a second, pulse racing, unsure whether or not to make a run for it, or confront him. 'I'm sorry, I—'

'Members of the public aren't permitted on college grounds during finals, Miss,' he declared, marching ever closer. 'So, if you'd like to follow me . . .'

'I'm not – I'm here to see the chef. I'm agency staff, called in for Parlour Evening.'

Of course, she had no idea what this was and so hoped to hell he wouldn't ask. But if he did . . . She watched uncertainty wrestling with complacency.

'All guests should register at the porter's office first.'

'Oh, I'm terribly sorry,' Scarlet simpered, adopting her most flirtatious look, tinged with a dash of ditsy. 'I didn't realize. I'm so silly. Shall I come with you now? Only I didn't want to be late . . .'

The porter returned an indulgent smile. 'That's all right,' he said kindly. 'Just remember for next time, all right?'

'Oh, yes, of course.' Scarlet offered a small curtsey. 'Thank you so very much!'

Then she turned and dashed off again, before he could change his mind.

Fortunately, the next corridor led to the dining hall. It was typical of all college dining halls: panelled with dark wood, hung with low chandeliers, adorned with oil paintings of illustrious old white men gazing austerely at the long tables below. Scarlet scurried along, mercifully finding the kitchen at the far end, through a final set of doors.

Upon peering in, she was met with a sight of unprecedented anarchy. In nearly fifteen years of working in cafés and restaurants, Scarlet had never witnessed anything like it: pans bubbling over, peelings carpeting the tiled floor, smoke billowing from ovens, fat spitting from abandoned roasting tins on the stoves, the air acrid with the stench of burnt oil and onions and spices.

And, at the centre of it all, a gargantuan man in chef's whites and hat, whose figure filled a good measure of the room and whose bellowing rebukes filled the rest: a string of expletives issuing forth that would've made a sailor blush. Around and about him raced a small handful of sous chefs desperately trying to stem the fountain of chaos.

Taking a deep breath, drawing upon every remaining reserve of confidence – most of it having been battered out of her by months of guilt – Scarlet strode forward, coming to a stop in front of the chef.

'Who the hell are you?' He glowered down at her. 'And what the hell do you want?'

'I'm your new sous chef,' Scarlet retorted. 'The agency sent me.'

'Which agency? I called four of the fuckers and—'

He paused and Scarlet froze, eyes wide.

'Oh, who gives a shit?' he answered himself. 'So long as you can julienne two hundred carrots and prep five trays of dauphinoise potatoes in three hours, you could be from Pluto for all I care.'

Having only worked with pastries and cakes, she hadn't a clue what 'julienne' meant, but she nodded anyway. 'Yes, of course, Chef. No problem.'

'Excellent.' He spun round to address a young man whose uniform was so splattered in various sauces he resembled a Jackson Pollock painting. 'All right, Smithy, you wanker, go and get this girl some whites.' The boy gawped at him. 'Now!'

*

With Scarlet mucking in, Parlour Evening passed without a glitch and the chef was, in his own acerbic way, so pleased he offered her a full-time position. She accepted, on the condition that she got room and board, plus fifty quid a week in cash. Chef was quite happy with this arrangement, especially since having Scarlet on-site meant he could call on her anytime he wanted. And she always came, since she had little else to do except sit in her room staring at the walls and reliving that awful night, or wander aimlessly around the city doing the very same.

And so she stayed at Exeter College, preparing lunches and dinners for the students and tutors in the Great Hall, and life continued on uneventfully. Which was exactly what Scarlet wanted.

Until, one day, someone found her.

Chapter Ten

6.33 a.m. – Luna

I didn't tell Ma what I did, because I know she'd disapprove. And then she'd forbid me from doing it again. Still, I don't regret it. I know I should, but I don't.

I often wonder what sort of man my father was. Ma speaks of him like he was some sort of saint, but I know he wasn't. He couldn't have been. I'm half of him and I'm nowhere near saintly. Anyway, I'm sure any goodness I have I get from Ma. *She's* the saint. The sort that sometimes makes you sick because they're so *nice* that you can never hope to measure up. Ma's an angel and, next to her, I'm a devil. So my father must have been pretty bad too. The only thing I can't understand then is why she fell in love with him. Perhaps she reformed him before he died. I wonder if she can reform me too.

1.03 p.m. – Teddy

He returns to Jack's Gelato again, telling himself it's only the ice cream he wants, but the sinking disappointment he feels at the sight of the empty booth testifies to the truth. He tells himself it doesn't matter, that he doesn't care. Then he orders three scoops: burnt sugar and salt; white miso and honey; bitter lemon and basil.

He eats slowly, tasting each delectable flavour, but even

this doesn't serve to take the edge off the disappointment. Irritated with himself, Teddy decides not to return tomorrow. He won't waste his time chasing a silly fantasy. He hardly knows her, after all. And that he found himself telling a virtual stranger things he's never told another soul is immaterial. She's simply the most exquisitely beautiful and elegantly dressed person he's ever seen. Teddy has always found it a great shame that people don't dress properly anymore, himself included. He longs for the days of tweed and silk, of men in waistcoats and everyone in hats. He'd dress like that if he could bear the looks he'd be certain to attract. Sometimes around town Teddy sees a group of students dressing as if they're members of the Bloomsbury Group. He's often wanted to thank them for aesthetically improving his day.

When Teddy reaches the Corpus Clock at the end of the street, he sweeps through the mass of tourists taking selfies, then turns left. By the time he's reached the Mill Pond, he's having second thoughts. And when he reaches the doorstep of the shelter – tucked down a little street off Newnham Road – Teddy has decided, reluctantly, that he probably *will* return to Jack's tomorrow. It'd be silly to avoid it, to allow some girl to deprive him of his favourite treat. He'll go and enjoy his gelato and won't think of her at all. Not at all.

Twenty-one months ago – Scarlet

Scarlet had woken to see the woman standing above her, regarding her with no small amount of curiosity. Startled, both by the stranger's presence and having momentarily forgotten where she'd fallen asleep, Scarlet scrambled to sit up. She was on a bench under a tree in the Botanic Garden.

She'd been working a lot of long shifts lately, which she enjoyed because it meant less time to dwell on mistakes, less time to steep in guilt. And she was always so exhausted at the end of the day that falling asleep was never a problem. Indeed, this was exactly why she'd collapsed on a bench after a stroll through the Botanic Garden and, under the soporific heat of the midday sun, promptly dozed off.

'Hello?' Scarlet said. 'Can I help you?'

The woman smiled and, perhaps only then realizing how close she was standing to the bench, stepped back. 'You're Scarlet Thorne, aren't you?'

'What?' Scarlet backed up further still. 'No, I'm not.' She stared at the interloper, expecting her, in true British style, to offer mumbled apologies before shuffling off. But this stranger, having not got the memo on manners, only smiled even more deeply – as if Scarlet was a film star rarely spotted in public – and shook her head.

'You are,' she said. 'I know you are. I was there that night . . .' She lowered her voice respectfully. 'The night our sister died.'

For a moment, pure shock pinned Scarlet to the bench. When she gathered herself, she leapt up and started striding across the grass.

The woman scurried after her.

'Please, go away,' Scarlet hissed. 'I don't know what you're talking about. You've clearly mistaken me for someone else. I don't have any sisters. And I'm certainly not *your* sister, so, please, leave me alone.'

'They say you've never been back since the accident,' the woman said, a little out of breath. 'I didn't believe them at first, but then I never saw you . . . They say you blame yourself, but I don't understand why. It wasn't your fault; you couldn't save her. No one thought so. I don't—'

Suddenly Scarlet stopped, causing her pursuer to double back. They were standing outside the glasshouses, flanked by spectacular tropical plants, though neither woman noticed the view.

'Look,' she snapped, voice verging on hysterical. 'I don't know who the hell you are, or who the hell you think I am, but I just want you to leave me the fuck alone, all right?'

'Wait.' The woman was crestfallen. 'I'm sorry, I didn't mean to upset you. I only wanted to help you.'

'Help me? Help *me*?' Scarlet was shrieking now. 'You're the one who needs help! Have you escaped from an insane asylum or something? Because I—'

'I don't think that's what they're called anymore,' the woman offered gently. 'It's not very politically correct.'

'Fuck political correctness.' Scarlet scowled at her. 'And get the hell away from me, now!'

As Scarlet started to run, the other woman reached out her hand and their fingers touched. It was only for a split second, but the sparks that sprang forth were bright as stars and emitted a crackle as if they were embers popping from a fire. A heat travelled up Scarlet's arm, flushing through her whole body and filling her eyes with tears.

It had been so long since Scarlet had felt the warmth of her own particular magic – the tidal waves of sorrow having drenched her flames and the sandstorms of guilt having smothered her desires – that to feel it now was like being hugged by another human after spending eighteen months hiding in a hole underground. She was so suddenly and completely overwhelmed by emotion that she couldn't contain it, dropping to the grass on hands and knees and sobbing like a woman in labour.

3.33 a.m. – the Sisters Grimm

Goldie patrols the ever-expanding glade. Thousands of sisters have gathered tonight. She wonders if, as in previous years, it's the approach of the summer solstice that's spreading the word and swelling the ranks. As she walks, giving a word of advice here, a smile of encouragement there, Goldie worries about Luna. Five days – well, four really, since it's already the middle of the night. Four days till the cursed appointment, till—

She hears Bea's voice in her head: *Do you ever not?*

You don't understand, she retorts, embarking on an imaginary conversation. *Having a baby means a lifetime of worry*. So she continues. She worries about what the specialist will say and what the social worker will do. She worries about care homes and fostering and what might happen to her darling girl. She imagines an empty flat, deathly quiet and lonely without Luna in it . . . Then she gives a vigorous shake of her head, trying to snap herself out of it. *Stop catastrophizing!*

Hearing sighs of frustration below her, Goldie glances down to see a teenager with sparks at her fingertips, repeatedly trying and failing to ignite a small dry stick.

'It's all right, Saskia, you're getting there,' Goldie says, stopping. 'Just focus. That's right. You can't think of anything else – no questions, no reasonings, no doubts. Expel every thought from your mind and channel all that energy into knowing that you can – that you *will* – light that stick.'

Watching the girl try again and again, Goldie thinks with a pang of longing, as she always does when assisting daughters of fire, of Scarlet and wonders, as she always does, where her sister might be. She watches and waits for a few minutes, saying nothing, only willing Saskia to succeed.

When the stick remains stubbornly unlit, Goldie bends down to whisper in Saskia's ear, 'Say this to yourself: *Validior es quam videris, fortior quam sentis, sapientior quam credis.* Over and over again. Until it works. I promise it will. You've got the power to do it; you only have to believe it.'

Saskia begins again, mumbling the words over and over: a chant, an incantation to bring forth fire – all the while focusing her gaze on the tip of the stick.

For a few minutes nothing happens, then, all at once, a spark.

Saskia cries out with surprise and delight. But the puff of her breath blows out the spark. Her face falls with disappointment, but then she laughs. 'I did it, I did it!'

The gust of the girl's laugh ignites the fire again and this time the flames surge as if the stick has just been doused in kerosene.

'Oh!' Saskia drops the stick, still laughing.

Goldie, laughing too, pats her on the back. 'Well done, Saskia. Well done.'

I should be at home with Luna, Goldie thinks as she walks on. *I shouldn't be here. What if something happens?*

She's asleep – she's fine. We're tuned in to her. Nothing's going to happen. This time it's not Goldie's imagination but Liyana.

'But she needs me.' Goldie sighs. 'And what if—'

Not right now she doesn't, but these sisters do. Now, come and assist me with the water witches. Her laughter is water on hot rocks. *They're getting a little out of hand.*

'All right,' Goldie says, doing her best to focus. 'Are they at the river?'

Soon she's standing on the riverbank, watching a clutch of sisters standing up to their waists in the cool river. They're giggling and splashing each other with waves, churning the water with their encircling hands. While Liyana's voice – humming through the mizzling rain – instructs them, Goldie watches on and lets her thoughts return to worrying again.

'I did it!'

Goldie blinks, returning her attention to the river. There, standing in the wake of what must have been a huge wave (judging by the fact that Goldie's toes are now wet) is a gleeful woman soaked to the skin, holding her arms high and sporting a huge grin.

'Fantastic!' Goldie claps and cheers along with the splashed women and girls standing in the river and on its banks. 'Well done!'

And then, in the ebb of the jubilant cries, Goldie hears a sound that chills her, though she's not standing in the cold river.

A scream.

Not the screams of excitement or delight but fear.

'Stop!' Goldie shouts. 'Listen!'

But she doesn't need to, since that's what every sister is already doing. All have stopped. All are still. All are listening.

For a split second there is silence. Blessed, relieved silence.

Then the scream comes again.

Chapter Eleven

4.37 a.m. – the Sisters Grimm

As Goldie runs, she thinks of Luna: *What if she came? Without my permission. What if it's her? Please, let her be okay.* Then Liyana: *It's happening, it's all happening again. Another accident, another sister dead.* Goldie runs faster than she ever thought possible, her heart hammering, her lungs stinging, her legs aching. Still, she pushes herself harder and faster, following the ribbon of sound. The screaming twists away from the river, taking her through a knot of willow trees. With a flick of her wrist, Goldie parts the curtain of leaves and is dashing through them, panting, sliding across the moss, nearly tripping on the stone, to land beside the girl.

Not Luna, is her first thought. *Thank God.*

The girl is young, perhaps ten, and bleeding profusely. She's covered in cuts, slices into her skin, clothes torn, bruises already blooming. Unconscious. *This is no accident. This is an attack.* Goldie doesn't recognize her, doesn't remember her name. But then there are hundreds, thousands of sisters, so why should she?

'Earth sisters!' Goldie screams. 'I need you!'

Women and girls are already crowding around the body, craning necks, emitting gasps of shock and despair.

'We need healers,' Goldie demands. 'Now!'

Five women dash forward, falling to their knees at the

girl's feet and her sides, until she's surrounded by a circle of women, with their hands on and above her, their eyes closed, their lips moving, mouthing silent incantations.

Goldie focuses on the girl's face, her glowing hands pressed to the girl's cheeks – binding her skin together, melding the cuts, smoothing the scratches – and then her neck, soothing her throat, restoring her spirit, breathing fresh air into her lungs . . .

Goldie feels the sisters at her side as she works – the crack of bones snapping back into place, the gasps of onlookers – and the two whose spirits hover above her, Liyana and Bea, each exerting the power of their elements into the circle of healing.

Beneath the girl, the moss thickens, fresh tendrils of ivy creep along the forest floor, sprouts of new saplings poke up through the soil wherever there's space to see. Everything touched by the elemental magic of the earth sisters is imbued with life. And so, they dearly hope, will be the girl at the centre of it all.

And then, at last, she opens her eyes.

'Are the soldiers back?'

'No,' Goldie says quickly. 'They can't be, can they? I mean, *he's* gone. We killed him. And he's never been back, not since he possessed Scarlet—'

'How do you know that?' a fire sister demands. 'How can you be sure?'

Goldie says nothing, just shakes her head. *Is it possible that a soldier might have wormed his way into Everwhere again? But why?* Wilhelm Grimm had created the army of soldiers to fight the sisters, forcing the young women to kill, thus turning them evil so he could have them for himself. When he'd died, the soldiers, with no more purpose or aim, had disbanded. Or so everyone had assumed . . .

'You can't be sure, can you?' the fire sister presses. 'Can you?'

Hundreds of Sisters Grimm are gathered together in the glade, sitting across the moss and stone. They gaze up at Goldie – who sits atop a fallen tree trunk, while three others sit at her feet, cradling the resurrected girl in their laps – waiting for her to say something, to explain everything, to reassure and comfort them.

'He might have been here all this time,' an earth sister says. 'His spirit haunting the place. He might've been waiting for more of us to come, to gather, so he could . . .'

Silence falls over the glade as she trails off, anticipation and fear in the air.

'Massacre us.'

Everyone looks around to see who spoke. A water sister rises from the crowd.

'We don't know, do we?' she persists. 'You can say everyone is safe and everything is fine, but it clearly isn't. If this happened, then it means that Everwhere isn't safe anymore – and someone must be responsible.'

A murmur sweeps through the glade, mutterings of anger and fear.

'Yes, I understand,' Goldie says. 'And we'll find out what's going on. We need to—'

'We need to fight!' A fire sister stands, holding aloft a branch that bursts into flames at its tip, like a flaming torch. 'If the soldiers are back, we'll fight them!'

A scattered cheer erupts in response.

'Wait.' Goldie raises her hand. 'Hold on, calm down!' When silence finally falls, she stands, gazing out into the crowd of upturned faces, some furious, others fearful.

'We mustn't jump to conclusions,' Goldie insists. 'We need to find out what's going on. And, until we do, I propose that we stay away.'

This statement evokes a rumble of discontent from the crowd.

'I know, I know,' she says. 'It's the last thing I want to do too. I know this place is a haven to many, but I'm only suggesting a few days, a few weeks at most. Just until we have a better idea of what's going on. In the meantime, Ana and Bea can keep searching and see what they can find—'

'And what if they don't find anything?' a water sister calls out. 'This place is infinite, after all – finding a single soldier here is like finding a needle in the proverbial!'

'I understand,' Goldie says. 'But I don't think we have much choice right now. And those of you who can investigate matters by means other than coming here, I urge you to do so.'

She listens to the murmurings, studies the sisters' faces: the heads turning to each other, the whisperings, the nods and frowns. Goldie catches the eye of one, a fire sister whose name she can't recall, who looks thoughtful and nods, as if she has an idea.

'I say we set fire to the place and smoke him out!' someone calls out from the crowd. Her voice is echoed by others:

'Hear, hear!'

'Hell, yeah!'

'All right!' Goldie raises a hand again, calling for silence. 'I can see that many of you want to fight and I agree that – in the relative safety of our homes – we *prepare* to fight, if that's what we need to do.'

'Of course that's what we need to do,' the fire sister shouts. 'And we need to do it now!'

'Okay, okay.' Goldie stands and paces, glancing down at the poor injured girl. 'Since it's clear we won't come to a unanimous agreement tonight, we need to put it to a vote and agree that the majority rules. Yes?'

She looks down at the rivers of faces, waiting to see every head nodding. It takes a little while, but eventually she sees bobbing heads sweeping through the crowd.

'Thank you,' Goldie says. 'Right, everyone who agrees to stay away – actually it'll be easier to count the minority. Everyone who wants to stay and fight now, please stand.'

The fire and water witches who spoke first shoot up, followed by twenty or thirty others who stand like trees surrounded by observant stones. Goldie waits. A few more stand. Everyone else stays seated.

'All right,' Goldie says. 'It's clear that the majority are in favour of waiting to fight till we know what's going on, and staying safe till we do.' She looks to each of those standing. 'Agreed?'

A few sisters fling up their arms in frustration. But, albeit reluctantly, they nod.

When all the sisters have gone, Goldie remains.

You made the right call.

Agreed. It's not safe here anymore.

'I feel bad, telling them to run and hide.' Goldie sighs. 'It's the opposite of what I usually try to teach. But I think—'

A breeze encircles her. *You know I always favour fighting, but courage is one thing and foolishness quite another.*

The rain starts to fall. *You won't let Luna come?*

'No, of course not,' Goldie says. 'And yes, I know she won't like it, but I'll explain everything. She'll understand.'

You're so sure? Laughter is carried on the breeze. *She's got a strong mind, that one. And an even stronger will.*

'Yes, but—'

Raindrops splash the soil at Goldie's feet. *When you return home, give Luna my little statue of Mami Wata, tell her to wear it always. Tell her to never take it off.*

'Okay,' Goldie says. 'But, believe me, she won't—'

Promise me.

Goldie sighs. 'All right, I promise.'

6.03 a.m. – Goldie

Goldie sits at the edge of her daughter's bed, watching her sleep. Gently, she touches Luna's blanketed foot and notices that her hand is shaking. *What if Luna had been there tonight? What if she'd been the one attacked?* If she could, Goldie would keep Luna locked in her room till she turned eighteen, keeping her safe, never letting her return to Everwhere. But how can she? Luna would never forgive her. Anyway, she'd also escape, that much is certain. Everwhere is in her daughter's blood and bones. Its magic pulses through her; it's the oxygen in her breath, the rhythm of her heart. If Goldie took Luna away from all that, then she might as well kill her, for she'd rather be dead.

She cannot believe that Luna will be turning ten so soon – fifteen days – how is that possible? Again, the dreaded fear that she won't be celebrating Luna's birthday with her – four days till appointment day – rises up inside Goldie. Squeezing Luna's foot, wishing for the thousandth time that her baby was ordinary. Not special, not different, not magical. *Not a Grimm, just an ordinary little girl.* She thinks of the other little girl, the one who hadn't been able to tell them anything, at least nothing that could help identify her attacker. She hadn't seen him – he had come at her from behind and in the fight she'd been too battered, too busy fighting for her life to pay attention to trying to identify him later.

But what Goldie can't understand is how and why.

How did a soldier return to Everwhere? Weren't they all disbanded upon the death of Wilhelm Grimm? She'd assumed, since she'd never seen another soldier again after they'd vanquished him, that the soldiers had lost both their powers and their ability to enter Everwhere. She'd assumed they'd all returned to being normal boys and men, perhaps with no memory of anything they'd done. But, of course, she had never known for certain. And assumptions, as well she knows, can be dangerous things.

The reason for returning is simpler. If a renegade soldier hadn't lost his drive to kill, then it made sense that he might return to fulfil his mission, even without the instructions of his captain. But why *now*? Why at no other time during the past decade?

That part didn't make sense at all.

'Why didn't you see this coming?' she'd accused Liyana last night. 'I thought you could see things. I thought you'd know.'

I can't see everything. Her voice came with a sprinkling of rain. *I sensed something, but didn't know what. Only fear, rising like a wave.*

Chapter Twelve

7.20 a.m. – Goldie

She's jolted awake by the wail of her alarm and tumbles out of bed, grabbing the phone and rubbing her eyes and wishing to hell she'd had more sleep. And then she remembers. As if the impending doom of the upcoming appointment wasn't agonizing enough, now she has the added burden of how to deal with a rogue soldier stalking Everwhere to overwhelm her already deeply troubled mind. One day till the appointment. *One*. Goldie's stomach churns.

Soon she's in Luna's room, gently rocking her daughter back into wakefulness. It is always Goldie's favourite moment of the day, when a drowsy Luna blinks blearily up at her and offers her a slightly grumpy smile. For a moment Luna is a tiny girl again, flushed with purity and innocence and an absolute, unequivocal love.

If only, Goldie thinks. *If only this moment could last forever.*

This is swiftly followed by another thought: *What if it could?*

Eighteen months ago – Scarlet

She spent a lot of time with Kavita after the incident in the Botanic Garden. Or 'Your Awakening' as Kavita liked to call it, though Scarlet favoured 'My Public Humiliation'. Or: 'The Afternoon I Totally Lost My Shit'.

'No, that was the day you found yourself again,' was always Kavita's retort whenever Scarlet said such things. To which Scarlet would roll her eyes, dismissing her friend's sentimentality, while always being secretly touched by it.

Kavita was a tutor in Medieval Literature at Balliol College and, after they'd known each other a few months, she confessed that finding Scarlet on a bench in the Botanic Garden hadn't been a coincidence.

'You were stalking me?' Scarlet had responded, mock-horrified.

'No!' Kavita laughed. 'Well, maybe just a little bit. But not in a creepy way.'

'I don't think there's a non-creepy way to stalk a person,' Scarlet said. 'By definition. Just like there's not a non-evil way to murder someone.' They were sitting side by side at the window table in G&D's – Oxford's oldest ice-cream emporium – sharing a tub of Daim-bar ice cream with crumbled chocolate brownies, and Scarlet held up her spoon. 'Hey, you're not planning on murdering me, are you?'

Kavita rested her chin between finger and thumb, as if considering it. 'Well, perhaps I was, but not now I've got to know you. Not only are you lovely, but you're also far more powerful than I am.' She laughed again. 'I only pick battles I can win.'

Scarlet's smile fell. 'I'm not as powerful as I wish I was.'

'Don't,' Kavita said, reaching across to rest her hand on Scarlet's wrist. 'It wasn't your fault. 'You tried to save her; you nearly died trying. You couldn't have done more.'

Scarlet said nothing, only dug her spoon deep into the tub to extract a large glob of crunchy ice cream and fill her mouth. For how could she admit what she really felt? *That she could've done more; she could've died, and wished she had.* Scarlet didn't fear death, not anymore. Now she feared life, since the agonies of life were far worse than the tranquillity of death. She longed to return to Everwhere, to spend an eternity as a spirit among the star-studded skies, meandering along the rivers and through the trees, listening to birdsong and chattering with her sisters without a care in the world. That one, or this. What bliss it would be. What a blessed relief.

'It's survivor's guilt,' Kavita said. 'Perhaps you should see a therapist?'

Scarlet shook her head. It was true that she'd been feeling guilty for a very long time, but lately the guilt had mutated into something else: regret.

2.49 p.m. – Teddy

He sits at the edge of the dilapidated sofa in the living room of the refuge, consoling the newest arrival at the shelter with a cup of Earl Grey and a plate of bourbon biscuits. Goldie had left to pick Luna up from school just five minutes before the woman had knocked on their door: a moment of bad timing since – understandably – battered women are often a little unnerved to entrust their safety to another man.

'Goldie won't be long,' Teddy says, glancing at his watch for the twentieth time in half as many minutes. 'So you don't need to tell me anything if you don't want to. Just drink some tea and eat some biscuits and—'

All at once, the woman, who hasn't yet told Teddy her

name, bursts into tears. Without blinking, he reaches for the open box of tissues on the coffee table. Her face is already so bloodied and bruised that it doubly saddens him to see her cry, knowing how painful it must be. He thinks for a moment about his own pains, and regrets: not going to Central Saint Martins; not asking the girl he met at Jack's Gelato (and thinks about too often) for her number. He'd put considerable energy into suppressing the regret of giving up Saint Martins and thought he'd succeeded in forgetting, but telling the girl seems to have unlocked and ignited his desire all over again. As if wanting her has made him start wanting everything all over again.

Stop obsessing, he tells himself. *Focus.*

'I know you're scared,' he says softly. 'Everyone is when they first arrive. But we will protect you. We've got our own measures in place and a direct line to the police—'

The woman takes a handful of tissues, shaking her head as she wipes her eyes and blows her nose. 'No,' she sniffs at last. 'You don't understand. You don't . . .'

Teddy leans forward in his chair, trying to catch the words before they're drowned by a fresh bout of tears. Failing, he waits. After several more long, wet minutes have passed, Teddy nudges another box of tissues towards her. Without glancing up, the woman reaches for a handful. Words are smothered by sobs, but Teddy doesn't try to extract them. He's learned to be patient.

'My husband,' the woman sobs, finally audible amid her misery. 'He works for the police, ten years now . . . so I ain't safe, and never will be . . .'

'Perhaps if you report him,' Teddy suggests gently. 'Then—'

The bark of her laugh cuts him off. 'And what bloody good would that do?'

'He should be punished for what he did.'

She snorts, wiping her nose. 'Raped by a man who'd been fucking me for ten months? They'll jump to prosecute that, won't they? Don't get me—'

'But . . .' Teddy is tentative. 'That doesn't mean you shouldn't try.'

'Put myself through an ordeal, through examinations and interrogations and God knows what else?' She sniffs again. 'Marital rape weren't illegal till twenty years ago – did you know that? Twenty fucking years! And, anyway, it's a bloody pointless law if ever there was one. No one'll get convicted by it. Never.'

'But come on,' Teddy says, struggling to remain calm. 'I mean, look at you! They can't deny what he's done to you.'

She glances up, meeting his eye for the first time. 'How long've you been working here?'

'Five years,' Teddy says, wondering what she means.

A look of disdain sharpens her face. 'Then how can you be so naive?'

8.39 p.m. – Goldie

'Becky's finally settled. She's had half a dozen cups of Earl Grey and I've had two dozen bourbons,' Goldie says. 'But I think she's feeling a little better.'

'And what about the policeman?' Teddy asks. 'What are we going to do about him?'

'You forget,' Goldie says, 'that we have protections other refuges don't.'

'Yes,' Teddy considers. 'But only so long as she stays in the house. What about out there? Cambridge isn't safe for her, is it? Not with her ex's mates patrolling the streets.'

'Not until she's stronger, no. But as soon as she's ready, I'll take her to Everwhere,' Goldie says, trying not to worry about the matter of soldiers and the like. 'And after we've trained her, she'll soon be able to defend herself.'

Teddy folds his arms, determined. 'We ought to report him.'

'True,' Goldie says. 'And if it'd do any good, we would. But she's right; there's no point. So, sadly, we've got to stick to more . . . unorthodox methods. Anyway, Becky's element is fire, so once she's a little stronger and a little braver, she'll be all right.'

Teddy sighs. 'She'll still need a shit-ton of therapy.'

'Yes.' Goldie nods, unable not to think of Leo and her own loss. 'Sadly there's no magical way to heal the heart.'

8.43 p.m. – Luna

She lingers outside her mother's office, ear pressed to the door. This is something she does every time a new resident arrives at the shelter – since, in her experience, eavesdropping on adults is usually the only way to get any real information. Thus, tonight she's learned that Becky's husband won't be seeing the inside of a court. *'Twas ever thus,* she thinks. It is a source of constant anguish and frustration to Luna that so few of the men who beat these women are ever subjected to any sort of justice.

Yet again, she thinks, *I shall have to deal with this one myself.*

Chapter Thirteen

9.29 p.m. – Luna

She knocks three times before he opens the door, scowling down at her. He's medium height, medium build, medium looks – blue eyes, scruffy brown hair – and, Luna thinks, rather resembles an accountant. She's surprised, having expected him to be a little rougher round the edges, a little tougher. She hasn't personally encountered many policemen but Luna had assumed that, as a race, they would look rather more imposing and intimidating.

'What the hell do you want?'

Luna smiles up at him, all sweetness and light. His scowl deepens.

'Shouldn't you be in bed, little girl?'

Still, she says nothing. 'All right,' he snaps. 'Whatever you're selling, I don't want it. Now, kindly sod off.'

Not moving, Luna nods. 'Good evening, Mr Metcalf.'

'It was all right till you interrupted it.' He starts to shut the door. It bangs against Luna's foot. At first he's shocked, then shock quickly shifts to fury. 'Remove your foot right now, or I'm gonna break it, you insolent little shit.'

'Actually –' Luna presses her hand against the door – 'my name is Luna. And you, I believe, are Alex. May I call you Alex?'

'No, you may fucking not,' he snaps, pushing back against the door. 'Now, fuck off back to your mummy before I—'

With one swift push, Luna bangs open the door. It cracks against the wall as she steps into the hallway. 'Before you what?'

The man stares down at her, incredulous.

'I'm sorry,' Luna says, as she closes the door behind her. 'I seem to have made a small dent in your wall. Oh, well. I'm sure you'll forgive me, won't you?' She clicks the lock, then turns back to him. 'I didn't mean it. No, that's a lie. I did. Just like I mean to do everything I'm going to do to you tonight.'

Finally, he finds his voice. 'What the fuck is going on? Get out of my house right fucking now.'

He reaches out to seize Luna by the scruff of the neck, but she grabs his hand and, with one motion, has twisted his arm and dropped him to his knees.

'Ah.' Luna's smile widens. 'There's that temper I've been hearing about . . .'

'Let go of me, you little bitch!' he shouts. 'Let me go or I'll make you regret it!'

'Oh, I've no doubt,' Luna says. 'But I'm afraid tonight I'm the one who'll be making you regret your behaviour. You're due a little lesson, aren't you, Mr Metcalf? It's been a long time coming.'

She twists his arm again and he emits a shriek of pain. Luna laughs and lets him go. He scrambles away from her, holding his arm, pressing himself against the wall.

'Who the fuck *are* you? Did she send you here?' he demands, his plain face contorted with fury. 'Do you have her? Did you take her? Cos if you did, I'm going to—'

Luna draws herself up to her full height of four foot nine, her smile unwavering. 'Do you mean your wife, Becky? Or are there a number of women you've beaten and raped?'

She looks him slowly up and down. 'I'd say not, but then it's hard to tell. Men like you are good at concealing your true natures.'

'Look here, you little freak,' he spits, cradling his wounded arm like a grounded bird. 'I don't know where you came from or why the fuck you're here, but I suggest you fuck off pretty sharpish, unless you want to get what's coming to you.'

'Oh?' Luna raises an eyebrow. 'So you hit kids too?'

Refusing to look at her, Mr Metcalf mutters into his chest, 'Just g-get the fuck out of my house.'

Luna steps forward to stand over him. 'Why don't you make me?' She presses her face into his so she can smell the whiff of onion on his breath. 'Isn't that what you like to do best?'

He raises his good hand to slap her but she's too fast, catching him at the wrist, her small hand gripping him tight. He stares at her, incredulous.

Luna grins. 'Stronger than I look, aren't I?'

Then, with a twist of his wrist, she shoves him back against the stairs. The piercing scream eclipses the crack of bone.

'You're insane!' Alex kicks out at her wildly. 'You're fucking insane!'

'Am I?' Luna advances upon him with small, deliberate steps. 'I suppose you'd know, wouldn't you, Alex? You can't have too many marbles up there if the state of Becky's anything to go by.'

'That's none of your fucking business,' he hisses, finally managing to strike his foot against Luna's hip, knocking her back. He laughs as she tumbles downstairs. 'Ha! You don't know anything about us, you don't know what she did, so you can fuck—'

'So she deserved it, did she?' Luna halts her descent and Alex's laughter fades. She picks herself up. 'She provoked you?' Luna scrambles up the stairs and seizes Alex's leg. 'Just like you're provoking me to do this.' With one hand, she presses his foot to the stair, then, standing over him, brings her shoe down hard on his ankle. 'So, have you learned your lesson yet, Mr Metcalf? Or will I have to keep teaching you?'

'N-no, p-please, please stop,' he begs. 'Please, don't, please . . .'

Luna leans down. 'Did she beg you to stop?'

He says nothing.

'Did she?' Luna growls. 'Alex?'

Reluctantly, he nods.

'And did you, Alex?' She pins him with her gaze. 'Did you stop?'

Slowly, he shakes his head.

'Not even when she begged?'

'N-no,' he splutters. 'N-no, I-I didn't.'

'All right then, Alex.' Luna stands again. 'Repeat after me: I will never touch a woman in anger again.' She waits. 'Now!'

'I-I will n-never touch a woman a-again,' he whimpers. 'I s-swear.'

2.17 a.m. – Goldie

She'd been so tired that she'd fallen asleep just after nine (enabling Luna to sneak out without being seen) on the dilapidated sofa, having polished off the rest of the biscuits.

When she dreams, she dreams of Leo. He's not alive as he was on Earth, but as he was when she resurrected him in Everwhere: his spirit and soul trapped in an ancient oak. Tonight, she's carried by her dreams to lie in his branches, to feel the brush of his leaves on her cheek.

'I miss you,' she whispers, blinking away tears.

His breath rustles the leaves. *I miss you too.*

'Do you?' Goldie asks. 'I thought you can't feel longing or loss. I thought you're free from all that now.'

You're right. I feel no sorrow, so perhaps I should only say: I love you.

'I look forward to no longer feeling sorrow.' She reaches out to hold one of his branches. 'Nor fear. All I seem to do is worry. I'm not sure I can take it much longer.'

You need a break.

'I do.' Goldie gives a wry smile. 'Though I don't see when I'm ever going to get one.'

Not yet, true, but soon, I hope. For now you're needed here, and our daughter—

'I know,' Goldie says. 'Don't worry, I'm taking care of her. And I'll fight social services tooth and nail, I can promise you that.'

—she's in danger. She needs you. She needs you to save her.

'Danger?'

Goldie wakes with a start.

Chapter Fourteen

2.48 a.m. – Goldie

As soon as she awakes, Goldie knows she has to take Luna and run. She knows it's madness, knows it will cause far more problems than it'll solve, but still she has to do it. Luna is in danger; that's all that matters. And Goldie knows what Leo meant by that; he'd reached across time and death to tell her to save their little girl from being taken away and brought up in care, unloved, neglected and abused. Of course, this isn't a certainty; perhaps some children have kind and loving foster parents. But Leo told Goldie this wouldn't be the case for Luna. And so, there's only one thing to do.

The appointment with Mr Lane is in six and a half hours, and the gates to Everwhere open and close in forty-five minutes, so Goldie has to act quickly. She can't tell Teddy, since he will only try to fight her, will tell her to be sensible and rational and, probably, to 'trust in the system'. But she doesn't trust in the system. Not anymore. Not at all. Goldie's trust in the system hasn't been strong at the best of times, given her experience with trying to gain legal protection for women in the shelter. Too often the police didn't bother and, even if they did, restraining orders didn't work. Which is why Goldie has taken things into her own hands.

And why she'll do it again now.

She's not telling Luna the plan. Which is to grab a clutch

of supplies – including a tent, sleeping bags, clothes and snacks, the little Mami Wata statue – and go to the nearest gate in Grantchester Meadows before 3.33 a.m. and walk through.

Simple.

Goldie's not certain how Luna will react, since she's never been a great fan of surprises, especially not ones that change her life dramatically. But Goldie has no choice. She can't risk Luna refusing to go. So she'll tell her it's just a fun little camping trip.

That the plan is not only unwise but also potentially quite dangerous, Goldie is choosing not to think about it too deeply. She'll write Teddy a short note, explaining and apologizing. She won't say goodbye. She'll promise to be back, as soon as she's got it all figured out. He'll be angry, of course. But, hopefully, he'll understand.

Anyway, it'll only be for a little while, she tells herself. Just a few days or so. What she'll do after that, Goldie has no idea, but she's deciding to trust in the evolutionary nature of life. Something will happen; an answer will come. Running away will certainly make everything far worse – what with missed social services appointments and unexplained school absences – along with the very real risk that everything on Earth will escalate so terribly that she and Luna will be forced to stay in Everwhere till Luna turns eighteen. Although Goldie is very tenaciously pretending that possibility doesn't exist at all.

Chapter Fifteen

3.33 a.m. – Goldie & Luna

'Why are we in Everwhere tonight?' Luna trots alongside Goldie, stopping now and then to pick up particularly attractive stones. She rubs them on her skirt, before discarding the ones not up to scratch. 'It's not Saturday. I thought I was only allowed on Saturdays. And anyway, I thought it wasn't very safe at the moment. You said there was a soldier back again.'

'I said there *might* be a soldier back again,' Goldie says as Luna chatters on. She quickens her pace, striding along, though the rucksack packed full of everything is heavy. She's heading towards the glade where she feels safest, the one containing her favourite oak and a circle of birch trees. She'd been in such a rush to leave that she'd almost forgotten Liyana's statue for Luna, and going back for it had nearly made them miss the opening of the gates. 'But we've just . . . We're only staying a little bit, while things get sorted out at home. Besides, Auntie Bea and Auntie Ana will watch over us all night, so we've got nothing to worry about.'

Am I crazy to come? Goldie thinks, even as she's speaking. *Am I protecting Luna from one danger only to put her in the way of another?*

Luna stops walking. '*Staying?*'

'Right,' Goldie says, reaching for Luna's hand and tugging her forward. 'Come on, I've got everything set up. I've found the perfect spot and we'll be fine here for a few days.'

'A few days?' Luna is incredulous. They've never stayed longer than a single night.

'Yes, yes,' Goldie says, as if it's nothing at all. 'That's not long, is it? And, before you say so, I've already got permission from your teacher; I told her we were going on a little holiday.' She hates herself for lying, but tells herself it's for the greater good. 'A little camping trip.' She hikes the rucksack up again. 'That'll be fun, won't it?'

'Yes,' Luna says, still suspicious. 'I guess so.'

When they reach the glade, Goldie sets down the rucksack with a thump beside a birch tree and leans against it to stretch out her back.

Welcome to our world. The breeze of Bea's voice blows through the tree's leaves. *Are you excited for your first Everwhere sleepover, Lu-Lu?*

Don't forget to wear Mami Wata. Ana sprinkles a little rain over her niece, though, as with the rain on Earth, it rolls off Luna like water off a duck's back. *We'll be spending all night working on incantations and chants, so you won't have to worry—*

Won't worry? Bea's laughter is like a miniature rumble of thunder through the air. *Don't you know who you're talking to? If she's breathing, she's worrying.*

'Shut it,' Goldie snaps. 'I'm not in the mood.' She fishes around in her pocket for the tiny, precious figure of Mami Wata and hands it to Luna.

Luna takes it. 'What's this?'

'She's your aunt's water deity. She'll help protect you.'

Luna frowns. 'How?'

'Wear her around your neck,' Goldie says, unclasping the cord, then scooping up Luna's hair and fixing it around her neck. 'She'll keep you safe.'

'I don't see how.' Luna raises a suspicious eyebrow. 'If soldiers are out here trying to kill us, then how will—'

'—*one* soldier, singular,' Goldie says. 'Not an entire army.'

'So you say.' Luna fingers the statue at her throat. 'But how do you *know*?'

'Because your aunties told me,' Goldie lies, hoping to hell she's not making the greatest mistake of her life. 'And since they can see everything here, I believe them. If there was more than one, they'd know.'

'Well then.' Luna folds her arms. 'Let's hope they're right.'

Two Days Ago: 8.29 a.m. – Scarlet

It's Kavita who tells Scarlet what's happening. She'd tried waiting for an opportune moment but when none presented itself – and she'd realized that Scarlet wasn't going to react well to the subject, no matter how happy the moment – Kavita decided to plunge in.

'I – I've got something to tell you,' she says, without catching her friend's eye. 'It's . . .'

They're walking through the main gates of Balliol College, heading towards the library, Kavita having enticed Scarlet with the promise of an exceedingly rare illuminated manuscript: the only one illustrated by nuns instead of monks. What she hasn't told her is that some of the illustrations bear a remarkable resemblance to Everwhere, which raises some interesting questions . . .

'It sounds ominous.' Scarlet pulls back, already bracing herself for impact.

'Well . . .' Kavita slows with her, until they've both stopped in the middle of the path.

'This is when you're supposed to say, "Oh, don't worry, it's nothing,"' Scarlet says, attempting levity and feigning nonchalance, though she feels anything but.

Kavita looks at her feet. 'Well, um, I know it's not a subject you want to talk about.' She forces herself to look up and meet Scarlet's gaze. 'But it's something you need to know.'

Scarlet folds her arms. 'I told you before, if it's anything to do with my sisters or that place, then you can save your breath, because I'm not listening.'

'Please,' Kavita pleads. 'It's important. *Really* important. A few nights ago, Goldie—'

'Don't.' Scarlet holds up her hand. 'I can't.'

'I know,' Kavita persists. 'I know it's hard for you to talk about this, but you'll regret it forever if—'

'I trusted you,' Scarlet interrupts. 'I asked you never to mention it again; after that afternoon, I begged you. I said –' she narrows her eyes – 'I said that if you ever did, if you ever insisted, then I wouldn't be able to hang out with you anymore. Did I not?'

'Yes.' Kavita nods. 'You did.'

'Well then.'

'But—'

'No,' Scarlet snaps. 'No buts, no exceptions. Never.' Then she turns and strides along the path back towards the gates of Balliol College.

'Wait!' Kavita calls after her. 'Wait!'

But Scarlet doesn't stop or hesitate or look back.

6.08 a.m. – Teddy

He's woken by a fierce banging on the door. With a groan, he falls out of bed, hunting around for a T-shirt, hikes up his pyjama bottoms and hurries out of his studio flat, along the corridor and down two flights of stairs. Only a new resident would arrive at such an ungodly hour and, after all these years, Teddy is used to being on call, day and night. Drawn by an impulse and intuition they can't explain, the battered and bloody Sisters Grimm turn up on the doorstep at all times of the night and day. Although they don't usually knock as violently as this.

As if on cue, the pounding resumes.

'You'll wake the bloody neighbourhood,' he mutters, hurrying along the hallway. Sisters' knocks are usually timid, apologetic, near silent. Often, they stand on the doorstep for hours before plucking up the courage to knock at all.

As Teddy opens the door, he wipes the annoyance from his face, rearranging his features into sympathy and concern as he fumbles with the bolts. When he unlocks and opens the door to see the two policemen, only concern remains.

'Good morning, sir.' The bulkier policeman steps forward, removing his hat. The younger, smaller policeman stays behind him.

At the sight of them, panic rises in Teddy's throat. 'What's happened? Is Goldie okay? Is it Luna?' He thought they were upstairs sleeping in their beds, but perhaps they took an impromptu trip to Everwhere and got hurt on the way home. 'What's going on? Please, tell me.'

'I'm Sergeant Preston and this is Sergeant Hil— Smith,' the policeman says. 'May we have a word, sir?'

'Um, yes, of course, I . . .' Teddy trails off.

'Shall we come in?' the sergeant says. 'It's a delicate matter.'

Teddy steps back, then catches the look in the policeman's eye. If he could articulate such experiences, he'd say that all at once the air takes on a darker, more ominous atmosphere, as if a sudden and violent storm is coming.

'No, I'd rather stay out here, if it's all the same to you.' He meets the policeman's eye, pulling himself up to his full height and finding, happily, that he's almost an inch taller than the officer and slightly broader.

'Suit yourself, sir.' Sergeant Preston takes a deep breath. 'I understand that you have a . . . resident staying here by the name of Becky Metcalf.'

'I'm afraid I can't answer that.' Teddy eyes him warily. 'As you know, that information is confidential.'

The sergeant glowers at Teddy, a muscle in his neck twitching. 'I'm not asking. We know she's here and she's wanted for questioning.' He steps back. 'We'll wait.'

Teddy frowns slightly, as if concerned. 'Is she under arrest?'

Annoyance flickers over the sergeant's face. 'Not as yet, but she's a person of interest and we— She needs to come to the station for questioning.'

'If she's not under arrest and you don't have a warrant,' Teddy says, 'then I'm afraid I can't help you.'

The air darkens and the clouds thicken.

'I could have you arrested for perverting the course of justice,' the sergeant snaps.

'Perhaps,' Teddy says. 'But then you'd need proof that your person of interest is indeed a resident here. Something which I can neither confirm nor deny.'

At this, Sergeant Smith steps forward. 'You'd bloody better start cooperating, sir, or we're going to—'

'Hush, Sergeant,' his colleague warns, before returning to Teddy. 'I apologize for my fellow officer, sir. I try to keep him on a tight leash, but he's very . . . zealous in his duties. And when he encounters civilians like yourself, trying to obstruct the criminal justice system, then he's liable to get a bit . . . testy.'

Teddy sets his jaw and meets the older sergeant's eye. 'Are you threatening me, officer?'

Sergeant Preston regards him with a look of mock shock. 'I'm doing nothing of the sort, sir. I'm only alerting you to the fact that we'll be returning very soon with a warrant.'

'Very well.' Teddy nods. 'Then you'll find me here, officer, keenly anticipating your return.'

The last thing Teddy sees, as he closes the door, is the furious face of Sergeant Preston glaring back at him. Teddy bolts the door twice, then leans back against it, breathing heavily, heart pounding in his chest.

'Shit,' Teddy mutters. 'Shit, shit, shit.'

Teddy, now sharply awake, shuffles towards the kitchenette, deciding he needs a black coffee with three sugars, maybe four, possibly five. Followed by a stack of toast, slightly burnt with too much butter. What he wouldn't give for a three-scoop cone right now. And the girl to whom he'd poured out his heart; what he wouldn't give to see her again too.

Reaching for the kettle, Teddy pauses to take a deep breath.

It's then that he sees the note.

11.19 a.m. – Goldie

When Goldie wakes, Luna is gone.

The shock of the empty tent is sudden and violent, as though she's just been woken by a fist slamming into her chest instead of the cry of a raven. Goldie is frozen for a moment, as denial collides with reality. Years ago, when Luna was only three, Goldie had let go of her hand on Brighton Pier and in a split second she'd vanished into the crowd.

Goldie screamed then and she screams now. *It's not possible. It hasn't happened.* Her panicked mind scrambles, as if sheer force of will can undo time, can unravel events and return her daughter as it had before.

'Luna!' Goldie shouts, struggling to escape from her sleeping bag. 'Luna!'

She seizes Luna's sleeping bag, praying that perhaps she is playing hide-and-seek, though she knows even before she touches it that it's empty. Has she run away? Perhaps she's returned to Earth. Or perhaps the soldier caught her first.

'Luna! Luna!'

As Goldie struggles with the tent flap's zip, she glances back at Luna's bedding to see that she's taken nothing with her, including the protective statue of Mami Wata, which lies discarded on her small pillow.

Chapter Sixteen

12.01 p.m. – Goldie

'Luna!' She hurtles through the glade, feet pounding the grass and stone, ears pricked for any sound. 'Luna!' Pushing aside the branches of the birch trees, she's slapped across the face as they spring back at her. Red welts swell immediately on her cheeks, but she hardly notices, running on. 'Luna!'

As she runs, almost slipping but never slowing, she sees that there are no footprints in the mud, so instead heads towards the river, only stopping at its banks.

'Luna!'

Goldie glances left and right, panic surging again at the decision she must make – which way was her daughter taken? The fear of choosing the *wrong* way, the fear of running away from Luna instead of towards her almost paralyses Goldie. But the knowledge that inaction would be the worst decision of all pushes her on. Praying for motherly intuition, Goldie chooses. Left – Luna would go left.

'Luna! Luna! Luna!'

Goldie hurtles along the path, almost slipping again as the mud thickens, scrambling over a fallen tree trunk when the path narrows and turns away from the river. All the while, she never stops screaming her daughter's name.

'Luna! Luna! Luna!'

Then, as the rush of the river fades behind her, she hears a sound and stops.

Laughter.

The wind picks up. *Bea.* A light rain starts to fall. *Liyana.* Goldie sprints forward, over moss and stone and fallen twigs, along the muddy path until she arrives at an enormous tree stump overgrown with lichen and ivy – in the centre of which sits Luna.

'Luna!' Goldie hurls herself towards the stump, tripping into it, and half falling, half catching her daughter in her arms. 'Luna.' She presses her face and words into Luna's hair. 'Luna, Luna, Luna.'

'Ma, stop – you're hurting me,' Luna says, wriggling free. Pulling back, she frowns. 'Ma, what's wrong? Why are you crying?'

3.33 a.m. – Goldie, Luna, Bea & Liyana

'You could've told me where she was,' Goldie snaps. 'You scared me half to death.'

She didn't go far.

We were looking after her.

'Yes, but I didn't know that, did I?' Goldie says, her voice like the crack of the twigs at her feet. 'I didn't know she was safe. And besides –' she drops her words to a whisper – 'you don't know if you could've saved her had the soldier attacked.'

'I can hear you, Ma,' Luna says, rubbing her hands together over the small campfire she insisted on setting alight. 'And I wouldn't need their help anyway; I can save myself.'

She's not wrong. The breeze whips up. *The* niña *can take care of herself.*

Waves splash against the riverbank. *She's the strongest sister I've ever seen, and only nine . . .*

'Nearly ten,' Luna says, without looking up. 'It's just over a week till my birthday now.' She breathes on the fire and it rises, spitting and crackling, ready to engulf whatever it can.

'Lu-Lu,' Goldie warns. 'You'll burn down Everwhere if you're not careful.'

Luna rolls her eyes. 'Like that's a thing. Anyway, if it escapes me, I can always put it out.' All at once, a crack of thunder sounds above, followed instantly by a flash of lightning and a brief heavy rain falls upon the fire. Snuffing it out. 'See.'

'All right,' Goldie concedes with a huff. 'All right.'

Grinning, Luna clicks her fingers and, despite the wet sticks, the fire sparks to life again. 'We should be eating marshmallows.'

'We don't have any marshmallows.'

Luna sighs. 'Then we should be telling ghost stories.' Another thought occurs to her. 'We're not still going to be here for my birthday, right? Cos ten is special and requires a proper party with cake, balloons, dancing—'

'You've not wanted balloons since you were three,' Goldie points out. 'Nor dancing.'

Luna shrugs. 'I'm mercurial.'

'Yes,' Goldie says, unwilling to admit that she doesn't know the word. One of the many curses of having a child prodigy. 'Yes, you certainly are.'

Luna sleeps and Goldie watches her, curled up in the sausage-wrap of her sleeping bag, flooded by an overwhelming desire to wake her and hug her. Luna shuffles, rearranging her bony little limbs, snuffling little snores. Oblivious to the dangers in this world and the other. Goldie watches, thinking how vulnerable Luna seems when she's asleep. No matter how clever or strong she is, no matter that she's a prodigy, a Grimm to best all others – asleep she's just a girl, thin as a sapling, who needs her ma to keep her safe.

'Would it be the same if I still had you?' Goldie wonders aloud. 'If you were still alive, would I be a little less scared?' She often conducts one-sided conversations with Leo, especially in Everwhere, when she can conjure the image of him so vividly that she can almost hear his replies.

'Yes,' she says, knowing what he'd say. 'You're right. I know you are.' She sighs. 'Why is it we're doomed to repeat the past, to make all the mistakes we promised ourselves we'd never make?' She feels her heart constrict, her eyes fill. 'Oh, Leo, I wish . . .'

Luna turns in her sleeping bag again and snores. Goldie glances at her, feeling another tug in her chest. Tears slide slowly down her cheeks.

'I want you,' Goldie whispers. 'I want you so much. And she's all of you I have left.'

6.39 a.m. – Scarlet

Since Scarlet doesn't have a phone, Kavita must resort to notes left at the porter's lodge. She leaves several a day, for several days. The notes oscillate between begging and pleading to cajoling and demanding.

Scarlet ignores them all.

Chapter Seventeen

8.39 a.m. – Goldie & Luna

For the first time, they've ventured slightly away from the glade – protected by enchantments and charms against malevolent intentions and invasions – and Goldie is even more anxious than usual, on high alert for any signs of attack. Although also anxious not to convey her anxiety to Luna, she's desperately trying to act as nonchalant as possible: as if nothing is unusual, as if they're simply on an ordinary camping trip in Cornwall. *If only*.

Now Goldie kneels by the river, washing clothes, while Luna sits on the bank, kicking her heels into the mud. The necklace of Mami Wata is back around her neck; every now and then Luna tugs at it, pulling it back and forth on the cord.

'This is so boring.' Luna sighs, digging up a clod of moss with bare fingers. 'I hate camping. I want to go home. I want to go to school.'

Goldie gives her a wry smile. 'Boring is good, boring is safe. Anyway, since when did you want to go to school?'

Luna rolls the moss down the slope.

'You can practise your skills here,' Goldie says. 'You can create waves or make rain, set fire to sticks, coax plants from the soil, climb trees and practise flight . . .' She lists these things as if suggesting Luna can practise piano scales, skipping or hopscotch.

'Boring, boring, boring,' Luna intones as she ticks off her muddy fingers. 'And boring.'

Goldie laughs while Luna hurls a stone into the river. Goldie's cheek is wetted by the splash, but she merely wrings out the shirt she's washing, then shakes it out.

'Why do you never talk about Dad?'

At the mention of Leo, Goldie feels her chest constrict. 'Because I don't want to upset you,' she says. 'But we can talk about him any time you want.'

Luna toys with another stone. 'Is he the reason I can control all the elements, not just one, like you and my aunties and all the others?'

'I don't know,' Goldie admits. 'I think so. You certainly are a rare and special girl.'

5.26 p.m. – Scarlet

'So, now you really are stalking me.' Scarlet strides past Kavita, who's leaning nonchalantly against one of the quadrangle walls just outside the dining hall. The wisteria is no longer in bloom in mid June, but a climbing rose scents the air with a heavy sweetness, and a profusion of marigolds fills the flower beds that run alongside every wall.

'Your college is prettier than mine this season,' Kavita says. 'The new head gardener is really going to town with all the colours, isn't she?'

Scarlet keeps walking, and Kavita hurries after.

'Wait!' Kavita calls. 'You can't just run away from this; you can't just pretend it's not happening!'

'Oh, I think I can,' Scarlet calls back. 'In fact, I think you'll find that's what I'm doing right now!'

'I can't believe you're doing this.' Kavita runs alongside Scarlet, who's on the path, careful not to step on the grass. 'I know you've been traumatized; I know you're suffering. I know—'

'No.' Scarlet stops walking. 'You know what happened, but you have *no idea* how it affected me. You throw around words like "traumatized" and "suffering", but you don't know what it feels like to let go of your sister's hand cos you're not strong enough to pull her from a whirlpool, to watch her drown; to realize too late that you should've let yourself drown too.' She glares at her friend, livid with rage. Sparks flicker at her fingertips. 'No idea. No fucking idea at all. Have you?'

Kavita is silent.

'That's what I thought,' Scarlet spits. 'And look what you've made me do – I never wanted to do this ever again!' She brushes her hands brusquely on her legs, then marches off again.

For a moment, Kavita is rooted to the spot. Chastised. Mortified. She should skulk away, should return to Balliol College and lick her wounds, repent her arrogance. But something propels her onward.

'I'm sorry,' she says, catching Scarlet up again. 'I'm sorry to do this to you, but—'

'Then stop it.'

'But I must,' Kavita barrels on. 'A girl nearly died last week. She was attacked and left for dead. Doesn't that bother you?'

Still walking, Scarlet doesn't answer.

'Girls are being hunted by soldiers again,' Kavita persists. 'You've got to help; you've got to go back.'

'No,' Scarlet snaps, juddering to a halt. 'I can never go

back.' She pauses, softening. 'I'm sorry for them, I truly am, but I came here to forget. Forgetting that place and what happened there is the only way I can stay alive; the only way I can survive. I can never think about it ever again.'

Kavita lets the words drift away before she speaks again. 'Don't lie,' she says. 'You think about it all the time. Every minute of every day.'

Unable to deny it, Scarlet says nothing.

'Look.' Kavita seizes her chance. 'I've been thinking about it a lot and I think something's been happening ever since Liyana died. I think her death shifted the balance of good and evil, slowly changing everything, like converging tectonic plates . . . It's no longer sealed against interlopers. So it's no longer safe. Goldie suggested we investigate what's going on, so I've been researching and—'

'Did you tell her what you're doing?' Scarlet interrupts. 'Did you tell her about me?'

'No, of course not! How could you think such a thing? I'd never do that, not without permission. I'd never betray you. Anyway, we've hardly ever spoken; I doubt she even knows my name. And I've not mentioned my research because I'm not certain I'll find anything and I don't want to get her hopes up.'

Scarlet listens to this speech, her face softening, her eyes glazing, her lip quivering, and, for a moment, Kavita is certain that she's about to surrender. And then, like tectonic plates, Scarlet's face suddenly shifts; the drawbridge is pulled up and she's hiding behind the fort again. Unreachable.

'You don't need me,' Scarlet says. 'You've got hundreds of other sisters better equipped to fight with you. Surely, they can defeat a soldier or two.'

'We don't know how many there are,' Kavita argues. 'And you – plus Goldie and Luna – are by far and away the most powerful sisters we've got. With Liyana and Bea, of course, the five of you would be invincible!'

At the mention of Luna, not having seen her niece since she was six years old, Scarlet seems to waver. But then she's intractable again.

'No.' She shakes her head. 'They don't need me. They'll be fine without me.'

And so the two fight on, like two opposing fires, each refusing to concede an inch of ground to the other.

8.39 p.m. – Luna & Goldie

'Do you remember the first time you flew?' Goldie asks as she strokes Luna's hair, her daughter, to Goldie's surprise and delight, having laid her head spontaneously and without coaxing in her mother's lap. Goldie's still on constant high alert, anxious about the possibility of attack, but she's managing – rather heroically, she thinks – to pretend that everything's fine. 'I do.'

Luna gives a little smile. 'Of course.'

'Do you remember the tree?'

Luna considers the question. 'It was an ash – no, an oak.'

Goldie nods, starting to plait Luna's hair.

'Don't,' Luna says. 'We don't have a brush to get the tangles out.'

'Good point.' Goldie stops. 'I did a bit of a rush job with the packing. But we can always pop back and get things when we need them.'

'Okay.' Luna absently plucks the shoot of a sapling

that's been growing beneath her fingers. 'But we're not staying much longer, are we? I miss Uncle Ted and everyone at the refuge.'

Goldie takes a deep breath. 'A little while longer, I think. I'm just trying to be safe, to keep us together.' She glances down at her daughter's face, nervous of catching her eye. 'You want that, don't you?'

Luna sighs and Goldie, realizing she's not going to answer, reaches for a tendril of ivy that's snaking across the ground and picks off a leaf, twirling it between finger and thumb. It wilts, shrivels and dries. Goldie crunches the remains to dust, scattering it over moss and stone.

'And are we safe here?' Luna asks. 'I thought—'

Before Goldie can answer, a breeze blows between them. *It wasn't an ash or an oak. It was a silver birch.*

Luna smiles up at the sky. 'Hello, Auntie Bea.'

Thunder rumbles in the distance. Goldie flinches, before Bea's voice fills the glade again. *When you were little, you loved their colour, how they glimmered in the moonlight.*

A rain falls. *You wouldn't even touch another tree in those days.*

'Auntie Ana,' Luna says with a smile.

'Oh, yes, you're right,' Goldie says. 'I'd forgotten . . .' She looks at Luna. 'And how old were you the first time? Three? No, four.'

Luna shakes her head. 'Three years and three months.'

'Really? As young as that? Are you sure?'

The breeze rustles the leaves. *Three years, three months and three days, to be precise.*

A very fitting age. The rain showers the leaves. *Why don't you tell us the story of the first time you flew?*

'You know it already,' Luna says. 'You were there.'

We've forgotten. The breeze makes the branches of the willow tree dance, causing Goldie to whip her head round, then breathe a quiet sigh of relief. *You'll have to remind us.*

Luna's silent.

Suddenly the rain falls harder. *If you make us wait much longer, you'll be soaked.*

'No, I won't.' Luna laughs as the rain rolls off her. 'That doesn't make me wet.'

'But it makes *me* wet,' Goldie yelps, covering her head. 'Stop it!'

Bea's laughter is a confetti of leaves. The rain stops.

'O-kay then,' Luna says, with mock reluctance. 'If you insist.'

Leaving Goldie's lap, she wriggles up onto a nearby tree stump, folds her arms and assumes a serious expression. 'So, it went like this . . . I was already climbing trees and making things grow and Ma still didn't know I could do anything else but that—'

'True,' Goldie says. 'I got an awful shock.'

'Shush, Ma. Don't interrupt the story.'

Goldie swallows a smile. 'Sorry, Lu.'

'Okay,' Luna continues. 'So, I was climbing birch trees and Ma was worrying, as usual, telling me not to climb too high, while Auntie Bea was telling me to go as high as I could.'

'Yeah,' Goldie says. 'Just like your Aunt Bea.'

Luna laughs. 'So, you were freaking out, but I kept climbing, pretending I couldn't hear—'

'I knew it!' Goldie exclaims. 'I *knew* you could hear me.'

Luna grins. 'Because I knew I was safe, cos Everwhere is different; gravity's more forgiving and all that. So, Ma was calling: "Lu! Come back! Luuu-naaa!" Even though it was only a little tree. But I didn't stop till I reached the highest branch. And Ma, gripping the trunk for dear life, kept calling: "If you fall, I'll catch you! But please, don't fall!" And I shouted back: "I'm not going to fall; I'm going to fly!" And then –' Luna unfolds her arms and holds them out like wings – 'I flew.'

'And I nearly had a heart attack,' Goldie says. 'And you all laughed.'

We did, we did. And their laughter echoes through the glade as the breeze dances over the water of the nearby river.

'And then you knew that I could control all the elements,' Luna adds. 'Not only one.'

'Yes,' Goldie says. 'And, terrified though I was, I must admit that I was a little jealous too. I mean, imagine being able to fly . . .'

Luna gives Goldie a sideways glance while she plucks three leaves from the ivy on the ground and, at a spark from her fingertips, they all burst into flame. She holds them, skin reddening, until the ash drifts to the ground. Then she slips down from the tree stump, reaches for her mother's hand and holds it tight.

'Don't worry,' she whispers. 'I'm never going to fly away from you, I promise.'

Goldie is so completely overcome with gratitude and love that, for a moment, she forgets to be scared, forgets to fear the rogue soldier roaming Everwhere, forgets to worry about social services waiting back home, forgets to fret over the well-being of the shelter's residents, forgets her anxieties over Luna's missed schooling, forgets her concerns on the sustainability of their future here, and . . . and . . . global warming, world poverty, the state of the nation. And, and, and . . .

For one blissful moment, Goldie forgets it all and is happy.

10.18 p.m. – Teddy

He hears the men before he sees them: the tap-tap of their boots on the pavement. He feels them before he sees them: the thwack of the bat against his skull. After that, he catches sight of them in fits and starts. A flash of a red glove before it smacks his jaw. The shiny black leather of a boot. A moustache. A thick muscled arm, the flesh of which he manages to bite into while it's locked around his neck, choking him.

When he's left on the pavement, mouth hanging open, dribbling blood and spit onto the stone, left leg broken in two places, wrist snapped, collarbone crushed, skull cracked, drifting into unconsciousness . . . the last thing Teddy sees is Sergeant 'Preston' – aka Metcalf, he realizes now – striding down the street with Sergeant 'Smith' trailing after him. And the last thing he thinks as his eyes close is, *I'll never do the things I wanted to do; now they will go undone.*

11.36 p.m. – Goldie

In Everwhere, Goldie wakes. Something is wrong. She sits up in her sleeping bag, palms sweaty, pulse racing. But Luna is there, curled up in a ball beside her, emitting little snores. Goldie exhales. *Thank God*. She cocks her head and listens, but she can only hear the occasional call of a raven and the rustle of the wind through the trees.

But something *is* wrong. Goldie waits. She glances about, wondering if she should step outside the tent and take a look. But that'd be foolish. The tent is further fortified by extra enchantments and charms, but the outside isn't. Outside, she's vulnerable to attack. No, she must stay inside.

Still in her sleeping bag, Goldie wriggles her way over to Luna, then lies down, curling herself like a crescent moon around her daughter, her little star. *Safe. Safe and sound.* As she's drifting back to sleep, Goldie thinks of Teddy and wonders if he's okay. If everyone at the refuge is okay.

Stop worrying so much, she thinks. *He's fine. Everyone is fine.*

Chapter Eighteen

3.33 a.m. – Goldie

Tonight she dreams of Leo again, of the time when her lover's spirit was trapped inside the tree and she sat every day and night in his boughs, when she could feel his touch and hear his voice. It's all she wants; it's all she's ever wanted. Even in her dream, Goldie knows it isn't really him, but she doesn't care. It's close enough. And, anyway, it's easier to pretend in dreams.

'Do you miss me?' Goldie asks. 'Tell me you do.'

Of course I do. Every hour, every day.

She snuggles into his branches and, in the dream, it feels as soft and warm as the embrace of his arms.

I see things, he says. *But they're always changing . . .*

'What things?'

You and Luna – but it never stays the same. Only I stay the same.

Goldie sighs. Leo reaches his branches around her body, swaying in the wind, rocking her gently. Goldie closes her eyes and lets herself drift . . . This way, she falls asleep in her dream and wakes with a start in Everwhere.

3.49 a.m. – Goldie

Goldie wakes, still curled around Luna, eyes open wide, heart thumping.

'Oh.' Goldie looks down at her daughter, for a split second thinking that Luna is her and she is Leo and she is being held by him. Her eyes fill. She blinks. A tear drops into Luna's hair. Goldie wipes her eyes, takes a deep breath and slowly exhales. 'Oh, Lu.'

Beneath her, Luna shifts in her sleep. Twisting away from Goldie, she mumbles incomprehensibly, then starts kicking and lets out a small scream.

'No,' Luna mumbles. 'No, no, no!'

Then she's screaming and thrashing and Goldie's holding her tight. This is one eventuality Goldie doesn't worry about: she's been soothing Luna at night since she was a baby. For Luna has always been especially plagued by nightmares.

'Hey, Lu-Lu. Hey, my little Lu-Lu,' Goldie chants, keeping her voice low and calm. 'It's all right, you're having a nightmare. It's just a nightmare. Ma's here. You're all right.'

8.18 a.m. – Goldie & Luna

'I need my hairbrush and my little mirror and my ear plugs – those ravens never shut up – and my pretty fountain pen – this one's running out – and my boots – my shoes are getting too muddy – and you're not expecting me to wear the same sets of clothes, day in, day out, are you? I've got so many wasted clothes in my wardrobe that I'm rapidly outgrowing and—'

'All right, all right,' Goldie says, interrupting the infinitely expanding list of demands. 'Point made. We'll go home. But not till tonight, after dark, and we're not staying more than an hour. Okay?'

'Okay.' Luna folds her arms. 'But if you'd have packed

properly in the first place this wouldn't have been a problem.'

Goldie sighs but says nothing.

9.15 p.m. – Goldie & Luna

'Can we return back through the gate at the Fitzwilliam? We could walk home from there; it'd be nice to see the city, don't you think?' Luna tries. 'I miss it.'

'No,' Goldie says, chucking an extra tube of toothpaste into her rucksack. 'It's too risky. We'll use the Botanic Garden's gate again.'

'Please, Ma,' Luna persists. 'It's nearly my birthday. Pleeeease.'

Goldie hesitates, all too aware of this looming problem. What on earth will she do if they're still in Everwhere then? 'Sorry, Lu-Lu, not today. Maybe another time.'

Procrastination is a fatal parenting move, she knows, since the child – especially a child like Luna – invariably remembers the promise and insists that the parent stick to it. However, right now she can't think of a better plan.

'All right, all right.' Luna sighs, trying to decide between two notebooks, then adds them both to her bag, along with a handful of pens.

'Only the essentials!' Goldie calls. 'We've got twenty minutes, then we're leaving.'

'Oh, Ma.' Luna snorts. 'Will you please stop panicking.'

'I'll try,' Goldie mutters. She pops into the kitchen to fetch a few cooking supplies and is stopped by the sight of her phone on the coffee table. She hadn't taken it to Everwhere – what would be the point? – but she now decides to call Teddy, having been surprised not to find him in his flat.

Goldie glances at the screen. Thirteen missed calls. Her heart constricts.

It's Teddy. Teddy's in trouble. Pulse racing, Goldie dials into her voicemail. Three calls are heralded by NO CALLER ID, the rest are from the refuge's number. The first voicemail is Becky, her voice thick with tears:

'*Goldie, where are you? We can't find you. Did you go somewhere? Why didn't you tell us? Teddy's been hurt – we think he's been mugged – it's really bad – he's –*' she breaks down, sobbing – '*not conscious . . . he's in a –*' the next word is lost to sobs, but Goldie guesses it's 'coma' – '*and they don't know if he'll . . . if he'll . . .*'

Goldie skips to the next: NO CALLER ID, a voice she doesn't know:

'Good morning. This is a message for, um . . . Gertie Clayton. This is Nick Collins from Addenbrooke's Hospital, Intensive Care Unit. I'm calling to advise you that your brother, Theodore Clayton, was admitted to us late last night. Please call us on 01223 805000 as soon as possible. Many thanks.'

'Luna!' Goldie shouts, every other fear now eclipsed by one. 'Luna, leave the bag – we've got to go!'

'But, what happened? I don't understand – what happened?' Luna hurries along the hospital corridor at Goldie's heels. 'Why would anyone hurt Uncle Ted?'

'I don't know,' Goldie says, breathless, feeling that she might faint if she doesn't reach her brother in the next five seconds. *Because some people are fucking psychopaths*, she almost says, but manages to swallow the words. 'I don't know, but—' Goldie breaks into a run, pulling Luna after her.

'Oh, God.' Goldie drops Luna's hand and puts her own to her mouth. The sight of her baby brother lying unconscious in a hospital bed – a hard plastic tube plunged into his mouth, and a face so bruised and bloody that he's barely recognizable – capsizes her and she crumples into the nearest chair. Luna crawls into her lap, sobbing so hard she's shaking. Goldie holds her daughter and together they weep, tears and rain falling in Teddy's room.

When Luna can't cry anymore, she wipes the backs of her hands under her eyes and her nose on her sleeve, then slides off her mother's lap and walks to her uncle's bedside.

'Lu . . .' Goldie looks up. 'Careful.'

Ignoring her, Luna tentatively touches the blanket covering Teddy's legs. Slowly, her hand begins to heat up, her skin pinkening at the fingertips, then flushing along the backs of her hands and up her arm. Goldie pulls herself from the chair and shuffles across the room to stand behind Luna.

'Come on,' Luna says, placing her left hand beside her right. 'We might be able to make him better.'

Goldie sniffs, wipes her own eyes and does as she's told.

'Stop, love,' Goldie whispers. 'Nothing's happening. It's not working.'

She lifts her own hands from her brother's body and presses them to her temples. Her head pounds with such ferocity she imagines her brain must have swollen to twice its size, perhaps soaked in tears. Her legs ache and she's so exhausted she could lie down on the cold, hard hospital floor right now and fall fast asleep. Except that she can't, since every nerve is on fire and her heart is thudding far too fast to settle. She's been ripped apart, hollowed out, utterly defeated.

When Luna doesn't move, Goldie places her hand gently on her daughter's shoulder.

'No.' Luna shrugs her off. 'No, don't stop; we can't stop.'

'Lu,' Goldie says, 'I'm sorry, my dearest one, but it's just not working.'

'It *is* working,' Luna snaps. 'It is!' She looks down at Teddy, who remains exactly the same. 'It is. It might be – you don't know . . .'

'Lu—'

'No!' Luna sobs. 'It has to! It must . . .' She drops her head to her chest. 'But why, why isn't it working?'

'Oh, sweetheart.' Goldie pulls her daughter into a hug. 'I don't know, I don't know why . . . I'm sorry, I'm so, so sorry . . .' She says this over and over, wishing against hope that some kind of miracle will bring her brother back to himself again. 'Why don't we have a nap and try tomorrow?'

At this, Luna just sobs louder, so Goldie holds her tighter, bending to scatter kisses atop her head and whisper reassurances into her hair. She's tempted to shuffle them both over to the chair or perch on the side of Teddy's bed, but she doesn't move. While her daughter cries, Goldie closes her eyes. She is so tired. So very, very tired. And not the kind of tired that can be extinguished by a good night's sleep, but the kind of tired that would mean stopping everything and stepping out of her life for a while. If only it was possible to stop time, to put everything and everyone on pause, while you spent a month alone just sleeping and reading and eating. *Imagine what a relief that would be.*

When, at last, Luna wriggles out of her mother's embrace, she wipes her face on her sleeves, then, catching sight of Teddy lying immobile in the hospital bed, lets out another cry.

'Who would *do* this?' she wails. 'Who could hurt Uncle Ted? He's the nicest man in the world! He spends his life helping people. He's the best, the kindest . . .' She trails off as sorrow shifts to fury, flushing her cheeks. Luna squeezes her hands into fists and sparks fire at her fingertips.

'Lu,' Goldie warns. 'Careful, you're—'

But, before Goldie can finish her sentence, an arc of electricity flares from Luna's fingers and cracks against the ceiling. The strip lights flicker, then go out.

'Oh, shit.' Goldie claps her hand over her mouth in shock. Luna tucks her hands under her armpits. Then, suddenly realizing what a power cut might mean, Goldie darts over to the ventilator beside Teddy's bed, checking everything, but mercifully the slow, rhythmic *beep-beep* still fills the small dark room.

'Oh, thank God,' Goldie exhales. 'Thank God for that.'

'I'm sorry, Ma,' Luna mumbles, looking and sounding as if she's three years old again. 'I didn't, I didn't mean to . . .'

'It's all right,' Goldie says, stepping back to her daughter, who pulls her into a tight hug. 'I know you didn't, I know.'

'Can we stay?' Luna presses her wet face into Goldie's chest. 'Please. I don't want to go back to Everwhere while Uncle Teddy's here. Please, please . . .'

Goldie is silent, stroking Luna's hair, her gaze fixed on her brother. 'Don't worry, Lu. We're not going anywhere.'

11.57 p.m. – Scarlet

After she'd finally stormed away from Kavita again, the sparks at Scarlet's fingertips kept firing. Increasingly infuriated, she does everything she can to stop them, but even plunging her hands into cold water only serves to extinguish the sparks for a few minutes.

It's while she's marching in circles around the Radcliffe Camera, waving her hands back and forth, that Scarlet changes her mind. It's nothing special that does it: only the chance sighting of two women walking hand in hand and the thought that follows it. She doesn't know if the women are lovers, sisters or friends, but their love for each other is clear even from fifty yards away. The pang of longing for her own sisters is instant, constricting her chest so acutely that she must stop to catch her breath. It's a moment before the physical sensation translates into a single thought: *This life without them isn't life; I'd far rather be dead with them than alive without them.*

Taking another deep breath, Scarlet hurries on. Not to march in circles anymore but to find Kavita. And, as she starts to run, another thought alights without fanfare: *This can be my redemption, my atonement, my salvation.* If she can kill this soldier, if she can make Everwhere safe again, then she will at last have absolution.

She will finally be free.

Chapter Nineteen

3.33 a.m. – Luna

When Goldie falls asleep in the chair beside Teddy's bed, her arm flung out towards him, her head lolling back, Luna crawls onto her uncle's bed. She's very careful not to disturb him, nor any of the wires and tubes, gently snuggling in beside him and resting her head delicately on his chest. She hates the sight of him with wires in his arms and a tube down his throat, so focuses instead on the rise and fall of his breathing, finding that the rhythm calms her.

She wishes that he was only asleep; she generally prefers adults when they're sleeping because then they're not talking – not making stupid rules or telling her off or saying irritating things. Luna's tempted to fall asleep on Teddy, except that Goldie – or a nurse – would then snap her awake and subject her to a furious lecture on what not to do in hospitals. Luna's wary of nurses, coming in every few hours to monitor Uncle Ted's 'vitals'. They check his breathing and monitor his blood pressure and make notes, like spies.

Luna doesn't want to admit it to herself but she's scared that her uncle won't wake up. She hasn't admitted this to Ma either, since her mother worries about *absolutely everything* and is probably already terrified and doesn't need another reason to be even more anxious about even more people. Still, Luna can't stop imagining what might happen: what if he stops breathing? What if he never wakes up? She desperately wants him to live, to open his eyes and sit up and say hello. And, even though Goldie didn't think that they could bring Uncle Ted back to life, like they can with plants, Luna hasn't given up hope on the possibility just yet.

Luna fingers the Mami Wata talisman around her neck. She finds it annoying, having to wear it all the time. She tried telling Ma it wasn't necessary, especially not on Earth, but Goldie had insisted. Luna doesn't like the necklace; it's heavy and constricting and makes her feel strange. As if she's under a blanket or stumbling through a fog, her senses dulled. She can't think so quickly, or act so quickly. But then she must admit that she doesn't feel as . . . frantic as she did before, nor so chaotic and churned up inside; doesn't feel like she's got constant itches she needs to scratch, and can more easily control the urge to cut her skin with blades and draw blood.

Still, she doesn't like it and wishes she'd never promised Ma she wouldn't take it off.

6.32 a.m. – Goldie

'Ms Clayton? Ms Clayton?'

Still half asleep, Goldie frowns and stretches, winces at the pain in her neck, then blinks into the concerned face of a kind-looking nurse. Goldie glances down to see Luna on the floor, slumped against Goldie's legs with her head in Goldie's lap.

Goldie blinks again at the nurse, wondering if she's missed something. 'S-sorry?' she mumbles. 'Did you— I didn't hear what you said.'

It's only then she sees a man standing at the head of

Teddy's bed. He's a tall, well-dressed, officious-looking man in his early forties. He is unsmiling, serious, cold.

'I'm Mr Christopher Pride,' he says without preamble. 'The neurosurgeon who'll be operating on your –' he glances at the forms in his hands – 'brother, yes? The surgery is set for eleven o'clock this morning, unless of course we get any emergencies coming into A&E. However—'

'I'm sorry, who are you?' Goldie asks. 'Are you a doctor?'

'I'm a surgeon,' he clarifies. 'Which—'

She frowns, not wanting anyone anywhere near Teddy who isn't fully qualified to operate on brains.

'Doctors go by "Doctor", but surgeons are "Mister",' he explains. 'At least they are in Britain.'

'Oh,' Goldie says. She's about to ask why this is the case, before realizing that she doesn't really care. In her old life, when her brother was still well, she would've been polite, would have smiled and made enquiries; now she simply doesn't have the energy.

'Anyway –' Mr Pride glances at Luna, asleep on the floor – 'we need you to fill out some forms. But perhaps it's better if we speak outside?'

'Forms?' Goldie asks, struggling to catch up. She still feels woozy, half drenched in sleep and thoroughly discombobulated. 'Surgery?'

'Yes.' He nods, looking graver. 'Would you like to come with me? We can bring a cot bed in for your daughter,' he adds. 'So she doesn't have to sleep on the floor.'

'Thank you,' Goldie says, gently lifting Luna's head up from her lap. 'That's very . . .' But she forgets the word and trails off, confused.

*

'What am I signing?' Goldie stares at the forms, trying to make sense of them while the words swim and sink into the page. She's standing at the nurses' station but desperately wants to sit down. 'Sorry, I'm not feeling exactly . . .'

'That's understandable.' Mr Pride speaks slowly, as if to a small child or dementia patient. 'These are the forms giving consent for Theodore's surgery this morning.'

'Oh. Yes. Right.' Goldie hates how this man says her brother's name as if he knows him, as if he knows her. As if he understands. 'But why . . . why does he need surgery?'

'Well . . .' Mr Pride shifts gear into recalling an oft-rehearsed speech. 'His skull was quite severely injured in the attack, which has now caused swelling to his brain. We were hoping this would go down, but it's been over twenty-four hours and, since we're not seeing a significant enough improvement, we need to intervene.'

'Intervene?' Goldie's heart pounds and a wave of nausea rises to her throat. She grips the sides of the desk.

Mr Pride nods. 'It happens in a certain number of cases and it's not unusual for the brain to need a little assistance. But sometimes, inevitably, there can be complications and so we always need to—'

'Complications?' Goldie asks, increasingly desperate to sit down but seemingly unable to form the words to say so.

'Yes,' he continues, oblivious. 'Naturally this is the case with any and all surgery – which is why it's always a last resort – but particularly with the brain. We anticipate that, since your brother is young and fit, everything will progress normally. However, of course—'

'So, so y-you're saying he could, he could . . .' Goldie feels herself start to sway. 'That he could . . .' She drops her voice to a whisper. She doesn't want to say it, but she has to say it. She has to know. 'That he could . . . die?'

Goldie stares at the surgeon, willing him to laugh at such a preposterous notion, to bat away the impossibility with a wave of his hand.

'It's unlikely,' he says.

'Unlikely,' Goldie repeats. She feels drunk. Might she be drunk? Of course not, what a ridiculous thought; she's not had a drink in months. 'Unlikely, but not . . . impossible?'

'No, not impossible,' Mr Pride admits, having the good grace to sound regretful. 'The human body is a complex and unpredictable thing, and so . . .'

Goldie releases her grip on the desk and lets herself slide slowly down to the floor. She folds her legs and sits on the linoleum of the hospital ward, no longer hearing or wanting to hear whatever the fucking neurosurgeon is saying. She needs to go to the refuge; she needs to reassure the residents, to tell them that Teddy's okay, that they're safe, that he'll be back soon. Except that she can't because she doesn't know if he is or if he ever will be.

11.33 a.m. – Scarlet

She sits beside Kavita at an ancient oak desk in Balliol Library, gazing down at the manuscript.

'It's incredible,' Scarlet says for perhaps the tenth time. 'I can't quite believe it.'

Kavita smiles. 'Isn't it magnificent?'

'I mean, it looks just like—'

'I know.'

The resemblance to Everwhere *is* striking: the leaves

and ivy, mist and fog, moonlight and ice, an infinite forest lit by an unwavering moon, ancient trunks stretching up to the marbled sky and everything as white as winter snowfall.

'The gates,' Scarlet says, pointing to a set of ornate gates at the edge of the manuscript illuminated by gold leaf. 'They've even got the gates.'

'Remarkable, isn't it?' Kavita says, her gloved hands hovering over the nine-hundred-year-old parchment as she lovingly traces the path of a river winding across the paper like a vein. 'It almost feels alive, don't you think? Like the picture has been imbued with the life of the place itself.'

Scarlet nods. 'I always felt as if Everwhere had its own heartbeat. Whenever I stepped onto its soil I could feel the ground hum beneath my feet.'

'Yeah,' Kavita agrees. 'And the pulse of its blood when you press your hand to a tree.' She pauses. 'It's a bit like this place, in a way.'

Scarlet glances out of the window overlooking the courtyard below. She takes in the stone walls, the unflowering wisteria that twists up and around the grand stone arches leading to the corridors that in turn lead to concealed rooms in which scholars have been gathering for centuries. 'Is this where you've been doing your research into Everwhere?'

'No,' Kavita says. 'I go to the underground library; it's where all the mystical manuscripts and magical reference books are kept. I'm working my way slowly through them, but I've not found anything yet.'

'An underground library?' Scarlet looks up. 'Sounds creepy.'

'Oh, no,' Kavita exclaims. 'It's one of the most enchanting places I've ever been. I want to take you there. I've been hoping you might help with my research . . .'

Scarlet makes a non-committal noise. 'So, when was this place built?'

'Sometime in the thirteenth century, I think,' Kavita says. '1263 or thereabouts.'

'Damn,' Scarlet exhales. 'That's a lot of history. No wonder it feels so . . . resonant and rich and spirited. Though I suppose it's a little strange,' she adds, 'that a place so full of the dead should feel so . . . alive.'

Kavita laughs. 'I guess it is, when you put it like that. But it's the reason I love being here so much – excepting the manuscripts – because I never feel alone. It's always been that way. I did my degree at Merton and had no friends, but I spent all my time in the library amid the books, or wandering through the grounds among the trees, and never felt lonely . . .'

While Kavita talks, Scarlet imagines herself as a venerable oak planted when the college was founded, or a gargoyle carved into limestone eight hundred years ago, solid enough to endure all weathers, destined to spend centuries gazing down at those below, gradually infused over the centuries with a hundred thousand different breaths and words, laughter and tears, silent wishes and whispered hopes. This is Scarlet's own secret wished-for future: this immortality.

'Don't you ever miss it?'

'What?' Scarlet turns back to Kavita. 'Sorry, what?'

'You've not been to Everwhere for three years,' Kavita says. 'Don't you miss it?'

Scarlet sighs and sits back in her chair. 'Of course I do. It's my home, isn't it? More than any other place in this world. I miss it every hour of every day.' She takes a deep breath. 'But that doesn't mean I'm not terrified of going back.' Wanting to shake herself free of the feeling, Scarlet returns her focus to the manuscript. 'What I don't understand is how these nuns – they were nuns, right?'

'Yeah.' Kavita nods. 'It's the only surviving manuscript of the Middle Ages that originates from a convent instead of a monastery.'

'Right,' Scarlet says. 'So, how did these nuns know about Everwhere? I always thought it was Wilhelm Grimm who created it, what, five hundred years or so later . . . so it's not possible that they could've seen it before that.'

'True,' Kavita says. 'Unless, of course, Grimm didn't create it but find it. After all, he appropriated the fairy tales from their tellers, so it's hardly surprising that he appropriated this land too.'

'Yes . . .' Scarlet considers this. 'I suppose you're right.'

A silence falls between them, echoed by the solemn, silent library, as the implications of this realization stir up their thoughts.

'Which means,' Kavita offers, 'that others can and could access it, not only Grimms.'

'Yes.' Scarlet stares fixedly at the manuscript, as if commanding it to surrender its secrets. 'And not only the good but the bad too. So whatever's happening, whatever's causing these shifting tectonic plates, might not be one rogue soldier, or even a dozen, but something else entirely.'

They are silent again as a fresh, more sinister implication settles between them: the something else might be something far worse than they'd previously imagined.

Chapter Twenty

10.33 a.m. – Goldie & Luna

Goldie sits on the hard floor of the empty hospital room while Luna is slumped in the only chair, staring at the closed door. Teddy's bed has gone, the orderlies having wheeled him out half an hour before.

'What are we going to do?' Luna whispers.

Goldie looks up. 'Wait.' She wishes she could say something more helpful, more comforting, but she can't lie. There would be no point anyway; Luna would know.

'What's going to happen?' Luna asks.

'I don't know.'

'Will Uncle Ted be okay?'

Goldie sighs a deep, sorrowful sigh. 'I hope so, baby girl. I hope so.'

'Can you ask?' Luna says.

'Ask who?'

'The cards.'

'Oh,' Goldie says. 'I suppose I could, but I don't have them.'

'I do.' Luna stands, pulling the pack of Liyana's Tarot cards from her pocket, and she walks across the room to deposit them in Goldie's lap.

Goldie gives her daughter a look of such gratitude that Luna, who'd been about to return to the chair, instead sits on the floor beside her. Instinctively, they hold hands, placing them above the cards while Goldie mumbles an incantation. She needs to get this right. It'll be the most important question she's ever asked.

Goldie takes a deep breath, then slowly exhales. She cannot bear to say the sentence aloud, so only asks it in her mind: *Will Teddy live?* Then she shuffles, very slowly, very carefully. And when at last she stops, ready to deal them out, the cards spring from her hands, scattering across the floor. 'Dammit!'

Luna meets Goldie's eye and they exchange an anxious glance.

Kneeling on the floor, Goldie scoops up all the cards, returning them to the pile, and resumes her shuffling, this time being more careful than before. Yet, even as she slices through the cards, cutting them together, in and out of their random order, they start to flick from the pack in fits and starts – as if making a bid for freedom. And, no matter how diligently Goldie picks them up and returns them to the pack, soon after another one follows.

'What's going on?' Luna asks, a note of panic in her voice. 'They've never done this before, have they?'

'No,' Goldie admits. She keeps shuffling and the cards keep jumping. 'Stop it!' she demands. 'Stop it!'

Then she hears Liyana's voice in her head. *Ask another question. They cannot answer this one.*

Yet it cannot be Liyana's voice, since they're not in Everwhere and Goldie has never been able to hear her on Earth. Still, she responds. 'Why not?'

'Why not, what?' Luna asks, confused.

Because the answer is not yet known.

Goldie feels a flash of panic. Her eyes sting with tears

and she squeezes them shut. *He will live. He will.* She doesn't need the cards to tell her this; she will make it true.

Ask another question. Deal five cards.

Goldie nods, roughly wiping her eyes. She must not surrender to doubt and despair; she must not lose hope. She must focus and be strong. Anger then, instead of fear.

'What is it, Ma?' Luna persists. 'What's going on?'

'Nothing,' Goldie says. 'It's fine, don't worry.' Then she returns to the cards. 'Who did this to Teddy?' she whispers. 'Who tried to kill him?'

This time the cards respond to her shuffle. They don't fight against her but follow her fingers, cutting and slicing together as if they're made of silk. And when she picks five cards and sets them out on the linoleum floor they come as easily as if they've selected themselves. Goldie looks down, studying each one, remembering what Liyana had written in the book of their meanings – though, Goldie now knows, that a Tarot reading is as much a matter of sequence and order as the meaning of any single card.

The first is the Five of Pentacles: two lovers huddled together in the snow, wrapped in a thin blanket and gazing out into the distance, five coins scattered at their feet. *Despair, loss, hardship, doomed relationships.* The second, the Devil: a man and woman chained together by their ankles. The woman is elaborately dressed in silk and fur. The man is naked, his skin green, his eyes red, his hair slicked into horns, his feet shaped into hooves. The woman turns away, but he gazes at her, as if he wants something that she doesn't want to give. *Greed, egoism, entrapment, danger.* The third, the Seven of Swords: a yellow-cloaked man, courted by snakes, points four swords at an unseen assailant who brandishes the other three. *Betrayal, deceit, violence.* The fourth, the Knight of Wands: a knight with a crown of flowers sits atop a wingless bird with a dozen legs who gallops across a desert towards a forest; he has two frail creatures with him and holds a flaming wand aloft. *Energetic, passionate, dramatic, the self-designated saviour.* The fifth, the Nine of Swords: a howling phantom haunts a terrified woman who vainly wields six swords in defence. The three remaining blades pierce her dress, pinning her to the ground. *Fear, doubt, psychic dreams.*

'Well?' Luna pipes up. 'What are they saying?'

Goldie glances up from the cards, having quite forgotten that her daughter was there. 'I'm not certain yet,' she says. 'Give me a minute . . .'

She stares at the cards and, when the answer comes, she's not sure if it's the Tarot that's telling her, or her intuition, or Liyana, or all three.

'Becky's husband,' Goldie whispers. 'The policeman.'

In that moment, for the first time in their lives, mother and daughter share the same thought: *I'm going to kill him.*

They don't mean it, of course. It's only an impulsive thought, conjured from fury and love and pain. But, even so, they want to hurt him. Twice as much as he hurt Teddy. Not kill him perhaps, but put him in hospital at the very least. However, Luna doesn't tell Goldie what she's thinking, and Goldie doesn't tell Luna what she's thinking. Both keep their thoughts to themselves, oblivious to the fact that they're thinking the very same thing.

At the knock on the door, they both look up. Without waiting, Mr Pride steps inside. Goldie scrambles to stand, gathering the cards and concealing them in her cupped hands.

'Doctor Pride,' she says, forgetting the correct terminology as she quickly passes the cards to Luna, as if they've only been playing a game to pass the time. 'How . . . is . . . h—'

'He's fine,' Mr Pride interrupts, putting her out of her misery. 'He's out of surgery and in recovery now.'

'Oh.' Goldie exhales a breath she didn't realize she'd been holding – for thirty seconds and three hours. 'Thank God.'

'Did it go well?' Luna pipes up. 'The surgery? Was it successful?'

'Yes.' The surgeon nods; if he's surprised by her precocious nature, he doesn't show it. 'It went quite well. We relieved the pressure in his brain, so the swelling is already going down and we hope that'll continue at a steady pace. Naturally, we'll be monitoring him closely, but we hope to see an improvement within the next twenty-four to forty-eight hours.'

Quite. Goldie fixes on that word. She doesn't like it.

'But that sounds good.' Luna looks to Goldie. 'That's good, right, Ma?'

Goldie nods, taking Luna's hand. 'Yes, that's good, darling.' She looks back to the surgeon. 'So, when do you expect him to wake up?'

Mr Pride glances at the folder in his hands. 'Well, as I say, we hope to see marked improvement within the next day or so. But we can't say for certain when he'll be conscious, or indeed if—'

'Wait,' Luna interrupts. 'You're saying he might never wake up?'

Mr Pride frowns. 'No, not exactly. I'm saying that it's impossible to speculate on such matters or predict the outcome of any—'

'Can you give us odds?' Goldie suggests, grappling wildly for some sort of definite answer. 'Can you tell us the *probability* that he'll be awake by, say, tomorrow? Can you?'

Mr Pride hesitates. 'Percentages aren't the best way of conveying the full picture,' he says, hedging his bets. 'They tend to give false hope, or else . . .' He sighs. 'But if you insist, then I'd say there's a thirty per cent chance that he'll regain consciousness by tomorrow and—'

'*Thirty per cent?*' Luna shrieks. 'That's not good! Give us a better number. Not that one. Higher, Doctor, now!'

Mr Pride gives Luna a bemused look. 'Well, I . . .'

'And what –' Goldie takes a deep breath – 'about the chance of him not waking up at all?'

Mr Pride doesn't quite meet her eye. 'I think that's unlikely.'

'Numbers, Doctor,' Luna snaps. 'Put a number on it.'

'I don't think that's a particularly helpful thing to do in the circumstances,' he replies. 'I, I . . .'

'Stop stalling.' Luna pins him with her gaze. 'Spit it out.'

'No, of course not,' the surgeon says, glancing from daughter to mother and back, clearly rattled. 'Well, again, if you insist, though, as I say, I don't think it's helpful.' He pauses. 'But if you really want a number then I'd say there's a seventy-five per cent chance . . . that's to say, twenty-five per cent chance of him remaining in a vegetative state—'

'*Twenty-five per cent?*' Luna squeals.

'Vegetative state?' Goldie clutches Luna's hand, feeling herself start to sway again.

'Well, as I say, I don't think it's wise to put figures on such things,' Mr Pride backtracks. 'And that's a seventy-five per cent chance that he *will* regain consciousness, so I think it's best to focus on the positive, don't you?'

Goldie lets go of Luna's hand, stumbles over to the chair and collapses into it. Luna follows, wrapping her arms around her mother's shoulders. They press their heads together, both closing their eyes.

Mr Pride glances again at his clipboard. 'Yes, well, I'd better . . . I have rounds to do and you have facts and figures to digest.' He edges towards the door. 'We'll continue to monitor Mr Clayton and I'll return tomorrow and we'll speak again then. Yes?'

'Yes,' Goldie says, without looking up.

With a final nod, Mr Pride turns and walks through the open door. He's done the right thing, he thinks, as he strides along the corridor. He stuck to the script, told them the usual spiel, omitted the small fact that they'd nearly lost the patient on the table, that for a few moments he'd been hovering on a hair's breadth between life and death. It was never wise to tell the family such things, only making them worry unnecessarily. Though he sometimes wished he could, since it'd give him the aura of a super hero he secretly felt he deserved. A mask and a cape. Like the one he wore every day for a year when he was five, until he swapped it for pigtails and a Cinderella costume. And he wouldn't at all mind having that Miss Clayton gaze at him adoringly. He never minds the adoring gaze of a pretty female. Still, by the time he's reached the end of the corridor he's entirely forgotten about both Goldie and her brother and is wondering if the canteen will be serving his favourite baked beans and mash today.

6.20 p.m. – Goldie

She knows who he is – the man walking down the hospital corridor – before she can properly see him. Her unconscious mind registers the information before her eyes do. Or perhaps it's simply her fears made manifest. *Fate*. The domino effect of events inevitably triggering each other, until they all topple down. Anyway, Goldie had known as soon as they'd stayed at Teddy's bedside that this moment would come. She'd put it out of her mind, refusing to think of anything else but her brother, but she knew it would only be a matter of time. She hoped though that they'd have more time.

She stands to meet him. She won't run. She won't cower and apologize for what she's done. She'd do the same again in a heartbeat. She'd do the same now, if only she could. She'd spirit Luna back to Everwhere in an instant, if only there was means and time.

'Mrs Clayton.' Mr Clarke stops in the open doorway. He nods curtly at Goldie, then looks longer at Luna, as if scouring her person for further signs of abuse – his eyes an X-ray searching for internal fractures. Then he steps forward.

'Luna,' he says gravely. 'We've been very concerned about you.'

Chapter Twenty-one

10.29 p.m. – Luna

She misses her mother. It's only been a few hours, but already it feels as if some essential organ has been ripped from her chest and held hostage while she lies in an unknown bed, in an unknown house, helpless. If she didn't have her notebook, she wouldn't be able to stop crying. Which she can't anyway.

Often, Luna doesn't feel like a child. Indeed, she often feels older than all the adults around her: teachers, family, strangers. But without her mother now, she just feels like a baby. Abandoned, scared, weak, powerless. *Maybe it's having Ma*, Luna thinks, *that makes me feel so strong*. She can't even imagine executing her plan to properly maim Alex Metcalf, after seeing what he'd done to Uncle Teddy; she's almost forgotten how violence and power feel.

She tugs at Liyana's necklace, wishing she could take it off. But a promise is a promise. Instead, she wipes her eyes, then starts scratching at the stupid scars on her shoulder blade. She hates them; she wants to tear them from her skin. Luna used to love them, despite the occasional pain, as the only link to her father. He bequeathed them; they're her only proof that he existed once. But now they're trouble; now they're what dropped her into this fucked-up situation in the first place.

She doesn't know what to do. She could escape, of course. She could hurt all the simpering social workers imprisoning her and force them to let her go. But Goldie told her not to. Luna doesn't know why, but she does know that her mother would die before willingly letting her go, so Luna supposes she has good reason. It's probably because they put at-risk children into care but lock magical ones in experimental labs.

So, of course, it's better they think she's a vulnerable, innocent nearly-ten-year-old. Not a Sisters-Grimm-star-soldier who could burn down this paisley-wallpapered prison with a single spark at her fingertips. Which, she's starting to feel, maybe she might have to do, promises or not.

11.28 p.m. – Goldie

It had been the hardest moment of her life – excepting only Leo's death – when she'd let Luna go. It'd taken every ounce of her will, common sense and faith not to simply let Luna electrocute Mr Clarke. And run.

But then they would've been on the run forever. Hiding out either in Everwhere – no Teddy, no shelter, no school; a feral life in a place without internet or supermarkets or houses or shops; a life spent in the shadow of a soldier out to kill them – or on Earth, which might not be worse but was unlikely to be much better.

No, it was an impossible choice to make but a necessary one.

Now Goldie sits in the chair beside Teddy's bed. He'd been wheeled back into the room an hour after Luna had been forcibly removed from it. The joy of actually seeing Teddy alive had momentarily – but only momentarily – eclipsed her sorrow at the loss of Luna. Her heart swelled, love surging at the sight of him. Tears filled her eyes and slipped down her cheeks before she could stop them. Despite the surgeon's reassurances that the procedure had been a (relative) success and Teddy had survived it, Goldie hadn't really believed him. Most of her life she'd believed in things she couldn't see, but, for this, only her eyes counted. No trust, no faith, no magic; only the cold hard fact of seeing him in the flesh.

Goldie had fallen on him then – before the orderlies had even finished clicking the brakes on his bed – sobbing while she clutched his hands, checking that the man in the bed really was her brother; holding on so tight that they could never take him away again.

She'd stood there for a long time, not letting go. Until she had a crick in her neck and an ache in her back. Until she had to admit that he was alive but not awake. If only Luna were there, then at least they'd be a family and that would be better, even if one of them was unconscious.

The absence of her daughter sits beside Goldie like a blaring siren that she can't switch off. It makes her head hurt and her heart ache because, powerful as she is, what can she do about it? Tomorrow she will call Legal Aid and hire a solicitor and try to get Luna back legally. However long it takes, however much it costs. But now Goldie does the only thing she can at this late hour. Which – after calling the shelter and checking on the worried residents within, reassuring them that all protections are in place so no one can enter unbidden – is to sit and watch and wait for Teddy to wake.

11.59 p.m. – Luna

She's writing stories, to keep herself from going mad in the room in the house they've locked her in. The people are okay; it's not like *David Copperfield* or anything like that. The woman in charge – Mrs Hicks – is all right. But she's not Ma. And, even when Luna's fighting with her ma, even when Goldie drives her crazy, she'd still rather have her than anyone else. She never had her father, so she doesn't know what he might have been like, but she certainly wants him more than no father at all. Without them, and her uncle and aunts, stories are all that stand between her and loneliness. But sorrow and fear make it hard to focus; thoughts and feelings tug her away from the page and then the words skitter across the lines. So she has to keep them short.

12.33 a.m. – Teddy

He can still hear everything. Not very clearly, but clear enough. Voices are muffled, as if he has cotton wool in his ears, or as if he's eavesdropping on people in another room. But he knows Goldie sits beside him. His sleep is shallow and he dreams intense, vivid dreams. Rather like the time he drifted in a punt along the River Cam at night. *So* peaceful. Wrapped in woollen blankets, he'd gazed up at the sky, turning his head to take in the stone spirals of the colleges in the moonlight or to catch sight of a passing swan. Teddy stayed away from the river in summer, when the tourists descended and commandeered every punt to zigzag from bank to bank in their blighted efforts to steer, turning the river into a clogged artery. In winter though, it was all his own.

Although he can't seem to make himself wake, nor speak, Teddy finds that he can direct his dreams. He doesn't understand how, since he's never had even an inkling of magic in his veins, but perhaps the why makes sense: having had all his other capacities and senses shut down, now the only ability left to him is heightened.

He dreams of many things: mostly strange and nonsensical things, as the stuff of dreams so often are. It's a while before Teddy realizes that he can take himself to the places he wants to go. Naturally, the first place is the little gelateria where he finds, as he never has again in real life, the girl. *Oh, how he's missed her.* In the dream it doesn't feel silly to have missed someone so much when you've only met them once. Nothing is wrong in these dreams because he is choosing it all; he is the god of all he surveys. They sit in the booth and eat infinitely regenerating tubs of ice cream. They sit for hours, never tiring of the ice cream, or each other.

And then that dream evaporates and another floats seamlessly into its place. Now he stands in a wooded glade encircled by willow trees. It is a wood, he thinks, except the trunks of the trees are not brown nor the leaves green; everything is white as if dusted with snow. A woman steps out from behind one of the trees. She is tall, elegant, with long dark hair and light brown skin.

'Who are you?' he asks.

Bea. She smiles, but her mouth doesn't move as she speaks; he simply hears her voice as if it's floating on the breeze. *I've come to try and shake you awake.*

Chapter Twenty-two

3.33 a.m. – Teddy & Bea

'I know who you are,' Teddy says. 'You're Goldie's sister. I've heard a lot about you.'

And you're Goldie's brother – yet we're not remotely related. Strange, eh?

'Stranger still that we've never met.'

And we never will.

'Why not?' Teddy's confused; his head is spinning and he feels a little like Alice tumbling down the rabbit hole. 'Because you're dead?'

Bea's laughter is the wind whipping through the trees. *That's the first hurdle.*

'And the second?'

Well, the state of my mortality wouldn't matter if you could come to Everwhere.

'I think I have.' He looks around at the woodland surrounding him, the trees overgrown with ivy and moss, the ground scattered with twigs and stones; and everything with a winter hue. Just as Goldie described it. Teddy will never forget the first time he saw her disappear through a gate; will never forget his awe at his amazing, magical sister and his disappointment that he couldn't follow her through.

I'm in Everwhere; you're only dreaming.

'Still,' Teddy says. 'We're meeting now, aren't we?'

Of sorts. And it's curious, because I've never been able to visit the dreams of a non-Grimm before.

'Curiouser and curiouser.' Teddy walks up to a tree and tentatively touches a leaf, rubbing it between his fingers. 'It feels so real.'

Can you feel this?

A warm breeze brushes Teddy's face. He puts his hand to his cheek. 'Yes.'

And this?

The breeze ruffles his hair.

'Yes.' Teddy laughs. 'That too.' He misses being touched, he realizes. And wonders when – if – he'll ever have another kiss. He thinks, with a pang of longing, of the girl in the gelateria.

You should've asked her on a date. You're handsome and sweet – she'd snap you up.

'How do you know about her?'

Bea's laughter brushes his face again and shivers through his body. *I'm in your mind; I know everything.*

'Oh.' Teddy blushes.

Don't worry, I'm not here to delve into your dubious little fantasies. The wind whips up the leaves into flurries and swirls that dance across the moss and stone. *I'm here to wake you up.*

Teddy frowns, confused again. 'And how will you do that?'

By telling you a few home truths.

His heart starts to race, anxiety flooding his veins. He leans against the trunk of a tree. 'Like what?'

Like this: you've fallen asleep in your life – metaphorically and literally – and I think that if you wake up your mind it'll wake up your body too. Win–win.

'What on earth are you talking about?'

You've been living a life of duty and it's been crushing you, smothering your breath and stultifying your blood, slowing your heart and turning your brain to dust.

'What . . .' Teddy trails off. He doesn't need to ask what she means when he already knows.

The shelter is our sister's calling, not yours.

Teddy sighs, sliding down the trunk. 'Yes, but she needs my help. And I want to help her. She's doing a noble thing.'

She is. But she's not alone; there are others out there who share the same calling. When you leave, she can find them.

The suggestion is so outrageous that it momentarily snatches away Teddy's breath. 'I-I can't do that, never. She gave up everything for me: her childhood, her education, her future. I owe her every— I owe her mine in return.'

That's one way of looking at it.

Teddy picks up a stone from the ground, clutching it tight. 'Is there any other?'

Well, you could stop being such a coward and have a little faith.

'Faith in what?'

In yourself, in your heart, in our sister. If you're honest with her and tell her what you really want, you might be surprised at the result. And if you follow the beat of your heart, then you might start breathing again.

Teddy squeezes the stone. 'And if I don't?'

Then prepare to die literally as well as figuratively, because you're already halfway there. Duty has already nearly crushed you to death. Your inspiration, your passion, your hope – your brain is already becoming dust.

3.33 a.m. – Luna

She tried; Luna really tried to keep her promise and stay all night in the stupid governmental institution, but she just couldn't. The temptation to set her intentions for Everwhere before she fell asleep was simply too great. It's too easy, that's the problem. She doesn't *have* to go through a gate, after all; she can simply travel on the coat-tails of her dreams. How can she possibly resist that?

Of course, her mother would be furious if she knew, but Luna's banking on the fact that Goldie won't leave the hospital until Teddy wakes; so chances of being discovered are slim. Feeling nostalgic, she returns to the glade where they'd camped and walks slowly round the circle of willow trees, reaching out to brush their white leaves with outstretched fingertips. As she touches them, they briefly brighten and shine and, one by one, each tree shivers, a shudder of delight running through them from root to tip.

And then she feels the dusting of rain.

Lu, why are you here alone? Where's your ma?

Luna smiles. 'Hello, Auntie Ana.'

Hello, dearest girl. Liyana's voice is as soft as the touch of the rain. *But you shouldn't really be here, should you?*

'Don't worry, I'm not staying long,' Luna says, stopping to sit at the base of a tree. She presses her bare feet into the moss and watches the fresh shoots of ivy curling up around her toes. 'I'll be back before they're awake. They won't even realize I'm gone.'

Who? I meant that it's dangerous out here, with the soldier attacking lone sisters. Bea and I can help protect you, but we can't be sure—

Luna folds her arms. 'I don't need protecting.'

Oh, my love, I know you're strong, but you can't be cavalier—

'Strong?' Luna snaps, feeling petulant. 'I'm stronger than any Grimm, and I'm not even ten yet.'

Only seven more sleeps to go.

'Right.' Luna smiles. 'Sorry, I didn't mean— I'm just missing Ma.'

What do *you mean?* Liyana's voice churns like a whirlpool. *What happened?*

'I forgot,' Luna says, 'that you can't see what's happening on Earth. Social services caught up with us and took me away last night.'

Oh, no. Oh, Luna. The rain ceases. *I'm so sorry.*

'Yeah.' Luna sighs. 'It sucks.'

I wish I could do something. Would you like a story to lift your spirits?

Luna's face lights up. 'Yes, please.'

I know it won't help, but distraction is something, I suppose. What do you fancy? Witches or demons or fairies or—

'Wait,' Luna interrupts. 'Can I tell you one of mine?'

You've written one? I'm so proud, dearest girl.

Luna grins. 'I've written a bunch, but I've never shared them with anyone till now.'

Then I'm honoured. Rain rustles the leaves, rolling away from Luna as if she held an umbrella above her head. *And I want to hear every word.*

Luna's smile becomes self-conscious. 'I hope I can remember it all.'

The Lonely Djinn

Once upon a time there was a djinn who lived in a secluded forest. She was the most powerful djinn in all the eight kingdoms and people came from miles around, travelling for weeks and months to visit this djinn and ask her to grant their wishes. They brought gifts with them, whatever they could afford, for the djinn was like a magpie and loved to furnish her home with pretty, shiny things. Fortunately for those who made this pilgrimage, the djinn didn't demand much and her needs were very few. She was exceedingly small – half the size of a magpie – and lived in a hollowed-out hole in a tree, which she furnished with moss for carpets and strips of silk for bedding. She stitched all her own clothes, ate al fresco and bathed in the river.

The djinn liked granting people's wishes. In fact, she loved it. She loved seeing how their faces lit up with disbelief and delight when they met her, knowing that all their efforts weren't in vain. She loved how they wept with relief when their pains and troubles were taken away. She loved how they looked suddenly whole again when a wish was granted and a hole deep in their hearts was filled.

Yes, granting people's wishes made the djinn happy, as happy perhaps as those whose wishes she granted. But when she had no wishes to grant, the djinn was sad. Sometimes she sat in her hollowed-out hole in the tree, on her soft moss and silk, gazing down at all the sparkling treasures the pilgrims had laid around the roots of the tree, and wept. Her tiny tears rolled off the golden trinkets and soaked into the soil and fertilized exquisite flowers that spread across the forest floor. But all this beauty didn't make the djinn happy, for she was alone.

The djinn hadn't always been alone. She once had a mother and father with whom she lived, many centuries ago, in the hollow trunk of a large tree. This tree was furnished with moss and silk and furniture her father had carved from fallen twigs. Everything in this tree came from the forest, for the djinn's parents favoured the things that Nature provided rather than the ornaments the pilgrims offered them. Back in those days, when the djinn had her family, she too didn't much care for or covet these man-made treasures either.

Then, one day, the djinn had fallen in love. A wizard came to the forest, hoping for his wish to be granted. He was the most handsome human the djinn had ever seen and seemingly the kindest and gentlest too. He offered to take her – once his wish was granted – on his travels across the world. The djinn child had always held a secret desire to travel the world, for she longed to see more than the forest she saw every day.

However, it soon transpired that, while the wizard was indeed the handsomest human in existence, he was neither as kind nor gentle as he first appeared. Indeed he was wicked and selfish, demanding that the djinn family grant him infinite powers and immortality. When they refused – for they would only grant good and well-meaning wishes – he turned his magic on them and cast the djinn father into a nearby willow tree and the djinn mother into a lake.

He could not kill their spirits, for they were immortal, but he took their form and their breath away and banished them for all eternity to blend with the forest they so dearly loved. Then, in a whirlwind of fury, he left the djinn child alone. She tried everything in her powers to separate her parents' spirits from the willow tree and the lake. But, even when she persuaded the pilgrims to make such wishes on her behalf, nothing worked. For djinn magic, though limitless, could only be cast for the benefit of others and never themselves.

As the years passed, the djinn grew used to her loneliness and a hard crust formed around her heart and over her eyes so that she hardly felt the hole anymore and only cried on occasion. Every day though, she saw the willow tree and the lake, and remembered her parents and wished that she'd never fallen for the wizard's tricks.

One day, a girl visited the djinn. This girl was as good and kind as she seemed and they fast became friends. Seeing a kindred soul, the girl loved the djinn and offered to take her on adventures all over the world. The djinn would be safe, she promised, and loved. The djinn wanted to go. She wanted to trust the girl. She wanted to believe her promise. But she could not. And so she granted the girl's wish and kissed her goodbye and wept once more, and for the last time.

Oh, my love. The sorrow in Liyana's voice is matched by the rainfall that runs in rivulets off every leaf and branch. *I wish I could hug you, so very much.*

Luna wipes her eyes with the back of her hand and sniffs. At the edge of the glade a twig cracks and Luna starts, suddenly alert.

It's all right – it's nothing. But I think it's time, little one, for you to go home. Liyana says the words without thinking, and when they're spoken she can't take them back. *I'm sorry, Lu, I wish you could stay, I really do.*

'I'm coming back,' Luna promises. 'Every night.'

I don't think that's a good idea, dearest girl. Not till we know what's going on.

Luna feels a great sorrow rise within her. Tears fill her eyes and she starts to shake. She wants to cry, to scream, to drop to her knees, to sob, to beg for her ma to come and take her home. She wants to be the little girl she is, to be held in Goldie's arms and rocked back and forth till she falls asleep. But it's an impossible wish. She doesn't have a home, nor her mother. Not now. Now she's all alone.

6.28 a.m. – Scarlet

'This place is incredible,' Scarlet whispers.

'I know,' Kavita whispers back. 'It's my favourite place in the world – this world, of course, not the other.'

'Yeah.' Scarlet nods. 'I see your point. I think it's rapidly becoming mine too.'

They're standing in an underground chamber carved out of stone and illuminated by lights scattered along the oak bookshelves which line every inch of the place from floor to ceiling. And upon the stone ceilings elaborate frescos create a night sky of midnight blue dotted with all the constellations of stars, which shine bright in silver paint like dozens of tiny diamonds scattered among sapphires. And beneath their feet, the frescos are exactly mirrored in rugs woven from lambswool, like the tapestries hanging in medieval castles. But it is the hundreds of books crowding those shelves which are the most striking thing of all: each one is about three inches thick, bound in faded leather with the titles embossed in a shimmering gold, the letters glinting in the soft light: *The*

Alchemy of the Waxing Moon, Diaries of the First Candle Bearers, Spells for All Seasons . . .

'When you told me it was underground, I thought it'd be sinister and creepy,' Scarlet says. 'But it makes me think of a hobbit hole. It's so dark and cosy—'

'—like a hobbit hole, but if Bilbo's pantry was filled with ancient manuscripts instead of seed cakes,' Kavita finishes.

'Yes.' Scarlet smiles. 'Exactly that. I just, I can't believe there's a secret library hiding under the streets of Oxford and nobody up there knows about it.' She reaches out towards a particularly twinkling book, then withdraws her hand again.

Watching her, Kavita laughs. 'You're allowed to touch it. This isn't the Bodleian, I told you. It's not run by ordinary Oxford University librarians who'll cut off your tongue if you breathe too hard near the specialist books. This is a place just for Grimms and we're permitted to pick these ones up, read them, take notes, do as we wish.'

'So . . .' Scarlet reaches out again, glancing back at a short blonde bespectacled librarian behind her, stacking shelves. 'I could take one home?'

'Not on your life,' Kavita snorts. 'They're all protected by charms – if you even so much as took them upstairs they'd start screaming.'

Scarlet turns to give Kavita an incredulous glance. 'The *book* would scream?' All at once feeling a little wary, she takes a step back.

'In effect, yes.' Kavita giggles. 'But don't worry, they don't bite.'

'Hum.' Scarlet folds her arms across her chest, unconvinced. 'So, do you really think one of these books might be able to help us fix whatever's going on?'

'I hope so,' Kavita says, stepping across the stone floor to slip a book from the shelf: *Magical Empires in the Middle Ages.* 'This is the greatest collection of esoteric manuscripts in the world, dating back to the early eleventh century. We even have a copy of Pym's *Encyclopaedia of the Mystical Arts*.' She looks expectantly at Scarlet, who nods impressively, though she's never heard of the thing. 'So, if any scholar has written anything illuminating about Everwhere, then this is the place we'll find it.'

10.28 a.m. – Goldie

The first twenty-four hours are crucial. It's the thought that haunts Goldie with every tick-tick of the clock. She tries not to look at it, tries to keep her eyes fixed on the floor – when gazing at her brother becomes too heartbreaking – but it's impossible to resist. She finds herself staring at its cruel, relentless little hands as she begs them to slow down.

'Stop,' she wants to say. 'We need more time.'

Goldie grips her brother's hands till both are so hot with healing energy she has to let go. She watches the energy coursing through his body, almost making his veins glimmer, but having no effect at all. She needs Luna. Together, they might be able to do it. Without Luna, she keeps trying anyway.

Nurses come and go. The surgeon visits to conduct his assessments.

Days pass. Still Teddy does not wake.

Chapter Twenty-three

11.18 a.m. – Goldie

She sits in the social services' waiting room, arms wrapped tight around her ribs, legs crossed left over right, right leg jiggling so fast her whole body shakes. She doesn't want to be here. She wants to be home with Luna; she needs to be at the hospital with Teddy. What if something happens when she's gone? What if he wakes? What if he *dies*? Nothing would take her away from his bedside, except for this.

This is your fucking fault, Leo. If not for those fucking scars, we'd never be— Tears fill Goldie's eyes. *Teddy and I would be at home with Luna.* As anger sinks into sorrow, the desire Goldie tries so hard to suppress rises up and fills her. She closes her eyes, imagining the scene she so rarely allows herself to imagine, the one that makes her entire body ache with longing: sitting on the sofa with Leo at one end, her at the other and Luna in between them. It is so simple, so ordinary, so commonplace. A scene experienced by millions of families every day, so boringly normal it's overlooked and unappreciated and forgotten by bedtime. And yet, if she could only experience this once, *just once*, Goldie would never ask for another gift as long as she lived.

Stop it, she snaps to herself. *Pull yourself together. You've got to show them you're responsible. You've got to show them you're strong.* The waiting room is empty save for one other woman who looks just as nervous as Goldie feels.

Every now and then, they catch each other's eye, then look away.

Goldie wishes she smoked; it'd be a helpful habit at times like these. She wishes she'd brought snacks. In lieu of cigarettes, KitKats would be an adequate substitute. She's been virtually subsisting on them for the past week, occasionally branching out with a Snickers or Mars Bar when she could stomach it. She tried to allow herself only one chocolate bar every three hours, but the vending machine is in the corridor just outside Teddy's room – visible through his window – and Goldie's willpower, weak at the best of times, is now non-existent.

Why is there no vending machine here? Goldie thinks. *They need one.* Biting her lip, she catches the other woman's eye again, then looks quickly away.

'H-have they t-taken your kids too?' the woman says. She's thin – too thin – and so sparsely dressed that she shivers in the air-conditioned room.

Reluctantly, Goldie nods. She doesn't want to talk. She doesn't want to cry. And if she talks, she'll cry. She twists her hands in her lap, desperately wishing she'd brought a Mars Bar in her bag.

'My Josh's been in care since he was four,' the woman says, as if Goldie had asked. 'I've been here every few months trying to get him back. Got myself sober, got a job, but they still won't let him home. It's always something with 'em. Now they don't approve of my new boyfriend, just cos he—'

Goldie is trying to nod, trying to listen, trying to think of appropriately kind and encouraging words to offer, when the hitherto silent receptionist calls out: 'Mrs Clayton!'

'I'm not married,' Goldie tells the woman as she stands. 'I don't know why they always . . .' She trails off, realizing that these aren't the comforting words that are called for, and wondering why on earth she offered them up in the first place. 'I'm sorry,' she says, distracted as she hurries across the waiting room and towards the door marked INTERVIEW ROOM. 'I really hope you get John back.'

'You're saying there's nothing I can do?' Goldie speaks slowly, carefully, vowing that she won't cry in front of him. She will not. No. Matter. What. 'So, I just have to wait while you keep my daughter and in the meantime, as you're carrying out these assessments to decide if I'm a fit mother, she's placed with a total stranger who might be a . . . a . . . a fucking werewolf for all you know and—'

'I assure you, Miss Clayton, that every single one of our carers goes through an extremely rigorous assessment process.' Mr Clarke sits forward, his chest puffing up with self-importance. 'And no one would ever be given a position of responsibility over a child without—'

'So you say,' Goldie interrupts in turn. 'But barely a week goes by without some stories in the papers about a –' she's about to swear but checks herself just in time – 'foster family who locks the kids in the basement or chains them to the radiators or—'

'Let me stop you there,' Mr Clarke interjects. 'Before you make another grossly exaggerated accusation. Yes, we've had some incidents in the past, but we've made significant changes to the systems since, with stringent checks to ensure that all caregivers meet the appropriate standards.'

'Appropriate?' Goldie's voice rises dangerously close to

hysterical. '*Appropriate?* Since I've spent nearly ten years taking care of my daughter to the *highest* standards, Mr Clarke, I'm afraid I'm not reassured by whatever you mean by "appropriate".'

'Forgive me, Mrs Clayton.' Mr Clarke raises an eyebrow. 'But, if that were the case, well, we wouldn't be here now, would we?'

Goldie, torn between the desire to drop to the floor and weep or lunge forward and rip out the man's throat, grips the arms of her chair. Instead of glowering at him, she casts her gaze to the floor and imagines burning a hole in the carpet instead.

'You do have another option,' Mr Clarke concedes. 'Should you wish to circumvent the foster system, you may appoint a family member as a guardian, who will of course need to be thoroughly vetted by us. But that's one way of . . .'

Instantly, hope blooms in Goldie's chest. A way out! A way – and then hope withers. Teddy, dear Teddy, her only remaining family member, excepting Luna. A stable, upstanding member of the community, former boy scout, who dedicates his life to charity work . . . and is currently in a coma.

She looks up to see that Mr Clarke is still talking, though she's got no idea what he's saying anymore.

'Yes.' She strives to keep her voice calm. 'Yes. Give me all the forms. I'll do that.'

'All right then.' Mr Clarke nods, opening a drawer in his desk and pulling out a folder.

'I have an exceedingly responsible sibling,' Goldie continues. 'He left school with eleven A stars, or nines, or whatever they are now. He runs the shelter with me, is totally dedicated to—'

'Put it in the forms,' Mr Clarke says, holding out an inch-thick stack towards her. 'Or you can do it online, if you prefer. Either way, I won't be the one who ultimately makes the decision, so there's no point in wasting your hyperbole on me.'

Goldie stands and steps towards his desk. She knows that the chances of Teddy waking are diminishing with each passing day; she knows it's a mad hope to expect a miraculous recovery and full guardianship, but what other hope does she have? Fixing a rigid smile on her face, she accepts the stack of forms with both hands, gripping them with the same force she'd like to apply to Mr Clarke's neck. If she'd been Scarlet, she thinks, the papers would surely have burst into flames.

3.33 p.m. – Teddy

Teddy and Bea continue to argue. It seems to Teddy that they've been arguing for an eternity, but Bea is fierce as a hurricane and quick as the wind and he knows she'll never give up. *That's one guaranteed way to win a fight*, he thinks. *Be the one who never stops fighting.* Particularly in this situation, when he cannot walk away.

'Look, I appreciate your intentions,' Teddy says, for perhaps the three-hundredth time. 'But I've told you, I cannot do it. I cannot betray my sister.'

So, you would rather be in this coma forever than tell Goldie you want to leave and go to Saint Martins? You're so scared of feeling guilty, you'd rather be dead?

'Don't be facetious.' Teddy sighs. 'It's only your opinion

that I won't wake up unless I decide to destroy my sister's life. You might be entirely wrong. A good many people lead lives of quiet desperation for ninety years or so without—'

Yes, and if they'd been beaten into a coma, I bet they wouldn't have bothered waking up.

'That's not fair. I want to wake up.'

So you say.

As always, whenever Bea visits his dreams, Teddy is in Everwhere. Now he sits in the bleached branches of an oak tree, legs dangling over the ground of moss and stone. This tree is so enveloped in ivy that it makes for quite a comfy perch and he nestles happily among the abundance of white leaves.

Anyway, most of those sorts don't know what else they'd rather be doing. The wind of Bea's voice whistles through the trees in irritation. *You have a passion, a desire – your heart's desire – that you're purposely giving up. That's what makes this such a dreadful decision.*

'But fashion is an utterly frivolous passion,' Teddy protests. 'What real good does it do anyone? It doesn't save lives or contribute anything; it only costs money and creates landfill.'

The great gust of Bea's sigh ruffles every leaf on the tree. *Stop being so obtuse! I'm not talking about cheap T-shirts stitched by exploited kids and thrown away after a few washes. What you'd do would be art.*

'Art!' Teddy laughs. 'And what's the bloody point of art?'

Now Bea's touch is a soft breeze on his cheek, a caress so gentle and kind that it shivers through Teddy and brings tears to his eyes. *How,* he thinks, *can any human live without touch?*

In the same way they can live without art, Bea says. *And books and films and everything creative and beautiful – but it's a much lesser experience of life. Don't you think?*

Teddy is silent. Because, as much as he'd like to, he can't argue with that.

Your world is a depressing place. We need artists to brighten it just as we need those who help us survive it.

Bea waits, letting her words echo in the stillness. For, like all good polemicists, she knows when to speak and when to shut up.

'I suppose so,' Teddy concedes as he puts his hand to his cheek. He wants to feel the warmth of her touch again but doesn't want to prove her right by asking.

And what about brightening the lives of the saviours? Bea presses her point. *Don't they deserve a little beauty, a little fun and frivolity? Who says fashion has to be wasted on self-obsessed teenagers, monied housewives and pop stars? Instead of wasting your gift on privileged bullshit like haute couture, you could bring beauty to all: nurses, teachers, carers . . .*

'Yes,' Teddy admits quietly. 'I hadn't thought of that.'

Choosing your heart's desire doesn't mean you suddenly become a selfish prick. You could set up a charity. You could give all the proceeds to Goldie's shelter, or to all the shelters everywhere – you can do whatever you damn well want, if only you'd bloody well wake up!

4.23 p.m. – Goldie

Goldie is watching him when it happens, her gaze resting – as it often is – on his hand. When she's not holding his hand, she's watching it and thinking of Luna, wondering where she is and what she's doing. She's dearly hoping that her little girl is okay.

Then she sees the twitch of Teddy's thumb.

Goldie stares, hardly daring to hope it might happen again. Several painful minutes pass and, increasingly desperate, she reaches out to tentatively take his hand. She thinks of Luna, of her little girl's fervent belief that they could use their healing powers to help bring Teddy back to life.

'All right.' Goldie sighs, dearly wishing that Luna was beside her now. 'We can but try.'

As she holds her brother's hand, Goldie thinks of all the times she's brought plants back to life. She imagines Teddy sitting up in bed, smiling, talking, back to his old self again. She imagines them both at the shelter, sitting in the office drinking tea, or on the dilapidated sofa talking into the small hours of the morning while Luna falls asleep in their laps. She remembers Teddy as a baby, when she stood vigil over his cot, when she took him for walks and pretended she was his ma; when he was six and their mother died and, too quickly, it was no longer a pretence. She remembers his skilful drawings and his raw excitement for everything, especially exquisite costumes. She remembers stealing posh clothes for him and all guilt fading at his squeals of sheer delight upon receiving them. She remembers descending into a fog after Leo died and Teddy going off the rails, throwing away his most cherished ambitions and . . .

Goldie removes her hands to wipe her eyes. She's about to pick up his hand again when, blinking through tears, she sees – as if through a dream – her brother starting to stir. His left leg shifts, ever so slightly and ever so slowly, towards the edge of the bed, as if making a snail-like bid for freedom.

Goldie stares, in astonishment and awe, as though Teddy is ten months old again and taking his first steps.

She watches, breath held as tiny tremors of movement shudder through Teddy's body, until both his legs jerk, then his arms and, at last, the muscles of his face start to twitch. A sob bursts from Goldie's throat, and she grips his blanket and presses her own face down onto his bed, hardly daring to look, muttering his name over and over again.

'Teddy, Teddy, my little Teddy boy . . . Teddy, Teddy, Teddy . . .'

At the sound of a spluttered cough, Goldie snaps her head up to stare at her beloved brother as he opens his eyes for the first time in a week. She doesn't know if his resurrection has anything to do with her touch or her incantation but, frankly, Goldie doesn't care. Tears fall down her cheeks, dropping onto the bed, as she watches her own Sleeping Beauty awake.

11.59 p.m. – Luna

She wonders if suicidal thoughts are normal. She can't ask because she'd get in trouble. She thinks everyone must have them sometimes, unless they're very lucky. But lately Luna spends hours imagining how to do it. And she has many ways at her fingertips. She could burn herself at the stake, like the witches of old. She could walk into a lake and create the currents to drown in. She could dig a hole and bury herself alive by coaxing the earth to tumble down and the roots of plants to grow thickly above her. She couldn't leap from a building or tree, since the instinct to fly would kick in, but she could do something creative with air, like creating a hurricane to rip her apart.

Luna knows it's morbid to think such things, but she can't help it. Because, awful though the thought of dying is, the thought of growing up without her mummy is even worse. And it's been five days. *Five days.* Every night she cries herself to sleep, and every day she tries not to cry – if she did that, the kids at school would have a field day. She's allowed to speak to Goldie on the phone, but it's not the same. In fact, it's even worse. After her ma says goodbye, Luna feels as if someone has opened her chest and torn out her heart. And she can't do what she'd usually do to make herself feel better: she can't touch her scars, can't cut her skin because there's not a razor blade in sight.

Luna has begged them to let her go home; she's told them a thousand times that she's not being abused. But, of course, no one's listening. They think she's protecting her mother; they think she's got Scotland – no, Stockholm – syndrome. It doesn't matter what she says, no one believes her. At first Luna was angry, so angry that it took all her willpower not to punish her captors the same way she punished the men who'd beaten the women they were supposed to love. But she felt too weak to exact vengeance on anyone, even the man who'd put Uncle Teddy in a coma. She felt sapped of all strength, all power, all will. Worst still, she was scared: scared that her mummy was gone and she'd never be allowed to go home.

And now she's sad.

So sad, so hopeless, so helpless, that it makes her want to die.

12.49 a.m. – Scarlet

They've been visiting the underground library at every opportunity for nearly a week now; they've carefully read, studied and examined almost fifty manuscripts, but have still found nothing to shed light on exactly what might be shaking up Everwhere. Which is not to say that they've found nothing. To Scarlet's shock, oblique and explicit references to the realm are scattered throughout nine hundred years of magical literature.

They've discovered a plethora of drawings, several diary entries that enable them to speculate as to what sort of malevolent element might have infiltrated the gates, but they find nothing definite or additionally revealing. Until Scarlet chances upon a small volume tucked between two great tomes: *Mystical Members of the Monarchies of Great Britain 1066–1605* and *Mystical Members of the Monarchies of Great Britain 1605–1952*. Its spine glitters as her hand hovers and, on a whim, Scarlet plucks it off the shelf.

She's flicking through its pages on her way back to the desk when she stops and starts reading slowly, carefully. Taking each sentence one by one, then going back to be certain she's not made a mistake. Closing the book to check the title on the spine, Scarlet makes a mental note of it: *Instructions for the Necessary Annihilation of Magical Realms in the Eventuality of the Infiltration of Maleficent, Malign or Malicious Forces.*

'Kavita,' she says, opening the book again. 'I think you should read this.'

*

'It's out of the question,' says Kavita. 'Surely you can't think— We can't destroy Everwhere. What would happen to all the sisters who rely on it as a safe haven now? Who learn how to empower and protect themselves? Who—'

'It's not a safe place for everyone,' Scarlet interrupts. 'It wasn't for Liyana.'

'Yes,' Kavita admits. 'Of course, but she was only one – not *only*. I didn't mean it like that, I'm sorry. I just meant to say that, compared to the hundreds, possibly thousands, of sisters who've had their lives transformed by Goldie, Bea and Liyana supporting and teaching them—'

'Yes, yes. And me too, once.' Scarlet leans across Kavita's desk to reclaim the book. 'I'm not saying it wouldn't be a great loss. But if something worse than a rogue soldier has invaded Everwhere, then we might need to consider more drastic measures.'

Kavita is silent. 'All right,' she agrees at last. 'But not until we've exhausted every other eventuality. Now, let's get back to reading. If we can pinpoint what's going on, then we can figure out the best way to deal with it.'

Chapter Twenty-four

3.33 a.m. – Everwhere

She knows she shouldn't be here, but she's never been able to resist doing something she's been told not to do. At six, she made herself sick eating twelve bags of stolen sweets. At fourteen, she was heartbroken by a boy her best friend told her never to date. At eighteen, she spent eight hours in a police cell after being caught shoplifting. It wasn't her first time, nor her last.

Every time she's done something ill-advised she's had cause to regret it. And when she feels the hands at her throat, she has cause again. Mercifully, she doesn't suffer long. A minute at most. Then her spirit is engulfed by the mists and her soul is sinking into the soil. Her death is the matter of a moment. After that, there's no trace. The only evidence: the white leaf.

It falls from a single spot in the sky and drifts to the ground, unseen.

1.18 a.m. – Teddy

'I'm not going anywhere,' Teddy whispers. With the breathing tube at last extracted, his throat is raw, as if he's been swallowing thorns, and though it hurts like hell to speak, it also feels like a small miracle, a victory he must embrace. 'So you can let go of my hand if you like.'

Goldie shakes her head, gripping him even tighter. 'I'm never letting go of your hand ever again.'

Teddy smiles, even though it hurts to smile.

Goldie glances down at the bag at her feet. 'I need to call Luna. As soon as she's awake, I'll try to catch her before she goes to school. If they'll let me.'

His smile widens. 'Th-then you m-might –' he swallows, wincing – 'have to let go of my hand, after all.'

'Stop talking,' Goldie says gently. 'You're supposed to be resting, remember.'

As soon as he'd woken, Goldie had called for everyone: her cries pealing through the hospital corridors to summon nurses, orderlies, doctors, cleaners, visitors, anyone within fifty yards of her cries. An hour after that, Mr Pride himself had arrived, pronounced mildly on the 'miracle' and advised cautious optimism regarding Teddy's full recovery, saying he had a 'long road' of physiotherapy ahead of him. Goldie nodded through all the clichés, unable to be anything but utterly overjoyed and wildly optimistic about everything, not just regarding Teddy but everything else in the world. Suddenly everything that'd seemed so relentlessly awful was now shiny and bright and hopeful. Even Luna, because now Teddy could be her guardian and everything would return to normal again.

'I-I'll stop,' Teddy says, swallowing painfully again. He should rest, of course, but if he waits to say what he needs to say, then he'll never say it at all. 'B-but first there's something I-I need to tell you.'

'Me too,' Goldie says, squeezing his hand. 'Well, ask you – anyway, you go first.'

Teddy shakes his head, relieved at the excuse to postpone the heartache. 'N-no, you,' he mumbles. 'Y-you.'

'Well.' Goldie sits forward. 'I know this is a little premature, till you're fully well again and all that. But I've got a rather enormous favour to ask you.'

7.09 a.m. – Luna & Goldie

'What is it, Ma?' Luna's heart thuds in her chest. 'Is Uncle Ted all right? Please—'

'Teddy's okay. He's better than okay – he's awake!' Goldie grips her phone, wishing with every cell of her desperate being that Luna was here, that she was holding her, hugging her, squeezing her tight. Without her, Goldie's joy is tempered and will be until she gets her daughter back.

Now, at the other end of the line, she hears Luna explode with simultaneous laughter and tears, gasps of shock and whoops of delight. Goldie grins.

'Oh, baby girl, how I wish you were here!' Goldie exclaims before she can stop herself. She'd promised that she wouldn't say such things, wouldn't burden Luna with her misery when the poor girl had quite enough of her own.

'Me too, Ma. M-me too.' Luna is silent for a moment before bursting into tears.

'Oh, Lu-Lu, please,' Goldie begs. 'It's okay, it's okay now. It is, it is . . .'

But Luna continues to sob and with every sodden breath Goldie's heart contracts in her chest till she can hardly breathe herself.

'M-my love,' Goldie manages. 'Please, don't cry. It's okay, everything is going to be okay.'

'N-not till we're t-together again,' Luna sobs. 'N-nothing will be okay till th-then.'

Goldie sighs, a deep sorrowful sigh. 'I know, my love, I know.'

'At night I dream of Pa,' Luna whispers. 'And you and me. We live together and we're happy and I'm safe. And then I wake up –' she sniffs – 'and I'm still in this prison and I . . .' She trails off, tears trickling down her cheeks again. 'I, I . . .'

'It's—' Goldie's about to say 'it's okay' again, but stops herself. 'I have a plan. I'm doing everything I can, Lu-Lu, and I promise, promise we'll be together soon.'

Luna sniffs again. 'What about the day after t-tomorrow?'

'Tomorrow?' Goldie asks. 'What's the day after tomorrow?'

'My birthday!' Luna squeals. 'I can't believe you forgot!'

'Oh, sh— I'm so sorry, Lu, I've . . .' Goldie curses herself. 'It's been . . . But, of course, I . . .'

'Ma, I want to come home,' Luna begs. 'Please, I don't want to be here. I just want to be normal. I want to come home.'

The desperation in her daughter's voice pushes Goldie towards the edge. She'd promised herself she'd follow the rules and do what's right; she promised herself that she'd stay sensible and safe and not make any foolish mistakes. But she can't bear to hear Luna's sorrow and longing, knowing she could make it better. If only momentarily.

'All right, baby girl,' Goldie whispers. 'Since it's your birthday, my love, let's break the rules this once and meet in Everwhere tomorrow night.'

11.57 p.m. – Scarlet & Kavita

'Ouch,' Scarlet moans, stretching out her back. 'I'm not used to all this sitting. It's murder on my muscles. I don't know how you do this all day. Don't you get bored?'

Kavita laughs. 'Just the opposite; I love it. I don't know how you cook all day; I'd be bloody knackered.'

'Yeah, that's what I like about it.' Scarlet pushes away from the desk to stand. 'It's totally all-consuming. When you're in the kitchen you can't think about anything else. Get distracted for a second and you've burnt a sauce. But with book reading it's so easy to drift off and think about other things . . .'

'I guess it's not the best activity if you're engaged in some serious avoidance and denial,' Kavita says wryly, 'I must admit.'

'Shut up,' Scarlet scolds. 'And I'm not anymore. At least, not as much as I was.' She glances up at the dim light bulb hanging above them. 'These lights aren't good for me either; they're making me squint like a mole. I'll be blind before the month is out.'

'I'm so used to it I hardly notice it now,' Kavita says. 'You could read by the sparks of your fingertips.'

'And risk burning all the books?' Scarlet laughs. 'I hardly think the librarians would appreciate that!'

'No,' Kavita says with a smile. 'Just do it like this.' She

raises her left hand in the air and, as the sparks start to fire, she draws her fingertips together to meet the thumb as she mumbles a string of sentences under her breath. Then, all at once, the sparks come together to form a little orb of bright light that hovers over her book, illuminating the pictures and words.

'Damn,' Scarlet gasps. 'How the hell did you do that?'

Kavita laughs. 'You don't know how to?'

'Of course I don't,' Scarlet says. 'I'm a Grimm, not a witch.'

'Then I suppose I'm a bit of both.' Kavita nods down at the illuminated book and gestures at those all around her. 'I guess you can't immerse yourself in medieval magical literature and not have a little of it rub off.'

Scarlet gapes at her friend. 'What else can you do?'

Kavita gives her a mischievous grin in return. 'Oh, I've got a few party tricks up my sleeve.'

'Show me.'

'I'd love to,' Kavita says. 'But you'll have to be patient –' she glances down at the book again, the orb of light still bobbing above the parchment inscribed with Latin words alongside intricate mathematical symbols and astrological images – 'because I think I've finally found something here.'

Scarlet leans down over the desk, peering at the manuscript. 'It looks absolutely nonsensical to me.'

'Here.' Kavita points to a collection of stars, tracing her finger over the lines without touching the page. 'You see . . .'

'What am I looking at?' Scarlet squints. 'It looks like a coat hanger to me.'

Kavita giggles. 'It's the constellation of Leo. And this –'

she indicates a series of squiggles and loops – 'looks to me like a mathematical representation of Everwhere.'

Scarlet holds her breath. This is the closest they've come to any kind of progress since entering the underground library and turning it upside down.

'So, what does it say?'

'Nothing yet.'

Kavita keeps reading. Scarlet watches as she turns the page, the orb of light levitating to avoid brushing against the page. Kavita mumbles the words as she reads, and a constant stream of whispered Latin fills the air.

Then she stops. 'Oh my God.'

'What? What is it?'

'Wait.' Kavita holds up her hand. 'Wait a sec.'

'What is it?' Scarlet echoes herself, bouncing up and down with impatience. 'Tell me!'

'Incredible,' Kavita mutters. 'Absolutely incredible.'

'What! What? What!' Scarlet squeals, unable to contain herself any longer. Sparks fire at her fingertips and the books all around her shrink back into their shelves.

'I can't believe it. I, I can't . . .'

Scarlet grabs Kavita's shoulders, causing her to jump. 'Read the damn book now or I'll set fire to your hair.'

'All right, all right,' Kavita says. 'Give me a moment to translate.'

Scarlet waits, thinking she might implode with excitement and fear. And when, at last, Kavita reads the words aloud, she can't believe them herself.

'*One day a Grimm will fall in love with a soldier and from them will be born a daughter of earth and sky*,' Kavita intones. '*And when she reaches her tenth year, she will . . .*'

'Yes?' Scarlet grips Kavita's shoulder. 'She will what?'

'Wait,' Kavita says, as she carefully turns the page. 'I've just got to . . . What the hell?'

'What is it?' Scarlet stares down at the manuscript, until she sees the long ragged edge where the page has been ripped out.

Chapter Twenty-five

6.33 a.m. – Scarlet & Kavita

They'd stared at the gap left by the missing page for far too long before finally accepting that it was indeed gone. Then they'd wasted another valuable few hours searching the shelves for extracts of manuscripts, then other books for loose pages or something else they might have missed.

'It's no good,' Kavita concedes at last, when the sun has long since risen. Not that they can see its light in the underground library, but they can feel the hunger for breakfast in their bellies. 'I've got to teach a lecture on Bede at nine. It's hard enough to stay awake through Bede at the best of times; I'm not sure how I'll manage it now.'

Scarlet yawned. 'And I've got bacon and eggs and toast and kippers to cook for a bunch of over-privileged ex-Etonians.'

Kavita smiles a sleepy smile. 'They're not *all* that bad, are they?'

'No,' Scarlet admits. 'Not every single one. I even heard a Birmingham accent the other day. It was quite a shock.'

Kavita laughs wearily. 'You should've been here when I was an undergraduate; white male privilege was like a plague that'd killed off every person of colour within a five-mile radius.' She sighs, pushing back her chair. 'Now it's only one mile. Meet me here after lunch service?'

'Sure,' Scarlet says, trying to remain patient. 'I've got a half-day; I might even be able to sneak a nap.'

8.28 a.m. – Teddy

He hadn't said anything, of course. How could he? His sister had asked *him* – her only surviving family member – to be the guardian of her daughter. She has no one else. He's the only chance she has of getting Luna back. So, what was he supposed to say?

Oh, I'm sorry – you'll have to leave her in the hands of social services, since I've decided to abandon you all and move to London to study fashion design. It's always been my dream; I'm sure you'll understand.

Surely even Bea wouldn't condone a move that callous.

So there it is; his hands are tied. He had his chance.

He had his chance and now it's gone.

9.57 a.m. – Goldie

She sits at her brother's bedside. His bed is empty now, a genial physiotherapist having wheeled him away for his first session of physical therapy. Goldie eyes the bed. The temptation to crawl into it, to curl up and fall asleep, is almost overwhelming. She could sleep for a week and, when she awoke, she'd feel so much more able to deal with her life, the life that currently sits on her shoulders like lead weights.

But, of course, she can't. Teddy, her beloved brother, her guardian angel, is on the road to recovery now, so Goldie needs to go back to the shelter and take over from the kindly volunteers. Then she needs to organize nearby accommodation for Teddy and Luna – since social services will no doubt insist that they don't reside at the shelter – and work through all the bureaucracy involved in getting her daughter back.

And then, once she's home, Goldie will need to care for Luna even more diligently than usual, working to ameliorate the traumas she'll have suffered from being taken away. On top of all this are the unfolding dangers in Everwhere that must be urgently addressed.

Goldie glances longingly at the empty bed.

Then, with a great effort of will, she pulls herself out of the chair.

She can sleep when she's dead.

10.28 a.m. – Luna

Luna glances out of the window, tuning out the wittering of Miss Walker, who's trying to enlighten the class on the finer points of fractions, and thinks of Everwhere. Tonight she's allowed to return. *Tonight!* When she turns ten. She can hardly believe that she's about to enter double digits. It seems to have happened so fast. So slow and so fast all at once.

She feels the itching at her shoulder blade again and tries to resist scratching. Another scar, another tiny star etched into her skin, had appeared overnight and now it prickles beneath her cotton T-shirt, sending tingles down her back that make her muscles twitch. Luna clenches her fists. If she succumbs to temptation now, it'll only build into an agony she won't be able to assuage, not without access to razors. It's always the same when a new scar appears; it begins with a terrible itch that, when scratched, burrows deeper and deeper into the skin till only the letting of blood will relieve the pain.

Luna still doesn't understand why the new scars have started materializing of late. She hopes it's to do with her father, that it's a message he's sending across the veil – although if it *is* a message, then Luna can't for the life of her figure out what it is he might be trying to say.

2.15 p.m. – Scarlet & Kavita

'Shit, I've been so stupid!' Kavita smacks herself repeatedly on the forehead, muttering 'shit, shit, shit' under her breath.

'What is it?' Scarlet grabs hold of her friend's hand. 'Stop maiming yourself.'

'I've been obsessing about the sentence,' Kavita says. 'But in all my obsessing, in looking for the most complex and challenging solution, I overlooked the simplest one.'

'What's that?'

'A finding spell.'

'Oh,' Scarlet says, none the wiser. She stands beside Kavita, leaning against the back of her chair. They're sharing the same desk as last night, the librarian having left everything exactly as it was, untouched.

'It's a way of piecing together something that was once there,' Kavita explains. 'It's only possible when you've got two reference points, so you can form a bridge between them and see an imprint of what the whole used to be. Does that make sense?'

'Not really,' Scarlet admits. 'But don't worry about me; do you think you can do it?'

Kavita shrugs. 'I can try. I've done it before, but never on something so ancient as this, and it'll depend on when the page went missing. These sorts of conjurings are impossible if something's been separated for more than a century or so – the bridge is too weak after too long.'

'Let's hope it was a thieving Victorian scholar then,' Scarlet says. 'And not a Georgian.'

'Better yet, an Edwardian.' Kavita holds her hands over the book, still open on the two pages either side of the missing one, and starts to chant.

'*Validor es quam videris, fortior quam sentis, sapientior quam credis . . . Validor es quam videris, fortior quam sentis, sapientior quam credis . . . Validor es quam videris, fortior quam sentis, sapientior quam credis . . .*'

Scarlet watches, breath held. She watches and waits and when after nearly half an hour has passed and still nothing has happened she leans in close to Kavita.

'Is it working?' Scarlet asks hopefully. 'Is it working but I just can't see it?'

'No.' Kavita sighs. 'It'll take hours.' She stares determinedly at the book. 'I'm essentially trying to stitch back together a page, molecule by molecule, using the imprint it left after being torn out.'

'Damn.' Scarlet echoes Kavita's sigh, sinking deeper into her chair. She stifles a yawn. 'Then perhaps I've got time for a nap, after all.'

'And we've only got one chance to bring it back,' Kavita says. 'If it works, that is.'

But Scarlet – who's been cooking for hundreds of scholars during the days and studying dozens of manuscripts during the nights, only snatching moments to pass out whenever she can – is already asleep.

11.38 p.m. – Kavita & Scarlet

Scarlet is woken by a sharp yelp.

'Quick! Quick!' Kavita is shrieking. 'It won't last – it'll disappear in a moment!'

'Shit, what?' Scarlet sits up, blinking rapidly. She frowns, then rubs her eyes. 'What is it? What's happened?'

'I've done it!' Kavita cries. 'Look!'

Scarlet sees what seems to be a hologram, flickering and guttering, the ghostly image of a page inscribed with scrolling sentences and scattered images of moons and midnight skies. The sight of it leaves Scarlet momentarily silenced.

'Bloody hell,' she gasps. 'I can't believe it. You've actually gone and bloody well done it! Read it, quick, quick!'

But Kavita is no longer listening; her gaze is fixed upon the flickering page as she tries to decipher the rest of the sentence. 'I wish it'd stop shifting,' she moans. 'Just for a few seconds. It's one thing to . . . okay, "validus" – or "fortis", "potens" – "powerful" . . . and "totus", of them both . . . more powerful than them both combined . . .'

All at once, the guttering page dies and disappears.

'Did you get it?' Scarlet says. 'Did you translate it in time?'

Slowly, Kavita nods. The expression on her face is grim.

'What is it?' Scarlet asks. 'What's wrong?'

Kavita turns her head to meet Scarlet's eye. '*Periculosum.*'

Scarlet frowns. 'What's "peri-co-sium"?'

Kavita turns back to gaze at the place where the holographic page had been. 'Dangerous,' she mumbles. 'It means dangerous.'

Scarlet's frown deepens. 'What's dangerous?'

'Not what,' Kavita says. '*Who.*'

'Then, who?' Scarlet persists, increasingly impatient.

Kavita doesn't raise her eyes from the manuscript. 'Luna.'

'Luna?' Scarlet stares at the book, incredulous. 'No, Luna's not dangerous. You must be mistaken. She's Goldie's daughter. She's not—'

'Exactly,' Kavita interrupts. 'There is only one child to whom this applies.' She shifts her tone, as if reading from a lectern. '"*One day a Grimm will fall in love with a soldier and from them will be born a daughter of earth and sky*,' Kavita intones. '*And when she reaches her tenth year, she will . . . become more powerful than both combined and more dangerous than either.*'

'No,' Scarlet says again. 'Are you sure? Are you—'

'Yes,' Kavita stops her. 'I'm certain.'

Chapter Twenty-six

3.33 a.m. – Scarlet & Kavita

With clear roads and no traffic (conditions rarer than dragons' teeth) the drive from Oxford to Cambridge is a shade over or under two hours. With its circuitous route, the bus takes around four hours. The train takes even longer since, despite fifty years' worth of promises, a direct line has yet to be built. Kavita, driving her Fiat Uno at maximum capacity and breaking speed limits in several counties, makes it in one hour and twenty-three minutes.

They arrive at the shelter just before three o'clock in the morning, to be told – once they've convinced her that they're Sisters Grimm – by a rather flustered Becky that Goldie has gone to meet Luna in Everwhere.

'It's her birthday tonight,' she says, sleepily. 'They're celebrating it together.'

She's hardly finished the sentence before Scarlet and Kavita are exchanging panicked questions about perils and birthdays and imminent dangers, before jumping back in the car and driving to the nearest gate which, as Becky helpfully informs them, is at the entrance to the Botanic Garden on Trumpington Road.

They park haphazardly, having no time to figure out the payment system on their phones, surrendering to inevitable tickets. They pace, impatient and desperate, along the path until the precise, glittering minute when the moon slips from behind the clouds and shines upon the gate and they push it open.

They're shouting Goldie's name before they've even passed through the gate.

3.33 a.m. – Everwhere

Luna, having escaped the confines of the foster home, is the first to arrive in Everwhere. Entering through the Botanic Garden's gate, she runs over moss and stone until she reaches Goldie's favourite tree and leans against it, panting. A few minutes later, when her mother enters the glade, Luna hurtles into her arms.

'Ma, Ma, Ma!' Luna cries, hugging Goldie tighter than she ever has before. 'Oh, Ma, I've missed you so much!'

'Lu-Lu, my precious, dearest Lu-Lu.' Goldie clutches Luna to her chest, burying her face in Luna's hair. 'How I've missed you. So, so, so much . . .'

They hold each other for a long while, long enough for Liyana and Bea to sense their presence and set out to find them among the infinite expanse of forests and lakes and fields.

Happy birthday, niña. Bea encircles mother and daughter in a breeze that envelops them both with the warmth of a summer afternoon. *Congratulations on your first decade!*

'Oh my goodness,' Goldie exclaims, looking down at Luna. 'I'm so sorry, darling girl, I-I can't believe I forgot to wish you a happy birthday!'

Happy birthday, my magical niece. Liyana sprinkles them with a light rain. *May all your wishes come true.*

'I've only got one wish.' Luna lifts her head from Goldie's chest but keeps her arms tight around her waist. 'And that's to never go back. And I *won't*,' she adds. 'I'm staying here and never going back. Never, never, never. And you can't make me.'

'Oh, Lu.' Goldie squeezes Luna tighter. 'Oh, my little Lu-Lu.'

It's a while longer before they finally let each other go, before they sit together on a patch of deep moss, before they speak again. Goldie leans back against the trunk of the tree, wiping her eyes and taking deep breaths in a vain attempt to calm herself. Luna snuggles up against her mother and closes her eyes. She yawns.

'You're tired, baby girl?' Goldie peers down at her in surprise. 'You're never tired.'

Luna gives a half-shrug. 'I haven't slept since . . .' She trails off, not wanting to pollute her happiness by thinking about the soulless bedroom in which she's been trapped for the past week.

'Oh, my love.' Goldie strokes her daughter's hair. 'Why don't you have a nap now? You can sleep on me. I'll be the lookout, so you've nothing to fear.' She says this as if she has slept well, when really she sports a constant ache in her temples from lack of rest and can barely keep her eyes open herself.

Luna smiles, curling her arms around Goldie's waist. 'Maybe just a little one.' She yawns again. 'A cat nap.'

Goldie kisses the top of Luna's head. 'Go ahead.'

They wait a few minutes, until Luna is safe and sound and emitting soft snuffling snores, like a piglet rooting for a late-night snack. Then they speak.

We don't want to rain on the birthday parade. Bea's words blow on a cooler breeze. *Or the mother–daughter bonding, but we've got disturbing news.*

Sad news. Liyana's voice ripples over the river that snakes alongside the glade. *Very, very sad.*

Goldie looks up, instantly alert. 'What is it?' she asks, even though she's sure she knows. 'Is— Has another sister . . .'

Yes. The wind blows and the rain falls in unison.

We didn't see it.

We, rather I, only felt it – afterwards, when her death trembled through the air and shivered through the tree I happened to be lingering upon.

Tears fill Goldie's eyes and she holds Luna a little tighter. 'Oh, no. That's awful. That's . . .' A tear slides down her cheek. She doesn't wipe it away. There is no way, of course, to know the identity of their lost sister. She will die unmarked, but not unmourned, as so many soldiers did in so many wars. 'Why did she come alone? I told them not to. Dammit.' Goldie sighs. 'What are we going to do?'

It's not easy.

Everwhere is infinite. And our vision is limited.

We might be intangible, hermana, *but still we can't be everywhere all at once.*

'I know, I know,' Goldie says, gazing down at Luna. 'But we've got to do something. We've got to figure out a way to catch him, or how can we keep letting them come here. It's too dangerous.'

4.14 a.m. – Scarlet & Kavita

'Where the hell are they?'

'How the hell should I know? This place is infinite!'

'Then we're f-fucked,' Kavita pants, stopping to slump against a fallen trunk to catch her breath. 'They might be bloody anywhere!'

'We came in through the same gate.' Scarlet staggers over to collapse against the same fallen tree. 'So we must be in the same radius. They won't have strayed too far – why would they? G-Goldie wouldn't think it safe. She's very sensible.'

'She can't be *that* sensible,' Kavita says, 'or she wouldn't be here in the first place.'

'Well, she has no idea about Luna, does she? So—'

'Come on.' Kavita stands again. 'We can't afford to chat. Let's go.'

'Where?'

'I don't know! But—'

'Goldie's favourite glade!' Scarlet cries as inspiration suddenly strikes. 'Somewhere near her favourite tree – that's where they'll be!'

And off she runs, across moss and stone, with Kavita on her heels.

4.28 a.m. – Goldie & Luna

'Wake up, darling girl.' Goldie shakes Luna gently. 'It's time to go ho— to go back.'

Luna snuffles and turns her head, eyes still tight shut.

'Please, Lu-Lu, if they find you gone, we'll be in even

bigger trouble than before.' Goldie kisses her cheek and, with another disgruntled snort, Luna opens her eyes.

'Come on, little one.' Goldie rubs Luna's arm. 'It'll take ten minutes to walk to—'

'I don't want to go,' Luna says, as she stretches and yawns again. 'I've decided; I'm staying.'

'I know how you're feeling.' Goldie starts to pull herself up from the ground, not as easily as when she was her daughter's age. 'But you can't; we can't—'

'Why not?' Luna interrupts. 'Give me one good reason.'

'I can give you a dozen,' Goldie says – though, not wanting to scare Luna, she decides not to mention the most important one.

'Not stupid practical reasons.' Luna springs up to stand beside her mother, arms crossed. 'Give me one *good* reason; one that actually matters.'

'Practical reasons *are* good reasons,' Goldie retorts. 'You have to go to school; you need an education, a job, a home. I can't raise you as a feral teenager.'

Luna kicks at the tree trunk. A small piece of bark whizzes past Goldie.

'And, one day, far, far in the future, you'll get a boyfriend or girlfriend,' she adds. 'If you like boys, you won't find any here.'

'And what if I don't want any of those things?' Luna scowls. 'What if I want to stay here. Don't I get a say in anything? It is *my* future, not yours.'

'Lu-Lu.' Goldie speaks in the soft voice she adopts whenever her daughter's being petulant. 'You might not want any of those things now. But one day you will, I promise. And when you do, you'll resent the hell out of me for not taking you back—'

Luna grits her teeth. 'No, I won't.'

'You *will,*' Goldie insists. 'And by that point, if we go back, I'll be put in prison for the rest of my life for abducting a minor – and then they'll never believe I didn't abuse you. I'll be locked up for decades.'

'So?' Luna pouts. 'Then you can just run away and live here for the rest of your life.'

'All alone in a tent?'

'You won't be alone,' Luna argues. 'I'll visit you every night and you'll have loads of other sisters visiting too, and during the day you'll have the aunties to keep you company.'

'Oh, well, that's all right then,' Goldie says. 'I'll just get a tent and live on rainwater and mushrooms and tree bark for the rest of my life, shall I?'

'You would if you loved me.' Luna digs her heels in. 'You'd stay if you loved me.'

'Oh, Lu-Lu, don't say that.'

Goldie steps forward, but Luna steps back.

'You know I love you more than anything in the world. And I'm working hard on getting you out of that bloody place and back to the shelter – or near the shelter – through the proper, legal channels. I've already set things in motion.'

'And how long will *that* take?' Luna demands. The maddening itch of the fresh scar on her shoulder flares as her anger swells. At her feet, tendrils of ivy begin to rise from the soil and snake across the ground.

'I'm not sure,' Goldie admits. 'Not long, I don't—'

'You don't have a fucking clue, do you?'

'Lu, please, don't,' Goldie begs. 'I'm doing everything I can. I couldn't do—'

'You could run away with me.'

Goldie shakes her head. 'What kind of mother would I be if I let you grow up without an education?'

Luna glowers. 'What kind of mother would you be if you let me grow up without a mother?'

Goldie stares at her daughter, incredulous. Luna glares back at her, looking so furious that, for a moment, Goldie thinks her daughter might be about to hurl a ball of fire at her head. Instead she bursts into tears. Goldie opens her arms and Luna stumbles forward to fall into them, pressing her face into Goldie's chest. She sobs and sobs, and Goldie holds her.

Neither of them notices the ivy that continues to slither across the moss and stone, creeping ever closer towards Goldie's feet.

5.24 a.m. – Scarlet & Kavita

When they stumble into the empty glade, both breathless and wild, Scarlet drops to her knees. 'Where are they?' she sobs. 'Where the hell are they?'

'Are we too late?' Kavita gasps, giving voice to the unthinkable. 'Do you think—'

'No,' Scarlet cuts her off. 'No, it's not happening again. Not after—'

It's then that she, having forgotten everything in the rush and panic, remembers her other sisters.

'Ana!' Scarlet throws her head back and screams at the night sky. 'Bea! Ana! Bea! It's me! It's Scarlet! Help me! Where are you? Where's Goldie? Where's Luna? Help! Please! Help!'

'Help!' Kavita joins the chorus. 'Help!'

5.43 a.m. – Goldie & Luna

What's happening? Goldie can't understand. *What's happening?*

She can't breathe. Something is strangling her – is it the soldier? But she was with—

'*Luna!*' she tries to scream, but the sound is only in her head, for her throat is too constricted to spit out the words and she can only splutter. Where's her baby girl? *What's happening?* Goldie is desperate, choked with panic. *Where is her daughter?*

She's still fighting for breath but dear Luna's face is in front of her now – yet, is it Luna? The girl seems to have the same features but she doesn't look the same; the mouth is cruelly twisted, the eyes inky black, the stare glassy, cold and unseeing . . .

Goldie seizes the small hands at her throat, tugging at the tiny fingers, trying to yank them apart. But the grip is so strong, like a mother gripping the wrist of a disobedient child. She cannot loosen the hands, cannot get any leverage, cannot force a shift. She tries to look into the face, to make contact with the eyes, to see something, to connect, to change what's going on – but her gaze slides from the glassy eyes and slips from the face, losing purchase on the precious little mouth and cheeks and brows she once knew so well.

She feels the puff of breath on her cheek, wondering if her daughter is bestowing upon her a kiss. *The kiss of life?* Hope rises. But, no, it must be the kiss of death for the grip tightens and Goldie is flailing, struggling and kicking, lashing out while the ivy laces itself around her ankles and slithers up her legs to wrap its tendrils around her waist and encircle her chest like a boa constrictor, squeezing the remaining breath from her lungs. She closes her eyes as she slips into the darkness.

Goldie's final thought, as her spirit starts to lift into the air and her soul readies to seep into the soil is: *Goodbye, my Luna. I love you, Leo.*

Chapter Twenty-seven

5.53 a.m. – Everwhere

The breath blows harder, colder. And somewhere in the darkness Goldie realizes that it isn't breath after all but wind. A Grimm wind. *Bea.* Harder it blows, harder still and colder. Goldie is knocked sideways – as if a blanket has been whipped from under her feet, flicking her from one place to the next so she's tumbling across moss and rolling across stone and colliding into the base of a tree, her body smacking hard against the trunk.

Yet still the hands are at her neck, slackening only for a moment during the fall, then tightening again. Goldie gasps, gulping a single pocketful of air before she's cut off once more. Thunder cracks above them and lightning strikes, briefly illuminating the starless sky.

And then, in the distance, she hears screaming. A rising alarm. A clarion call. Then closer it comes: a battle cry. Suddenly she's thrown again, tumbling across the ground with bodies atop and beneath. A melee of fists and slaps and scratches and screams and shrieks and chaos and confusion.

And then Goldie is gulping air at last, as Luna is wrenched from her throat; she's gagging and gasping, seizing breaths, snatches of oxygen . . . She's face down in the dirt, reaching her hands up to her throat, stroking her skin tenderly as breath starts to flow.

Still, the wind roars and the thunder claps and the screams split the air, and when at last Goldie lifts her head a strike of lightning illuminates the glade and she sees her little Luna lying on the ground, her head smashed against a rock.

'Lu!' Goldie cries, but her cry is only a whisper. 'Lu!' She scrambles across moss and stone, too weak to stand and run but never stopping, not for a second stopping, until she's reached her daughter, until she's scooped her up, cradling her baby girl, as fiercely close as a newborn. Luna's hair is matted with blood, her head flopped to the side, her eyes rolled back in her head.

Chapter Twenty-eight

6.03 a.m. – Everwhere

The wind has died, the air is silent, and the night dark.

In the aftermath of the storm and the crescendo of screams, the air seems ever more silent and stagnant, and the sky darker and denser, suspended so low it smothers the trees, which hang their heavy heads like mourners at a graveside.

Goldie stares down at her daughter's face, returned to the sweetness she knows so well, yet too pale and too still: *sleep without breath*. Goldie turns her tear-stained face to the sky and shrieks at the moon, at the stars, at their Creator.

'No!' she screams. 'You took him; you cannot have her too! I will not allow it. Do you hear me? I will not!'

Then she's opening her daughter's mouth, blowing her breath into the little lungs, pausing only to pump her chest; doing the same over and over again. Then pressing her hands, her life-giving hands, over Luna's heart. Watching her face, with all the hope she can hold, willing her with all the strength she has to wake.

Nothing. I want nothing else, only this. Whatever you want in exchange for her life, I will give. Anything you ask, I will do. Just return my daughter to me.

But Luna does not open her eyes nor move a single muscle. Not the flutter of an eyelid nor the twitch of a lip.

All is still. But Goldie won't move. She will stay with her child; she will stay until she joins her, until they are both dust and air. Together their spirits will lift into the sky; together their souls will sink into the soil.

It's then that, at the corner of her eyeline, Goldie sees the two women. In shock, she lifts her hands from Luna's heart and puts them to her mouth, concealing her gasp.

Scarlet takes a tentative step forward. 'I – I'm so, so sorry,' she says. 'I didn't mean— We were only trying to save you, to stop her from . . .'

It takes a moment for understanding to dawn.

'*You* did this?' Goldie screams. '*You?* Why?'

Scarlet hangs back. 'T-to save your l-life.'

'My life?' Goldie grips her daughter's chest. 'My life? What do I care about *my* life? Without hers, it's nothing!' Her tears fall with the rain. 'What did you do? What did you *do*?'

Now the other woman steps forward. 'It wasn't S-Scarlet's fault,' she stutters. 'Sh-she was trying to kill you.'

'I don't care!' Goldie's screams are hoarse but loud, the breath scraping her raw throat. 'She's my daughter; I gave her my life. She can take what she wants! But she cannot die!'

The breeze blows again. *She's not only your daughter; she's a soldier too.*

'I don't care what she is,' Goldie snaps, once more pressing her hands to her daughter's heart. 'She's my baby. She's my—' She drops her face to Luna's chest.

Suddenly Scarlet darts forward, dropping to her knees at Luna's side. She puts her hands beside Goldie's and pushes down hard; sparks spray from her fingertips as a jolt of electricity shoots through Luna's tiny body. She waits a few seconds, then does it again. Again, Luna's arms and legs jerk from the ground, then drop back. Lifeless.

Scarlet shocks Luna again and again and again.

When, at last, she draws her hands away, Goldie cries out in anguish.

'No! Don't stop! You cannot stop!'

Sister . . .

The trees sway, the rustling leaves a gentle chorus. Of love, of letting go.

Sister. Sometimes a tragedy prevents an even greater—

'No!' Goldie seizes Scarlet's hands and presses them back to Luna's chest. 'Do it again. Now!'

The rain picks up. *Goldie, dear, you must listen—*

'No!' Goldie silences Liyana. 'You cannot tell me what I *must* do – none of you know what I must do! And why didn't you tell me? You must have known. You must have seen, or you surely must have sensed it – I could have done something! I could've saved her!'

We didn't see – we cannot see everything.

We didn't sense – we cannot know what she did not know herself.

'Come here,' Scarlet calls to Kavita, who's still standing frozen, horrified, by the tree. 'Now!'

Shaking herself from her stupor, Kavita is beside her before Scarlet can say another word. Her fingers are already sparking before her hands are on Luna's chest, and when the three of them are simultaneously shocking Luna's heart and heating Luna's body and breathing (once more) into her lungs, the girl's whole body begins to shudder and twitch and shake. They try again and again, until Goldie shouts at them to stop.

'Wait.' She lifts Luna's limp hand from the ground, encircling her daughter's wrist. 'I saw— Don't. You might hurt her.' She gazes at Luna's face as she feels an almost imperceptible fluttering beneath her fingertips.

'What is it?' Scarlet leans forward.

'Shush!' Goldie hisses, not looking up.

And then, sure enough, there is the slightest shift: a minute rise of her chest; a trifling breath slips from her lips. Goldie holds her own breath, every muscle taut, every thought strung into a prayer: *Please, please, please . . .*

Luna's eyes don't open; her body is still.

But slowly, surely, with each rise of her chest, breath returns to her body.

'Oh, God,' Goldie mumbles. 'Oh, thank you, God.'

She wraps her arms around Luna's tiny frame as tenderly as if she's not touching her at all, then cradles her like a newborn babe. And she cries, tears of relief and gratitude and love – great, great love – that bathe Luna like rain.

Chapter Twenty-nine

6.33 a.m. – Everwhere

All is still and all is quiet, excepting Goldie's muffled sobs, until the breeze picks up again to rustle the leaves of the surrounding trees. *What will you do?*

'I don't need to do anything.' Goldie strokes Luna's hair. Her daughter now sleeps in her lap, her breathing shallow but regular. 'I'll teach her to control herself. She'll be fine.'

She nearly killed you.

'All right, Bea,' Goldie snaps, not lifting her gaze from Luna's face. 'I don't need you to point out the bloody obvious.'

A light rain joins the breeze. *I'm afraid I must take her side this time; you cannot let her kill again.*

'We don't know it was her who hurt the other girls,' Goldie protests. 'We can't be sure.'

Scarlet lets out a gentle cough and Goldie looks up, scowling. 'Kavita and I discovered a prophecy about her,' she says softly. 'Warning of how powerful, and how dangerous, she would become when she turned ten.'

'Dangerous? Don't be ridiculous.' Goldie cups Luna's cheek, brushing her finger across her closed lips, feeling the blessed puff of her silent little breaths. 'Anyway, where did you see this thing and how on earth do you know it was about Luna?'

Now Kavita, who's sitting beside Scarlet, a few yards

away from Goldie and Luna, speaks up. 'We read it in the underground library at Oxford University, accessible only to our sisters,' Kavita says. 'And there aren't any other Grimms born of a sister and a soldier, are there?'

'I've never heard of it.' Goldie sniffs. 'And, anyway, how do we know that? Everwhere is infinite. There might be quite a few kicking around.'

No one says anything in response, and even Goldie doesn't pursue such a wildly absurd postulation.

What will you do? Bea asks again. *How will you curb her? How will you protect all the sisters in Everwhere?*

Goldie sighs. 'I'll talk to her, all right? I'll make sure it never happens again.'

'That won't work,' Scarlet says. 'She cannot control herself.'

How can she? Rain dusts Goldie's cheek but leaves Luna dry. *When she doesn't even know what she's doing?*

Goldie is silent, since she can't deny it. She can still see her daughter's beautiful face twisted into something unrecognizable: the cruel mouth, the glassy, unseeing eyes.

'As she grows, she'll become stronger and increasingly dangerous,' Kavita says, deeply apologetic. 'With every year, she'll be both more powerful and less able to resist her own destructive impulses.'

We cannot allow it. A light thunder rumbles over the trees above them. *Everwhere will no longer be a sanctuary; it'll become a place of death and peril again.*

'I'll think of a way,' Goldie says. 'I'll figure out a way to protect Luna and everyone else. I don't know how yet, but—'

What will you do? The wind grows colder. *Lock her up so*

she can never escape? What good will that do? And how will you stop her from falling asleep? It's impossible!

Goldie tightens her jaw, clenching her fist. 'There will be a way,' she mutters. 'There is always a way and, whatever it is, I will find it.'

'Please.' Scarlet shuffles along the ground, reaching out towards her sister. 'You've got to consider the safety of the others. You've got to be—'

'Don't tell me what I've got to be!' Goldie turns on her, spitting out her words with such venom that Scarlet pulls back. 'When Ana died, you abandoned us all – you didn't give a toss for all the other sisters then, did you? You didn't care about any of us at all! You only cared about yourself; you only cared about your own guilt and your own grief. Well, what of Ana? She didn't give up, did she? She dedicated herself to helping and supporting her sisters – and she was the one who died! And what about me? I had just as much reason to grieve as you – far more so, since I'd lost Leo too. But I didn't run away, did I? No, I swallowed my grief and carried on. So forgive me if I don't think you've got any right to tell me anything at all!'

Scarlet says nothing, only hangs her head, tears falling into her lap.

Kavita slips her arm around Scarlet's waist and gives her a gentle squeeze. 'But she came back, didn't she?' Kavita offers. 'She came back just in time to save your life.'

Goldie huffs, conceding the point.

And Scarlet is right, the wind roars.

She is, the thunder cracks.

'I don't care.' Goldie cradles her daughter closer to her chest. 'I will find a way.'

Chapter Thirty

6.58 a.m. – Luna

'I can sit up, Ma. I'm strong enough.'

'Are you sure? Don't hurt yourself.'

'I'm fine,' Luna says, rubbing the back of her head. 'Can't you see?' She gives her mother a little smile. 'I'm stronger than you think.'

'Clearly,' Goldie says, managing to smile back, though her heart is still hammering in her chest, her hands shaking. 'Stronger than any sister I've ever seen.'

Luna sits up. 'What's wrong, Ma?'

'I . . .' Goldie rubs her temples. 'I'm fine. Nothing wrong with me.'

The wind picks up, whispering through the leaves. Goldie ignores it and Luna, with her hand still pressed to the back of her head, doesn't seem to notice. Before she'd woken, Goldie had dismissed Scarlet and Kavita, then told her daughter a story about a game of chase and a slip and a fall.

'How about you?' Goldie persists. 'You had a pretty nasty fall – how's your head?'

'I'm fine, Ma,' Luna says. 'You're the one who's acting weird.'

'Okay, that's a blessed relief.' Goldie starts to stand. 'Then I guess we'd better go, if you're going to get back into bed before they find you gone.'

'Go?' Luna groans. 'Do we *have* to? Can't we stay? It's my birthday! Come on, Ma, please!'

'Oh, my love, I wish we could, but we can't.' Goldie reaches down to pull Luna up. 'We already talked about this, remember?'

Luna pouts, but nevertheless stands. As they walk out of the glade, following the winding river towards the nearest portal, Luna studies her mother curiously.

'Are you sure *you*'re okay, Ma?' she asks. 'You seem even more anxious than usual, and that's saying something.'

'I'm fine, Lu-Lu.' Goldie reaches for her daughter's hand. 'I'm fine. I was just worried about you, that's all. You had quite a bump.'

'Yeah.' Luna rubs her head again. 'It hurts like hell.'

'Ouch!' Goldie pulls back her hand. 'What—'

'Sorry, Ma.' Luna frowns down at the sparks at her fingertips. 'I don't know why – I can usually control it. Sorry.'

'No worries,' Goldie says, glancing at the sky with a warning look. 'Let's go.'

7.14 a.m. – Luna

She'd made it back just in time. She was in bed just before Mrs Hicks opened the door to wake her. Fortunately, her guardian hadn't noticed her matted, bloodied hair, and she was able to wash it before anyone else saw.

Luna still can't really remember what happened in Everwhere, though a question tugs at the edges of her mind and she's got a sneaking suspicion that her mother isn't telling her everything. Also, she keeps crying and doesn't understand why. She feels different too: softer, calmer, less angry, less vengeful. Right now she can barely summon the energy – or desire – to punish someone who deserved it. Perhaps this change was caused by the blow to her head, which still throbs from hitting the rock. Or perhaps it's the fact that, after last night, she misses her ma even more than usual. Or perhaps it's because it's her tenth birthday today and she's having the worst day ever, away from home and everyone she loves.

Luna doesn't know. What she does know is that she's knackered and aching and miserable and at least – if nothing else – wants a birthday cake. Even a slice. At least that'd make things a bit better. Cake makes everything better.

The other thing that Luna doesn't yet know is that half a crescent moon has etched itself onto her shoulder blade to sit among the constellation of scars.

11.11 a.m. – Goldie

She sits at Teddy's bedside while he sleeps, recovering strength after a gruelling hour of physiotherapy. She hasn't yet told him anything of recent events. Though she can hardly believe it's only been a day since she's seen her brother. Having endured such an avalanche of catastrophes, Goldie feels as though she's lived a dozen lifetimes and died a dozen deaths in the past twenty-four hours.

Now she sits cross-legged on the hospital chair, slowly shuffling Liyana's cards. She doesn't want to. She wants to plunge her head into the soil and wait until all this has passed. She wants to become a tree, an ancient oak that will weather any crisis, that will stay solid through the centuries, unmarked and unharmed, witnessing every fleeting drama with a benign and ever-patient eye. And yet, of course, she cannot. She cannot escape. Goldie must find an answer, a solution, to her daughter's devastating condition, and fast.

And she can't ask any of her sisters, since they've all made their deplorable positions horribly clear. And she can't talk to Teddy about it, since she doesn't want to cause him any more anguish than the great deal he's already suffering. Similarly, she can't talk to any residents at the shelter, since they've also got quite enough on their plates and she's meant to be taking care of them, not the other way around.

So, slowly, reluctantly, Goldie deals. And, with every new card that appears, her spirits sink and her hopes dwindle.

The first to appear is the Moon: a purple-haired wolf standing at a river's edge howls up at a fat yellow moon. Towering white trees flank the river, their trunks encircled by a pair of two-headed snakes. *Prophetic dreams, illusions, the unconscious mind*. Then comes the Five of Wands: four winged, sharp-toothed, long-beaked creatures with snaking tails clash their wands like swords in battle. A fifth, filigreed wand rises up between them. *Discord, conflict, struggle*. Followed by the Three of Swords: a girl sits on a stone holding her own heart in her hands, the swords pierce her heart, blood dripping from their tips. *Heartbreak, sorrow, betrayal*. Finally, the Tower: a growling stone beast guards the crumbling tower, flames roar from the windows, licking the sky. Blown by a ferocious grey wind, vultures soar above the people tumbling to their deaths. *Loss, sudden change, devastation*.

The message of the cards is clear. And, even if it hadn't been, Goldie already knew it. She'd known what they would say even before she dealt them. She cannot explain how, but there it is. The knowing has weighed on her since last night, since she saw the truth, since her sisters spoke, since she felt the shift. Goldie knew.

She didn't want to know, but she knew.

To save her daughter from turning into a soldier, to protect all the other sisters, she must destroy Everwhere.

Chapter Thirty-one

11.33 a.m. – Goldie

She stares at the cards for a long time. She'd feared the worst and here it is. The cards are telling her that to save the person she loves most she must sacrifice the place she loves most. The place where she is at her most powerful, the place where she is at her most free, the place that holds her most beloved memories of Leo and her dead sisters.

Yet she knows it was ever thus; one cannot achieve the near-impossible without great personal cost. The universe requires balance and the gods demand a tribute; neither will give a gift without receiving one in return.

Still, the cost will be borne not only by Goldie but by all the Sisters Grimm. She will be taking from them the one place where they can be all-powerful, where they can be free, where they can be entirely and wholly themselves: accepted and unjudged.

It is a tremendous loss.

And yet it must be done.

Goldie gathers the cards, slicing them back into the pack. *How*, though, will it be done? How does one destroy a world? Indeed, is it possible? Can it be done? Goldie glances up at the clock on the wall above Teddy's bed. She doesn't have much time. Scarlet, though Goldie hates to admit it, was right. The multiplying scars. The fresh wounds. Luna is destroying herself and, according to the cards, this self-destruction will rapidly accelerate. If Goldie doesn't act fast . . . she sees an image of her little girl committing suicide, killed by the soldier inside her: her spirit lifting into the air, her soul seeping into the ground . . .

Goldie pinches the bridge of her nose and blinks back tears. She doesn't have time to dwell, doesn't have the luxury of such reflection. She racks her brain for what to do next. The cards can't tell her. They only lay out the tragic state of things; they do not provide solutions. Her sisters don't seem to have any answers, except for the one thing Goldie will not contemplate. And Luna doesn't even know what's going on inside herself, let alone anything else. Who, then, can help?

Suddenly, in a blank mind and a bleak state, one name rises.

It's the last person Goldie wishes to talk to right now, but she has no other choice.

4.54 p.m. – Scarlet

It hadn't taken Goldie *too* long to find her. She'd only called twenty-three colleges before finally alighting upon the one in which her sister had been hiding out these past three years. Then she leaves the hospital, telling Teddy she's returning to the shelter for a while, before jumping in the car and driving straight to Oxford, without stopping.

Two hours and six minutes later, she arrives in the city centre, parks the car outside Trinity College, then sets about trying to locate Exeter College.

*

'I got the impression you didn't want anything to do with me,' Scarlet says.

They're sitting in a tiny café on Turl Street, tucked into a corner table. Goldie is stress-eating a plate of chocolate macaroons, while Scarlet lets her coffee go cold.

'I didn't.' Goldie nibbles on a macaroon. 'But needs must.'

Scarlet studies her coffee. 'Look, I'm sorry, all right? I didn't mean . . .'

'What?' Goldie drops the macaroon. 'You didn't mean to run away and never let us know if you were okay, or even alive? You didn't mean to abandon us all for three years? You didn't mean to forget you even had sisters or—'

'I didn't forget you,' Scarlet says softly. 'I thought of nothing else. That's why I couldn't come back, because I was being consumed by guilt. I couldn't bear it; I *can't* bear it. Every night I dream of her death and every day I wish that it'd been me who'd died instead.'

Goldie, having already prepared a retort, is about to snap it back, but the sincerity of Scarlet's words stops her. All at once she can feel the sorrow coming off her sister in waves, soaking the air, dampening her fire. Scarlet is drowning, just as Ana drowned, choking on her own tears.

'I'm sorry,' Goldie mumbles, reaching across the table for Scarlet's hand. 'I didn't realize how much . . . It wasn't—'

'—my fault,' Scarlet finishes. 'Yeah, I keep telling myself that too. But it doesn't seem to make a difference, nor shake the feeling that it should've been me that day.'

'You can't think like that,' Goldie says. 'Life and death, it's not up to you; it's fate.'

Scarlet shrugs. 'Perhaps.'

They sit in silence a few minutes, Goldie toying with the remaining macaroons.

'So,' she says eventually. 'I've got a question I think you can answer.'

Scarlet looks up. 'I've been wondering when you were going to ask. What is it you want to know?'

Goldie mutters the question amid a mouthful of crumbs. Scarlet leans forward.

'What?'

Goldie repeats herself.

Scarlet stares at her, incredulous. 'You want to *destroy* Everwhere?'

Goldie nods, still not looking up. 'Can it be done?'

Scarlet pauses, as if it's surely not a matter of how but why. Why would anyone ever wish to do such a thing? Eventually, she nods.

'Yes. I can't think why in hell you'd contemplate doing it. But, yes, it can be done.'

3.33 a.m. – Everwhere

We won't do it. We'll never do it. The wind picks up.

Lightning strikes and rain falls. *We will not. Absolutely not.*

'It's the only way,' Goldie says. 'Scarlet told me; she's been studying with that friend of hers and—'

There must be another way. You said it yourself: there's always another way.

The words fall light as mist, as if they're simple, ordinary words. As if they mean nothing; as if they don't denote the end of everything. Do her sisters not think that she wished for another way? Do they think she did not rage against it? Do they think that she would leave her daughter so easily?

From the moment Goldie gave birth to Luna, she was terrified. She'd been charged with protecting this little life and, to carry out this task, she had to keep herself alive too. These were the two essential things. And now she will have to do the former at the cost of the latter. There's no other way. It will break Luna's heart and yet it will ensure she lives. And Goldie can only hope that the love of her uncle will help to heal her fragile heart. And at the shelter she will have a revolving door of doting honorary aunts. One day, she will mend. And, most importantly of all, she will be safe.

The wind howls. The rain soaks the earth.

Please, don't make us do this. Not yet. Give us more time to find an alternative.

'We don't have more time.'

For Luna's sake, there must be another way.

Goldie shakes her head. 'Sometimes there's only one way.'

The spectre of Luna hangs between the sisters, but the killing of their little girl is no longer considered. Goldie has made that clear. Silence hangs heavy in the air.

Goldie sits on the sodden moss, oblivious to the wet and the cold. She presses her hands to the ground, watching the fresh shoots of ivy wiggling their way through the soil and into the open air: bright white against the dark.

All right, if this is what we must do, then we will do it.

Goldie looks up, into the night sky, into the rain, into the tops of the trees.

'Thank you,' she says. 'Thank you.'

*

The life of one sister. This is the price; this is the gift required. And, in return, Everwhere will be extinguished.

'If a sister dies at the hands of another,' Scarlet had said. 'And if she does so willingly, this will destroy Everwhere.'

'How?'

Scarlet had shrugged. 'I don't know. The text didn't explain. But Kavita thinks it might be the meeting of death and life, of good and evil, murder and sacrifice, in a single act. Somehow they cancel each other out and, in doing so, extinguish the place that exists to sustain that precarious balance . . .'

'I don't understand,' Goldie said, finally forgetting the macaroons. 'I don't—'

'Nor do I,' Scarlet admitted. 'But I don't think that matters. You don't have to understand a thing for it to be true. Didn't you once say that to me?'

Goldie stared at her cup. 'I don't remember.'

'There's a real risk that you won't be the only sacrifice,' Scarlet repeated. 'Given the way it must be done, it's likely that Bea and Ana will be extinguished in the explosion too.'

'I'll warn them,' Goldie promised. 'And if they refuse, will you—'

'Of course,' Scarlet interrupted. 'I'd take your place altogether, if only you'd let me.'

'No. She's my daughter. This is my sacrifice.'

Chapter Thirty-two

3.33 a.m. – the Sisters Grimm

That night, Scarlet returns to Everwhere to talk with her sisters a few minutes after Goldie leaves them. She doesn't have time to execute her plan; only to tell Bea and Liyana what to do. Without hesitation, they agree.

Luna closes her eyes on Earth and opens them in Everwhere. She doesn't realize at first what's wrong; she doesn't realize at first that anything *is* wrong. But then, as she walks along the path, feeling older and taller, delighting in the rush of the river and the rustle of the leaves, Luna feels the start of something: a shift that quivers through the earth and sky like the shudder of a distant earthquake and the rumble of distant thunder.

Luna stops and glances about her. Everything looks the same as it always did: the unwavering moon, the midnight sky, the trees towering above her, the moss at her feet, and everything all in white. Yet there is something. And there it is again: a flicker across the landscape, like a skip on a cinema reel – as if everything disappeared for a millisecond, then returned.

Luna frowns. 'What the hell?'

And then she feels the jolt. As if *she* disappeared for a second, then returned.

In that instant she knows: she's in danger. Worse than that, so is her ma. And so is Everwhere.

*

Luna runs towards the gate Goldie will have come through – *if* she came through a gate – hurtling over soil and moss and stone, levitating over fallen trunks. When she slips in the mud, she lifts her small body high enough to fly above the trees, still fixing her gaze on the ground like a bird of prey for any sight of her mother.

In the distance, Luna is struck by the sight of light emanating from behind a copse of trees, as if the sun had snuck into Everwhere and was rising in defiance of the moon. When she crests the topmost leaves of an ancient oak, Luna sees the fire. Then, as if in a dream, she sees her mother standing on a tree trunk, which burns beneath her feet.

'Ma!' Luna shrieks, as she swoops to the ground. 'Ma! What the hell are you doing?'

The flames are rising, licking and spitting at Goldie's feet as Luna runs towards her. 'Luna!' Goldie cries. 'No!'

'Ma! No!' Luna's voice is a siren, eclipsing every other sound. 'Maaaa!'

Her cry is a simultaneous earthquake and storm, sending tremors through the ground and air. The trees quiver and shake and, all at once, it feels as if Everwhere is being upturned. Then, just as suddenly, everything falls silent and still. Even the flames at Goldie's feet are static, as if time has stopped.

'Luna, go!' Goldie screams, as the air shifts again, reigniting the fire. 'You can't be here! It's not safe – you've got to go!'

'What are you doing?' Luna shouts. 'Ma! What are you *doing?*'

'Lu, please!' Goldie shouts. 'It's not safe! You cannot be here when—'

But Luna is already lifting her hands above her head,

already bringing down a great torrent of rain to extinguish the fire.

'No!' Goldie screams. 'Stop! You don't underst—'

A biting wind whips up, curling around Luna's hands and dragging them back to her sides. Suddenly the rain stops.

'Aunt Bea?! No!' Luna struggles, trying to break free. 'Stop! You need to help her!' She flings her head back. '*What's going on?*'

It's what she wants. It's what must be done.

There's no other way.

'What?' Luna stops struggling and stares at her mother. 'What do they mean? *What* must be done? Why are you setting yourself on fire?!'

'To save you.' The flames fall low beneath Goldie's feet and she breathes a little easier. She gazes at her daughter and Luna looks back. And for one seemingly infinite moment everything is suspended: the fire, the wind, the fact of what is now and what is to come. And then time begins again.

'Save me?' Luna steps forward. 'How? Why? Why do I need saving?'

'The new scars on your shoulder,' Goldie says. 'Those are from the girls you killed. The same happened to your father and—'

'Killed?' Luna laughs at such an absurd notion. 'What are you talking about? I've never hurt anyone in my life . . .' She trails off, recalling all the men she's maimed over the past few years. 'Well, no one who didn't deserve it, anyway. And I've certainly never killed anyone! Even if they did deserve it.'

'Last night,' Goldie whispers. 'You'd have killed me if Scarlet hadn't stopped you.'

'What?' Luna is incredulous. 'What? No, that can't be . . .'

But even as she speaks, half-memories, and what she'd thought were dreams, are slotting themselves together like pieces of a puzzle – and all becomes clear.

'Oh my God.' Luna drops to her knees. 'Then I am the one who should die, not you.'

Ignoring her, Goldie calls up to her sisters. 'Take her,' she screams up at the sky. 'Take her away! Now!'

A sudden wind rises around Luna, a wind so fierce and wild that it lifts her from the ground and suspends her, kicking and flailing, in the air. Beneath Luna, the currents in the river start to swirl before a great wave breaks the banks, surging over soil to buoy Luna up.

'Put me down!' Luna demands. 'Put me down!'

She fights the wind and water with her own elemental weapons, whipping up hurricanes about her and whirlpools beneath her and strikes of lightning that crack the air.

'Lu! No!' Goldie cries. 'Go! Let them take you! Please!'

But Luna fights with all her might and all her heart and, just as she's gaining control, Scarlet steps into the arena.

The sight of her third aunt, standing with her hands and hair aflame – illuminating the bleached landscape like a human torch – shocks Luna into submission. Her paralysis enables the combined forces of wind and water to carry the little girl away and cast her out of Everwhere.

And then, as planned, Scarlet turns to Goldie with a well-aimed throw of a well-aimed stone, knocking her sister unconscious.

Having left Goldie in the loving arms of Luna, who cradles her mother as her mother has so often cradled her, Scarlet returns to the scene and, before she has a chance to let herself be stopped by fear, she calls upon her remaining sisters to do what they'd promised to do.

She sets the lightning strike herself; the hurricane and whirlpool do the rest.

It is quick.

'Thank you' are her final words. Then: *I'm home.*

Chapter Thirty-three

In explosions, particles are scattered, but they do not disappear; energy is mutated, certainly, but never extinguished. For nothing that existed can ever be fully erased; always something remains. And so, from the ashes of Everwhere, a new place took root, created in the firmament of destruction.

It's not ancient, of course, nor lit by an unwavering moon. It has no trees to speak of yet, but they're growing. Saplings are scattered across the fresh soil, and seedlings are sprouting. Instead of darkness and winter, the new place is lit by the sun and infused with the essence of spring. It's not written of in ancient manuscripts, nor yet charted in any mystical texts, and few – excepting the sisters throughout the world – know of its existence. But those who've visited it are already enchanted.

They call it Elsewhere.

ENDINGS & BEGINNINGS

Kavita

It was Scarlet's idea, after Goldie had finally confessed everything, over cold coffee and chocolate macaroons at the corner table in the tiny café on Turl Street, about Luna being taken away.

Scarlet had looked grave and then suddenly brightened. 'If the scars disappeared, would they have to give her back to you?'

'I don't know,' Goldie said. 'I suppose so.'

'I mean, that's their whole case, isn't it?' Scarlet warmed to her subject. 'So if Luna woke up one day without the scars – they wouldn't be able to explain it, but they couldn't object. Right?'

'I guess . . .' Goldie frowned. 'But what does it matter? Unless you've turned into a witch while you've been away, then—'

'I have a friend,' Scarlet said, 'who can do pretty amazing things. I bet she'd be able to conjure up some sort of spell to, I don't know, conceal them or something, even if she couldn't actually make them disappear. But that'd be enough, don't you think?'

They'd had to meet in Elsewhere to execute the plan, since Goldie hadn't been permitted an unsupervised visit with Luna, and Kavita's particular skills didn't extend to rendering herself invisible. Fortunately, however, Scarlet had been right and Goldie watched in astonishment while Kavita made the scars disappear.

'Are they gone forever?' Luna asked regretfully. 'Will I never see them again?'

Goldie took her daughter's hand. 'Don't worry, my love, you won't forget him. His blood still runs in your veins, so to speak; your heart still beats with his rhythm . . . As long as you live, your father is always with you.'

Luna hesitated. Goldie squeezed her daughter's hand, flinching at the sparks as Luna's fingertips sent little electric shocks up her arm. 'We'll talk about him more often,' she promised. 'Every day, if you like. You can ask me anything you want and I'll answer.'

Luna's eyes widened. 'Really?'

Goldie nodded, gravely. 'Truly.'

Still, Luna hesitated. Then she looked to Kavita. 'All right then. You may do it.'

Goldie smiled, always surprised how Luna could be so childlike one minute and so grown-up the next.

Six months later, long after Luna was home again, Kavita applied for a tutorship in Medieval Literature at St Catharine's College, Cambridge. She moved into the shelter to support Goldie and become an honorary aunt to Luna.

All went well until, one night, she caught her niece shimmying down a drainpipe, having climbed out of her bedroom window. Under interrogation, with the combined scrutiny of Kavita and Goldie, Luna had confessed.

'Sometimes, I, um, inflict a little, um, righteous punishment on those who otherwise wouldn't see justice,' she admitted, sounding more like a veteran vigilante than a nearly-eleven-year-old girl. 'I got the arsehole who hurt Uncle Teddy, but don't worry,' she added, seeing the look of horror on her mother's face. 'I only maim; I never kill.'

'Oh.' Goldie stared at her, incredulous. 'Well, that makes it all right then.'

'Really?' Luna asked, relieved. 'Does that mean I can keep doing it?'

Goldie folded her arms. 'Absolutely not.'

While mother and daughter glowered at each other in a stand-off, Kavita stepped between them. 'Perhaps we can come to a compromise,' she suggested. 'Since, I think, we can all agree that these abusers deserve to be punished, and since the legal system is so inadequate, and Luna has certain . . . proclivities that make her perfectly suited to carry out a particularly apt style of justice . . .'

'Absolutely not!' Goldie echoed herself with even greater vehemence. 'The sisters seem to be safe in Elsewhere, at least for now, but—'

'Come on, Ma!' Luna protested. 'I've never turned into a soldier again since Auntie Vita erased my scars; I can control my impulses now – you know I can. I just—'

'No,' Goldie interrupted her daughter in turn. 'I don't care. Besides which, it's too dangerous. One of these men might have a weapon; you might get hurt.'

'You're right,' Kavita agreed. 'Which is why I'm suggesting that we don't let her go alone. We go with her.'

'Oh, yes!' Luna exclaimed, releasing her inner child by jumping up and down while squealing with delight. 'Please, Ma, can we? Pleeeease!' She grins. 'We'll be a feminist version of the Three Musketeers.'

Teddy

He's still walking with a cane when he sees her, hurrying out of the gelateria in the direction of King's Parade, hastily licking what looks to be a cone of basil-and-passionfruit sorbet.

'Oh!' Despite himself, he calls out. 'Oh! It's you!'

But they aren't alone on the street and she doesn't hear him, or see him, but only hurries on. *Late for work again,* he thinks with a smile. Then: *If only I knew her name!*

'Hey!' Teddy calls out again, stumbling along after her. 'Wait!'

And then she turns and sees him.

At the sight of her smile, his heart lifts. As she walks towards him, it thuds.

'Hello,' she says, still smiling.

'Hello.' He nods at her sorbet. 'Good?'

Her smile widens. 'Superb.'

Teddy nods. 'I'm going to miss it.'

'Oh?' Does he dare detect a note of disappointment in her voice? 'You're leaving Cambridge?'

Now it's his turn to smile. 'I'm starting at Saint Martins in September.'

'You are? How wonderful! I'm so glad.' She licks her sorbet thoughtfully. 'So you told your sister you were leaving and she didn't mind?'

'She . . .' Teddy trails off, unable to form coherent sentences when all he can think is: *She remembered! She's been thinking about me too!* 'Yes, well, she . . .'

'Are you all right?' She nods at his cane, tactfully changing the subject. 'Did you hurt yourself?'

'No, no.' He shakes his head dismissively. 'It's nothing; I'm fine. Look, I've been wondering . . .'

'Yes?' she asks, as she glances down at her watch. 'Oh no, I've got to go! My boss'll kill me if I'm late, and I'm already late!' She gives him one last kindly look. 'It was lovely to bump into you again; I was hoping I would.' Then she turns to go.

Struck dumb, Teddy watches her hurry along the pavement, darting in and out of the groups of tourists crowding the street.

'Wait!' Teddy calls out, all at once coming to his senses. 'Please, wait!'

She stops and hesitates, and Teddy hobbles towards her as quickly as his leg will allow him. 'Sorry, I'm sorry. Sorry . . .' He punctuates each step with an apology, as is the usual British way when navigating crowds. 'Sorry, I'm sorry, I'm— Thank you for waiting,' he says, reaching her. 'If I'd had to run, I'd have been scuppered.'

'I'm sorry,' she says in turn, glancing again at her watch. 'I'm sorry, but I've really got to—'

'Yes, sorry, of course.' Teddy stumbles over his words, then takes the plunge. 'I was hoping . . . I was hoping that perhaps we could keep in touch.'

She laughs. 'You don't even know my name!'

Teddy blushes. 'True, and I would've liked to discover it in a less obvious, more naturalistic way – rather than in a way that puts me on the line for abject humiliation and mortification, but if I don't ask now, then I might never see you again. And that . . . that would be . . . shit.'

'Would it?' she says, still laughing. And for one torturous moment he waits for the inevitable brush-off. 'Well, after such an eloquent request, how can I say no?' She reaches out her hand, fixing him with a brilliant smile. 'Ella Khara Latimore, a pleasure to meet you.'

'Ella,' Teddy repeats, forgetting, in his delight, to offer his own name in return. 'The pleasure is all mine.'

Scarlet, Liyana & Bea

I don't think I'll ever tire of this.

Of what?

Being weightless, being formless ... of drifting hither and yon, without a care in the world. This one or the other.

The breeze shivers through a sapling, rustling its few leaves. *Who says hither and yon nowadays? How old are you?*

Sunlight sparkles on the water. *I'm timeless, immortal, no age at all.*

A current eddies along the riverbank. *The very best age to be.*

And the very best place to be.

The breeze curls across the water and through the light, three sisters coming together for a moment, before dancing apart again.

Not too shabby for a place to spend eternity, I'll give you that.

Luna

'Okay, if you don't want to play cards or puzzles, then I'll read you a story.'

She sits on the floor of room 8 with Tallulah, a little girl who arrived with her mother last night.

'Yes!' Tallulah grins. 'A story, yes!'

Luna smiles. 'Would you like one from the bookshelf? Or one I wrote myself?'

'One you wrote,' Tallulah says without hesitation.

'Well,' Luna admits, 'I didn't write it *all* myself. I wrote it with my auntie Ana. She's dead,' Luna adds. 'But she still writes the best stories.'

Tallulah brightens, intrigued by the notion of tales written by ghosts.

'All right,' Luna says. 'I know the perfect one. For you and your ma.'

Tallulah turns to her mother, who's sitting by the window gazing anxiously outside, biting her thumbnail. 'Mummy! Come here, Luna's going to tell us a story.'

'Oh,' her mother says, sounding confused, but still she slips off the chair and steps over to the floor where her daughter sits. Tallulah slides into her lap and settles herself. With her audience gathered, Luna folds her hands in her lap and assumes her special storytelling voice.

'This one is called "Cinderella",' Luna intones in her favourite storytelling voice. Then adds in response to Tallulah's frown. 'Don't worry, it's not like the one you know.'

Tallulah sits back, satisfied, and her mother smiles, grateful.

'All right. Are you sitting comfortably?' Luna smiles. 'Then I'll begin . . .'

Cinderella

Once upon a time, there was a girl born with hair and eyes the colour of cinder ash, and so her father called her Cinderella. Her mother favoured another name and so her parents fought. This time, her father won.

Unfortunately, for poor Cinderella, the fight that greeted her arrival into the world was neither the first nor the last of a great many arguments between her mother and father, who seemed unable to agree on anything and unwilling to let any perceived slight pass. And so, the little girl with the ash hair grew up in a house full of sorrow and regret.

Every night Cinderella cried herself to sleep, then dreamed of growing up safe and secure in a happy, harmonious home with parents who truly loved each other, and lavished praise and attention upon their adored daughter. Upon waking, Cinderella would remember how distant her dreams were from the world in which she lived. And so, every morning, she vowed that one day, when she married, she would create for herself the happiness she so longed for.

And it came to pass, when Cinderella finally came of age, she left home. She travelled across lands and oceans, going as fast and as far as she could until, like Dick Whittington before her, she arrived in London, not to seek her fortune but to find a husband with whom she would be truly happy for the rest of her life.

However, having no experience of romance, nor of men in general, or husbands in particular, Cinderella did not know how to go about finding the perfect one, the one who would fit just right. She soon found that waiting, wishing and hoping produced no discernible results. And, sadly, she seemed to have no fairy godmother to resolve the situation in an instantaneous and effortless way.

Fortunately, Cinderella's disappointment was exceeded by her determination. And so, she didn't give up but instead decided to become her own fairy godmother, buying a beautiful bridal dress of silken lace as a good-luck charm while she continued the search for her groom. One day, Cinderella's faith and fortitude were rewarded and she found him.

At least, she thought she had. However, as the years passed, it started to seem that perhaps he was not quite the perfect fit that Cinderella had at first thought. She didn't care that he was so tall her neck ached when they kissed, or that he insisted on sleeping on a mattress that was so hard it hurt her back, or even that he favoured food so piping hot it burnt her tongue. No, Cinderella soon adapted to all these minor quirks, including his big bushy beard in which pieces of his piping hot food would frequently find a home. What she found harder to accommodate was that he didn't listen but instead talked only about himself and held strong opinions, to which Cinderella often secretly objected, on a great many subjects.

However, Cinderella was a determined woman who dearly wanted her dream of happiness to come true. So she never complained about her sore back or her burnt tongue, never said anything when he dominated every conversation or stridently voiced his various offensive opinions. But Cinderella noticed that the less she said, the sadder she felt until, one day, she felt far more sorrowful and lonely than she had ever been, even as a child.

And so, finally, Cinderella was forced to admit that this husband was not the perfect fit, after all, and she needed to continue her search. Heartsick with disappointment but still determined, Cinderella thought that, since it had all gone so wrong with this particular man, perhaps it would go right with a man who was entirely the opposite.

Fortunately, her search was soon successful and Cinderella found a man who was very short, causing her neck to ache on the other side, who favoured a bed so soft it curled her spine and food so tepid it had no taste at all. But he listened to everything she said, rarely talked about himself, and never seemed to have an opinion on any subject at all. At first, this was a great relief to Cinderella. Yet before long it began to bother her. This new husband was cold and distant and frequently left her feeling rejected and hurt. But still, Cinderella resolved to make it work.

So, she told herself that everything was okay, that he loved her in his own way, and that at least they never fought like her parents had done. Again, the days passed and Cinderella spent several more years struggling to force this new relationship to fit into her fantasies of the perfect romance. Until, one day, Cinderella realized that she was again as sorrowful and lonely as she had been as a child. And so, she left.

Now heartbroken with disappointment and too beleaguered and battered to be determined anymore, Cinderella gave up. She would never find her perfect husband; she would never have the fairy-tale marriage of which she had always dreamed. Thus, as well as giving up, Cinderella let go. She let go of her dream, of yearning, of true love.

In that moment, a space opened in her heart. Hitherto, craving had choked the atriums, longing had clogged the arteries, desire had snapped shut the valves. But now they were clear; now she could breathe again. And, in that moment, in that space, love rushed in.

'So?' Tallulah sits forward eagerly. 'What happened next? Did she—'

'I don't know.' Luna smiles, as she speaks in her superior, storytelling voice. 'I don't know if Cinderella ever found the fabled husband,' she says. 'But I do know that from that day forward she was truly happy for the rest of her life.'

Goldie

Having promised her sisters to take a break now and then, she visits the Botanic Garden every Monday and Friday morning for a few hours, wandering through the hothouses in the winter and sitting on her favourite bench beside the lake under the willow trees whenever the weather is fine enough.

Now she sits, on one particularly fine Friday morning, reading the story that Luna and Ana have finally finished for her: 'Little Bird Beauty'. One day, Luna vows, she will sell their stories, making Liyana the first posthumously published author who's still writing new novels.

Goldie turns the page to read, in Luna's neat scrawl: *There was once born a baby girl so uncommonly beautiful – her hair and skin the colour of a raven's wing, the movement of her arms like a bird in flight – that her mother named her Little Bird Beauty . . .*

Kicking off her flip-flops, she presses her bare feet into the soft cool grass, glancing down to see the fresh bright green shoots wiggle out of the soil, stretching and unfurling into fresh daisies that push up between her toes, opening their petals to the sun.

Goldie smiles, thinking: *New life, yes. It's never too late to live a new life.*

The End

For those who've got this far and would like to know how that particular tale ends:

Little Bird Beauty

There was once born a baby girl so uncommonly beautiful – her hair and skin the colour of a raven's wing, the movement of her arms like a bird in flight – that her mother named her Little Bird Beauty. As Beauty grew, it became clear that her temperament matched her name: that she was as good, kind and true as she was beautiful. As she grew, her goodness only grew too, until she was famed throughout all of London and beyond. So it was that when she came of age, every bachelor wanted her for his wife. By the time she was eighteen, Beauty was keen to marry, for, universally adored though she was, loved by everyone who met her, she still felt a sense of loneliness at her core, a longing for something, though she didn't know for what.

'True love is what you want,' her mother told her. 'For, while it is extremely pleasing to be loved a little by a great many people, true happiness lies in being loved completely by one.'

And so, being a dutiful daughter, Beauty heeded her mother's ill-conceived words and married the man who seemed to love her more than any other. She would, she was certain, come to love him in turn, because it would surely be easy to love someone who adored you so completely. Unfortunately, before the first year of marriage was out, Beauty found that she'd been wrong.

But her husband was both successful and attentive, showering her with attention and adoration, and so, because she did not know what else to do, Beauty stayed.

One day, Beauty's father-in-law died, and her husband inherited the most prestigious legal firm in London, in all of England, making him the king of all London society and Beauty his queen. And while this might have made her happier, she found that it did not. As the months wore on, Beauty found her loneliness returning, along with her sense of longing for something she still couldn't quite place. Her sorrow permeated everything, taking the smile from her lips, the shine from her hair and the light from her eyes. Until, one day, no one spoke of her beauty anymore and even her husband's words of love began to feel empty and false.

That day, Beauty had every mirror in their six-bedroom Notting Hill home covered with thick velvet cloths and forbade the maid to polish any window or silver plate too well, so she'd never again have to catch sight of her reflection.

The following year, on her twenty-first birthday, a great feminist author arrived uninvited to the celebrations, demanding to meet Beauty. At first, Beauty was nervous, since the writer had a fearsome reputation, known throughout London, especially to the misogynist establishment and media, as the Beast. But she found, once they began talking, that she rather liked her.

'I have a gift for you, my queen,' the writer said. 'An invitation.'

'Yes?' Beauty asked, no longer fearful but intrigued.

'I invite you to play a game,' the writer said. 'I invite you, for a year, to pretend that you are me. Or only for a day, if you wish,' she added, upon seeing Beauty's reaction.

'What sort of a gift is that?' Beauty frowned. 'I think

I'd prefer something like the secret to Everlasting Happiness or Eternal Youth, please. Or even a recipe for an excellent chocolate cake.'

The great feminist writer laughed. 'Oh, but, my dear, the gift I'm offering is far better than either or, indeed, both of those things,' she promised. 'Even including the chocolate cake. Trust me.'

Beauty didn't believe the writer for an instant, but found, curiously, that she trusted her, though she couldn't say why. And so, she took the writer's invitation, just for an hour at first, then a day, beginning to stride about the house, then her neighbourhood, then all of London, acting as she'd heard that the writer herself did. With a few minor modifications.

Beauty visited the Tower of London, standing at the very edge of parapets and screaming into the wind, for so long and so loud that the tourists below began fearing dragons. She went on a tour of the Houses of Parliament, only to be ejected for taunting a clutch of stuffy MPs and accosting the Prime Minister. She caught a train to Scotland and went to Edinburgh Castle at lunchtime, knocking out the Lieutenant General with a stolen scabbard, then firing the booming one o'clock gun, grinning down from Mills Mount Battery as the gunshot echoed over the Scottish hills. In her attempted getaway, Beauty ran along the stone passageways wielding a ceremonial sword, terrifying the tourists and four policemen, who leapt out of the way once they saw she wasn't going to pay them heed. Beauty spent the night in jail, until her well-connected husband was able to set her free. During those days, Beauty had such fun that she forgot to feel either longing or loneliness.

After that, Beauty stopped saying 'of course' when

she wanted to say 'piss off', stopped smiling at someone when she wanted to slap them, stopped staying silent when she needed to scream. In short, Beauty began, for the first time in her life, to please herself and act as she wished. And she found, much to her surprise, that the great writer had been right: her gift had been far better than the Eternal Youth or Everlasting Happiness (and even the chocolate cake recipe) that she had asked for.

Soon, Beauty asked her husband for a divorce, which he gave her and honoured the very generous pre-nup. A few weeks later, Beauty attended a reading of feminist fairy tales given by the great writer at the British Library. Afterwards, they went to dinner. After that, they went to bed.

What's more, one evening Beauty was striding along the hallway of her Notting Hill home, on her way to the roof terrace from where she planned to scream long and loud into the wind, when she saw a mirror draped in a thick velvet cloth. Having entirely forgotten her decree, and no longer fearing her own reflection, Beauty tore off the cloth. Upon seeing herself – the spark of brilliant light in her dark eyes – Beauty realized that her lover's gift had not simply been better than the gifts she had asked for but had, in fact, given her those things too.

From that day forward, and for the rest of her life, Beauty never again felt either loneliness or longing for something she couldn't quite place or, indeed, for anything else at all.

And so, BlackBird was born.

Acknowledgements

Well, we've reached the end! Who'd have thought it? And now I must offer my deep gratitude to all those who've been with me from first to last, supporting me in creating this trilogy of which I am immensely proud. Any novel – let alone three – is the result of marvellous teamwork and thus I give great thanks (again and again) to the following: Simon Taylor (editor extraordinaire), Beci Kelly (creator of the MOST splendid covers), Chloë Rose (most wonderful publicist), Wendy Shakespeare (loveliest and most eagle-eyed copy editor I've ever had), Vivien Thompson (superb production editor), Hugh Davis and Rebecca Wright for more brilliant catches and Holly McElroy for generous mercy in a pinch. Also, my utterly amazing agent, Laurie Robertson, who cheers me on, cheers me up, gives very insightful feedback and is superb at brainstorming plots! What more could an author want?

Infinite thanks, of course, to Alastair Meikle for the spectacular illustrations and to Naz Ekin Yilmaz for the marvellous map.

Gratitude every day to the dearest friends who do what authors need and appreciate so much: ask how the writing is going, buy the latest novel and attend all the bookish events. I am deeply touched by all who go above and beyond in this regard. You each occupy a cosy nook in my ever-expanding heart.

Thank you to: Ova (for unflagging encouragement and

faith in the darkest hours, for loving my writing as much as I love hers); Al (my forever editor – who, this time, caught fifty-six errors the rest of us missed – thank you! And I still miss you every day – when are you coming back to Cambridge?!); Emily (for being the best partner, in both business and creativity); Ruth (for the beautiful letters, delicious cakes and marvellous adventures); Virginie (thousands of miles away but ever-present in my heart); Ash (for always believing everything will be wonderful); Anita (for never failing to make me laugh); Sarah (for the best bookish chats); Alice (fellow collector of inks, pens, stationery and *objets d'art*); Amy (bookseller-turned-friend and best interviewer I've ever had); Colette (no one I'd rather eat pizza with); Holly and Bex (for the cake and laughter and putting it all in perspective); Natasha (for expanding my fantastical education and still believing in fairies); Kelly (gorgeous cheerleader with the kindest heart); Tanya and Ella (dear friends and family both – Ella, I hope you like your cameo); Chris (I hope you don't like yours ☺ – you've taught me to be more discerning about whom I befriend at the school gate) and Jo (for all the delectable cakes); Laurence and Naz (who've both taught me so much and are always at the other end of the phone whenever I need advice); Natalie (fellow writer and dear friend); Amanda (fellow witch, so generous and beautiful); Clara (for always understanding); Rachel (lovely long, happy lunches at HNs); Ella Wolfnoth (artist extraordinaire); Helen (for marvellous memories); Miriam (still my oldest friend: remember V96?); Maggie (newest friend and one who understands the supreme importance of pie – I hope I'll know you forever!); Hazel (looking forward to that afternoon tea); Sarah M (fellow writer and bookish friend); Al P (for always asking, never forgetting); Roopali (for loving the light books and still buying the dark ones); Yvonne (for wonderful trick-or-treating memories); Marta and Jorge (for being the best company in the parenting trenches); Vanessa (for being at every event); Emma (fellow foodie and barrister extraordinaire) and Gio; Regula and Sacha (for a wonderful month talking and writing – I'm looking forward to Basel!); Steve (for that day, seventeen years ago now – can you believe it?!); Barn (always late but always there) and Dave: 'Eat Cake Productions!' – one day.

And, of course, to my beautiful and brilliant family, who do all the above and more: Artur, Oscar and Raffy, Mum and Dad, Jack and Mattie – you give it all meaning. And to my adopted family: Idilia, Christine, Fatima and Manuel. Thank you for your unfailing unconditional love.

Acknowledgments

[illegible]

Menna van Praag has lived in Cambridge all her life, except when she was studying at Oxford. She is the author of nine novels, including the acclaimed Sisters Grimm trilogy, of which *Child of Earth and Sky* is the third and final volume.